She had hung her clothes on a thornbush.

She was playing in the shallows when I caught sight of her—wading waist-deep and lifting the sea water in her cupped hands to shower it on her shoulders and breasts.

"Afraid of the water, Mr. Douglas?" she taunted.

Knowing she had stripped naked like any child of nature, I had my clothes off in a trice and entered the cove in a long, raking dive.

A saint on a pedestal would have turned to watch her emerge from the sea. Like all perfect things, her naked loveliness was beyond describing. I simply let my eyes feast on her.

And as I stood near the shore, I felt the hunger of the flesh. Above the hammer blows of my heart I knew that once I had changed this girl to a woman, she would be all mine.

Books by Frank G. Slaughter

Air Surgeon
Battle Surgeon
Buccaneer Surgeon
Code Five
Constantine
Convention, M.D.
Countdown
The Curse of Jezebel
Darien Venture
David: Warrior and King
Daybreak
The Deadly Lady of Madagascar
Devil's Harvest
Divine Mistress
Doctor's Wives
East Side General
Epidemic!
Flight from Natchez
Fort Everglades
God's Warrior

The Golden Isle
The Golden Ones
The Healer
In a Dark Garden
The Land and the Promise
Lorena
Pilgrims in Paradise
The Purple Quest
A Savage Place
The Scarlet Cord
Shadow of Evil
Spencer Brade, M.D.
The Stonewall Brigade
Storm Haven
Surgeon, U.S.A.
Sword and Scalpel
That None Should Die
Tomorrow's Miracle
A Touch of Glory
Women in White

Published by POCKET BOOKS

The
Deadly
Lady
of
MADAGASCAR

Frank G. Slaughter
(Originally published under the pseudonym C. V. Terry)

PUBLISHED BY POCKET BOOKS NEW YORK

THE DEADLY LADY OF MADAGASCAR

Doubleday edition published 1959

POCKET BOOK edition published July, 1960

5th printing.......................August, 1976

This POCKET BOOK edition includes every word contained in
the original, higher-priced edition. It is printed from brand-
new plates made from completely reset, clear, easy-to-read type.
POCKET BOOK editions are published by
POCKET BOOKS,
a division of Simon & Schuster, Inc.,
A GULF+WESTERN COMPANY
630 Fifth Avenue,
New York, N.Y. 10020.
Trademarks registered in the United States
and other countries.

ISBN: 0-671-80749-8.

Contents

The
Deadly
Lady
of
MADAGASCAR

CHAPTER 1

The Star of Bengal

THE strange tale I have to relate could open at several points —and I hesitate over the proper beginning, since it is my wish to compel belief. Let the reader be warned: I am no scrivener with the Muses at my beck and the tricks of rhetoric at my elbow. In sober truth (I can see it clearly now) I am but a seafarer who missed respectability by a whisker, a man whose education in worldly ways leaves much to be desired, though I still beg leave to call myself a gentleman. Already my pen hesitates to drive on, lest I paint too black a picture of my mission to Madagascar. Words are tyrants, when one is unaccustomed to their use.

Let me make one thing plain at once: I can never call myself the hero of this narrative, though I am one of the two principal actors. Indeed, there are some who may dub me villain long before I have done—and yet, given a second chance, I would not have acted otherwise.

I can only throw myself on the reader's mercy (assuming, as I do, that this manuscript will eventually find its readers). I can but hope that he will judge me with both mercy and tolerance. And, since I pretend to no narrative skill, I will begin, willy-nilly, at the moment when the course of my life was changed beyond recall.

The time's a summer morning. The place, the Lower Bay of New York, where the *Resolute* rode at anchor while she awaited the dawn. Richard Douglas (your servant) is discovered *solus*, pacing the deck at the end of his night watch, his eyes sweeping the murky sky for some hint of daylight.

That June morning—how well I remember!—was hot beyond belief.

Merely by closing my eyes I could bring back the East again, and all its misty splendors—pretend, while the spell

1

endured, that I was in the Madras anchorage of the Company, or drifting in a calm off Java Head. Certainly there were no danker fogs in the Spice Islands. India itself had never boiled with a deeper, more sinister mist than our present roadstead.

For want of a useful occupation I had been circling the decks for the past hour, pausing now and again to study the idle canvas of the ship I had captained from Glasgow, in fact if not in name. Until the fog lifted, there was little point in whistling for a breeze. . . . When it was full daylight, I would waken the actual master of the *Resolute* and resign the deck, certain that I had acquitted myself well on the crossing. It was but fitting that Captain Greene should con his ship to her berth in the New World.

Daylight would be time enough to wonder about the future—to ask why I must cross an ocean to receive my orders from Sir Luke Metcalf himself.

I could take a certain comfort in the pea soup that surrounded me. While it lasted, it was a blanket that smothered thought. It was easier still to ignore the stab of conscience when I admitted I could no longer picture Anne Sinclair's face too clearly—nor bring back more than a forlorn echo of the vows we had exchanged so ardently when we had parted six weeks ago at Clydeside.

It was quiet on deck that daybreak—too quiet for a young man's peace of mind. Save for the gulls in the white void, and the creak of our blocks, I could call myself alone on earth—though there were lookouts at the bow and others in the waist. All were fully armed (I had given the order myself when the hook was dropped). America was a strange bourne to me: I had fully expected to find red aborigines roaming the meadows that had begun to take shape on the larboard bow . . . Captain Greene would laugh at the precaution when he came topside—but Greene was a veteran of the Atlantic crossing. I had learned my own seamanship in the Orient, along with a healthy respect for marauders.

If only to distract myself anew, I moved to the rail to study the East Indiaman riding at anchor to starboard. Like the *Resolute,* she had come into this mooring with the sunset, a victim of the dying offshore wind. She had secured her cables with a *brouhaha* of furling sails and a prodigious scolding among the lascars who made up her crew. Now, like ourselves, she had lifted her canvas again, and was straining at her hawsers in the outgoing tide. There was a show of light in the master's cabin—but her poop deck was empty, though it was apparent she was ready to move with the first breath of air. Already her stern had swung dangerously close to us in that uncertain light.

The crews of these blunderbuss argosies of the East India Company are adept at routine maneuvers. This particular Indiaman, however, was no longer the property of the vast merchantile empire I had served so faithfully. The flag at her peak was Portuguese—and there was an un-English air about her, a kind of deshabille no British captain would condone. Only the crew seemed in character—and the double row of gunports that had once protected this salt-caked Argo from the Mocha sultans and the freebooters of Malabar. It was not the first time that the Company (seeking alliances everywhere) had sold one of its overage carriers to a rival.

Speculating on her present port of origin, I watched the Indiaman swing with the tide, until her ornate afterhouse was in view, looming like the segment from some Chinese pagoda in the wan promise of dawn. A splinter of sunlight, cutting the fog, picked out a name plate beneath her stern window: STAR OF BENGAL.

The label rang no chime in my memory (and I knew most of the Company's merchantmen by heart). Obviously, she had been rechristened after her sale. In the East the gods of chance wear other faces: it is not considered bad luck to rename a vessel after her transfer. . . . *The Star of Bengal,* completing a lazy circle with her mooring as the axis, presented her poop deck to my view a second time. To my astonishment, I saw that a woman had appeared at the rail.

I would never know if she had come from the captain's quarters or the companionway that adjoined it. She was tall and slender—and, even at that mist-shrouded remove, exuded a special strength that belied her sex. Her hair (it was dark as the retreating night) spilled over the peignoir that covered otherwise bare shoulders. The costume, together with the lady's most unladylike yawn (a feline stretch, suggesting a cat rising from a dream), told me she had left her bunk only a moment ago.

Thanks to the uncertain light and the hair that wrapped her in its sabled cloud, I could not discern her features.

But I observed that she was studying both me and my ship intently. Resenting that easy scrutiny, with its suggestion that a woman's eyes could be keener than my own, I felt an impulse to greet her with my famous bellow—a stentor's shout that had flung commands into the teeth of hurricanes. Without knowing why, I was certain that this woman gave orders—but seldom received them.

The sound of our ship's bell (followed instantly by the bosun's pipe that summoned the morning watch) was enough to break my thralldom to that piercing glance. It was time to waken Greene, to snatch what rest I could before my interview with Sir Luke Metcalf. Certainly this was no moment to yield to pique. Did it matter that the first woman I had glimpsed after six weeks at sea suggested—however briefly— that she was the stronger of the two?

Opening the door to our afterhouse, following the corridor that led to the captain's cabin, I was aware of a great, brazen clangor that filled the whole seaway outside. When I knocked at Greene's door, I realized it was the ship's gong aboard the *Star of Bengal,* speaking a language a whole world removed from my native tongue.

Captain Jeremy Greene, already completing his morning ablutions, acknowledged my knock with a snort of welcome. Rinsing his jaws and blinking at his image in a shaving mirror, he could have been a drowsy monkey, beginning to go heavy in the legs. The fact that the captain wore only small clothes completed the image—which was, of course, but skin-deep. Despite those bulging thighs and a tufted chest that resembled a sprung mattress, the master of the *Resolute* was the flower of his species—a superb mariner with a mind that pierced most frauds. We had approved of one another from my first day aboard.

"Ready to go in with a breeze, sir," I said. "I've left your first officer in charge. Will you take over?"

"Consider yourself relieved, Mr. Douglas," said Greene. "And, while you're about it, log yourself out. It will be your last act aboard."

"I trust I've given satisfaction, Captain."

Laughter rumbled in the mariner's massive chest. "My report is signed and sealed: it goes to Metcalf the moment we dock. If you'd composed it yourself, it could hardly be better."

I moved on toward the chartroom, cheered by that brief exchange. At Glasgow, I had boarded the *Resolute* as a passenger—but it was no accident that I was soon asked to handle the ship in all kinds of weather, with Jeremy Greene as a critical observer. This (as we both knew) was an essential part of my testing for the task Sir Luke Metcalf had in mind—even though that task had not yet been announced in detail.

A veteran of the sea lanes despite my youth, I had met my testing head on. At first I had served as Greene's mate, while the real first officer snored in grateful slumber below. . . . Later I had taken a whole watch, while the skipper himself sat drinking in his afterhouse with Dr. Thomas Hoyt, our only other passenger. These duties had included heavy gales off the Banks, and a hard fight to make westing outside the Nantucket shoals. It was good to know that Sir Luke would have no cause to fault my seamanship.

The log lay open in the chartroom. When I had made my final entry I signed and sanded it. For the last time, I shook off a conviction that I stood between two paths, with a foot in each and my heart in neither. . . . While that cloud rested on my spirit, it was no less dismal than the mist that still boiled outside the ports:

> *June 23, 1701: Windless night.*
>   *Rode at anchor outside New York Harbor, just below a channel (the Narrows) leading to the Upper Bay.*
>   *At sunset a former Indiaman, the* Star of Bengal, *dropped anchor to starboard.*
>   *Posted lookouts and stood watch until dawn. At sunup, resigned deck to Captain, who relieves me of further responsibility for the crossing.*

When that log was filed in London (among the endless ledgers of the East India Company) my entry would make an odd footnote to our voyage. I wondered what the historian would make of it. My doubts dissolved in a wave of drowsiness; fumbling my way to the cabin I shared with Dr. Hoyt, I fell into a sleep without dreams.

Hours later, wakening with the knowledge of time and place all seamen possess, I saw it was well past noon. There was no hint of sun, and the dank heat was still unstirred by the faintest zephyr, but the fog had lifted. Across the cabin Tom Hoyt was seated tailor-fashion in his bunk, nursing a jug of Jamaica. At first sight he seemed to be lifeless as a Chinese idol. Experience told me that the brain behind those half-closed eyes was wide awake.

"You've just enjoyed the sleep of the just," said my friend the doctor. "Only the sleep of the drunkard is sounder. Unlike myself, I'll wager you've wakened with a clearer head."

Dr. Hoyt and I had been friends before he joined the ship at Liverpool: the fact he was also en route to New York to take orders from Sir Luke Metcalf was an added bond. Today, studying my cabin mate with candid eyes, I admitted that I could have chosen my friends more carefully. At thirty Tom Hoyt was already a tosspot gone to seed—destined for debtors' prison, the block, or a drunkard's grave. Yet I found it impossible to dislike him. There was real courage under his moldy exterior, a gallantry that a peer of the realm might have envied.

In his way Tom Hoyt was a link between my own somewhat reckless past and a much more austere future. When he proffered the jug, I drank down an ounce of the fiery rum without demur. (Eye-openers are traditional on all Company ships: I could hardly refuse one now.)

"Were you dreaming of your Jeanie, Dick?" asked Tom. "She of the light brown hair and uncontested virtue?"

"Her name is Anne—not Jeanie."

"True. Anne Sinclair, of the Aberdeen Sinclairs. There's no more proper name in all Scotland. It's still beyond me how you got past her father's door. Let alone the promise of her hand in marriage."

I moved to the porthole without attempting to parry his thrust. I had told Tom Hoyt no more of my engagement to Anne than seemed needful. I had not said that it was more promise than betrothal. Anne's father, a blue-nose bigot, had laid down two ironclad conditions to our union. First, I must quit the sea and continue my studies in Admiralty law. Second (and this was really vital), I must bring a thousand English pounds to the altar, and not a farthing less.

It was because of old Sinclair that I was now prepared to cast dice one more time with fortune. . . . Watching the

green shore line that opened beyond our porthole, I wondered if my reason for accepting Sir Luke's offer was so
simple. Was I about to risk my life in far places for Anne's
sake alone? Or was this voyage to Madagascar but a flimsy
excuse to embrace a life I still hankered after, despite my
best resolves?

"The meadow to larboard belongs to Staten Island," said
Tom. "Look to starboard as the bow swings, and you'll see a
land mass the natives call Long Island. The town of Manhattan's dead ahead—the finest plum England ever stole from
a Dutchman. Shall we go on deck and suggest that Greene
put us ashore by longboat? I'm eager to match wits with
Metcalf."

"You don't match wits with Sir Luke," I said. "Either you
take his orders or you cut him down. So far, no man alive
has bested him with dirk or cutlass—far less with brains."

"How well d'you know this martinet, Dick?"

"I've yet to meet him—and I'm forming no advance judg-
ments."

"You've said he was a tryrant—and a master duelist."

"*That's* common knowledge."

"Any notion why he sent for us?"

"I can guess. So can you, Tom."

Our orders from London were to the point. We were to
sail from this port on the *Pilgrim Venture,* an armed merchantman outfitting in a Jersey shipyard. The *Venture* was
booked to call at the Cape, at Fort Dauphin on Madagascar
—and, finally, at both Goa and Madras. There had been no
hint of the part we would play in that voyage. Sir Luke
would give us the details in New York.

"Why are you risking your neck?" asked Tom.

"Why are you?"

"It's a scurvy trick, answering a question with another,"
said my doctor friend. "A Scot has no right to use it. However, I'll try answering for us both. *I'm* here because London
is too hot to hold me: I'd prefer sudden death off Africa to a
slow extinction in jail. *You're* here to make yourself a man of
property—assuming, of course, that fortune heeds lovers'
prayers and sends you home alive. What fee did they promise
you if our mission's a success?"

"A thousand pounds, Tom. I've told you often enough."

"I'm worth but five hundred," said Hoyt. "But then I

can't nurse a ship through a typhoon, or talk back to a Trucial corsair in his own tongue." He lifted the jug and toasted me gravely: "To you, Dick Douglas—and your Aberdeen lady. Let's pray you return to Scotland with enough hard cash to prove you're a laird, for all your salty ways." He put down the demijohn: we had both heard the screech of capstan bars. Greene, who could smell a breeze in the making, was about to end his voyage.

"On deck, lad," said my cabin mate. "And the devil take the future. A first view of Front Street is worth waiting for."

When we emerged from the afterhouse, I observed that a rain squall was building rapidly to the east. Its breath had already sent whitecaps dancing in the Lower Bay. The Indiaman (still far too close to our bow) had lifted her anchors and was easing into a tack as her brown-skinned sailors swarmed to man the braces. Greene, his own yards braced, had just begun to come about. Mounted on his starboard rail, a speaking trumpet at his lips, he was barking a warning at the *Star of Bengal*. Before I could reach his side, I felt the wind freshen. In that flash the sky turned to ink and a curtain of rain descended on the bay. The captain's oaths were whipped into space in the keening of the squall. The Indiaman, taking full advantage of the first puff of air, was bearing down on us like a waterborne juggernaut.

"Does she mean to ram us, Dick?"

Mounting the ratline, I only half heard Tom's shout. There was still no sign of an officer on the poop—though the helmsman was taking orders from some source. For an instant (so furious was the pounding of the rain) I could barely see; when the white curtain lifted, I was positive a collision was imminent.

Greene, still bellowing above me, had thrust a foot into space, as though he could fend off the juggernaut single-handed. Obviously, with his own canvas taut, he had no time to change course.

"Hell and molasses, Indiaman! Put up your helm!"

A babble of jeers from the *Star of Bengal's* rigging was his only answer. The rain stung my cheeks while I leaned far out to join my bellow to the captain's. . . . Then, stopped in mid-flight as though by a sorcerer's wand, the *Resolute* lost her weigh. Her canvas collapsed impotently as the

Indiaman ran abreast, taking our wind in her fat-bellied sails. For so ponderous an argosy she handled well. Long before she could level her course with ours, I saw that her unseen skipper had courted this risk deliberately. The maneuver, after all, was only an expert flourish of seamanship—and a gamble that the squall would hold.

For an instant the two ships measured each other's length. Then the *Star of Bengal* cut smoothly across our bows—and the girl rose from the shadow of the larboard rail. Thanks to my perch in the ratlines, her eyes were level with mine.

Her hair was still unbound, beneath a pea jacket that she had tented to protect her from the downpour. Because of that double shadow I had but a fugitive glimpse of her face— but it was enough to stab my heart with wonder. Her skin was only a little less dark than a Malay's, her eyes as jet-black as her hair. Yet even then I saw this was no foreign houri—and that, for all her brazen airs, she could be no more than twenty.

Her shouted taunt, in Portuguese, was meant for me alone. "Way for a sailor, senhor!"

She was gone with the shout. The *Star of Bengal* with every inch of canvas straining, had already set an easy course down the Narrows.

CHAPTER 2

Duel in an Alley

"TAKE an even strain on your cables, Mr. Douglas," said Captain Greene. "She's warped into McLane's wharf—and she won't fly away. We'll know her name before the sun is down —and why she's here."

Our skipper had been more amused than angered by the theft of our wind, now the danger of collision was past. Following the Indiaman down the Narrows, he had dismissed my speculations (and my curses) with a philosopher's shrug. The girl, he said, had had every right to laugh at us: in her place he would have hooted as lustily when our bows just missed scraping. The *Star of Bengal,* in his view, had had a harmless joke at our expense. In the end there had been ample searoom for both vessels and no damage done. . . . Now, bowling down the Upper Bay with the rain squall lifting, he dismissed our brush with disaster as he pointed out each new landmark.

"Look well at New York," he said. "A city on an island, thrust like a fat finger into the finest harbor in the colonies. Give Manhattan another century: we'll make it the rival of London."

I will confess I but half heard this prediction: my eyes were fastened on the *Star of Bengal,* swinging easily with the tide while her mooring line snaked home in the slip ahead. My mind was still whirling with half-formed resentments. I could not escape the conviction that I—and I alone—had inspired the dark-eyed charmer's mirth.

"Who can she be?" The words had escaped without my wish: I felt myself blush as I uttered them.

"The ship—or the lady?" asked Greene. "The former is unloading at McLane's—so that rogue will have answers to both. There's little on earth or sea that Bob McLane can't explain, with chapter and verse."

"Amen to that," said Tom Hoyt. Raising his jug, he drained it and tossed it overside. He had not troubled to study the scene taking shape under our bows: Tom had visited this compact, steepled town when it had scarce forgot it was once Dutch New Amsterdam. He could afford to turn his eyes from a waterfront I had heard described as a latterday Gomorrah. Viewed with a westering sun behind it, Front Street seemed worthy of the name.

The mooring that awaited us (it was more slip than dock) lay on a flank of Manhattan Island, cheek by jowl with McLane's own warehouse empire. This was a side of the island washed by a tidal estuary known as the East River—and its Front Street was famous to sailors the world over. Bowsprits and martingales of a hundred ships loomed like monstrous insect antennae above it. Its brick store fronts, at first glance, seemed an endless tavern, echoing with song and shaken (at frequent intervals) by explosions of blows and cursing.

Here and there befuddled mariners had come to rest in the gutter, careless of the thundering drays that fought for space on the cobbles. Other roisterers weaved drunkenly among the wheels. I saw lascars, black-browed Spaniards with earrings and flaring sideburns, tattooed, near-naked savages from Oceania, tar-headed sailormen who could only be British, even without their varnished boots and flaring pantaloons. Here and there, local merchants walked proudly, resplendent in broadcloth and flowered waistcoats, always with a Negro slave or footman in attendance.

By daylight the scene was more ribald than dangerous. Even the drabs who hunted at the edge of the crowd (flaunting uncorseted hips and rolling kohl-dark eyes) were part of its gaiety. It would be a different story when darkness fell and knives were out. . . .

I counted some twenty sloops and ketches at the wharves, all of them discharging tobacco from Virginia or the Carolinas. There were pinks laden with molasses and crude sugar from Barbados, or kegs of rum. There were coasters redolent of naval stores from Southern backlands, and galiots from Curaçao with dyestuffs and salt. Fat barges from the Massachusetts Colony unloading bricks and lumber. On the Long Island shore there were still other barges, white with fresh-milled flour from towns upriver. No man in his senses would call such commerce dishonest. As Greene had said, it insured a noble promise for New York's future. Yet even a newcomer like myself needed no second sight to look deeper.

McLane's shuttered warehouses—and their counterparts at other landing slips—were the true reason for Manhattan's aura of gold. Some years ago that king of buccaneers, Sir Henry Morgan, had turned respectable with his title and had driven his former companions from the West Indies. Today these same gentlemen of fortune hunted in the Orient rather than the Caribbean. Man's eternal lust for plunder had merely found a wider hunting ground—and the plunder had grown infinitely more varied.

Regardless of the source, middlemen like Bob McLane would always take their profits—even as they continued to play both sides in the endless, ravenous war between the East India Company and the pirates who now worked from the Gold Coast of West Africa to the bayous of Mozambique and Madagascar. It was no accident that I had been asked to report first at McLane's own warehouse office. This same factor was outfitting the *Pilgrim Venture* for her impending voyage to India. McLane would also sign her crew and guarantee her safe passage. As the New World factotum for the Company, Sir Luke Metcalf had been wise enough to make his peace with the devil. This much was common gossip in both London and Glasgow. With the Atlantic between, I had shrugged off that implication of surrender. This afternoon, watching the *Resolute* ease into her berth, it seemed an insult too galling to accept tamely.

It was a worse affront to my own pride when I reflected that one could be both a Scot and a scoundrel if the price was right. . . . I came out of my musings when Tom Hoyt glared down at Front Street—and shook a fist at Bob McLane's roof tree, where an English standard whipped bravely in the breeze.

"Should he fly the black flag?" I asked. "Is that what you're thinking?"

Tom shrugged off the query. "Don't let a Calvinist viewpoint feaze you," he said. "Sir Luke's a canny hunter, I'm told. Certainly he's learned to run with the wolves."

"What does that mean?"

"Just this, my young innocent. Metcalf's paid a fortune in bribes to McLane—but I doubt he's been sold short weight so far. And Greene is quite right. Ask that damned factor what you like about the *Star of Bengal*—and the lady passenger who's charmed your eyes from their sockets. You'll get a reasonable answer."

I glanced amidships, happy to observe that our sharp-tongued skipper had gone forward to give orders to the wharfingers who had begun to swarm aboard. "A reasonable answer, Tom—or a true one?"

"Truth's a big word, lad. But I'll warrant that whatever he tells you will provide food for thought."

"Do you suppose that girl owns the Indiaman?"

"Since when have women owned property, Dick?"

"She ordered the helmsman to blanket our sails today. I'd take oath on that."

"Women rule us in many ways," said my doctor friend. "They've yet to give orders from a poop deck."

"Why was the deck empty then? Why did she hide below the rail—and laugh at us when she took our wind?"

"Ask her yourself," said Tom. "She's near enough to hail."

I looked down again at Front Street: prepared though I was, I felt that same odd stab of pain at my heart when I saw her—a *malaise* sharper than hunger and deeper than mere desire. The girl, and a three-man retinue, had just emerged from the shadow of the moored Indiaman and turned into the cobbles with regal unconcern. She was in black silk now, with a great, belled skirt and elbow-length gloves of mesh. A tip-tilted parasol shaded her proud profile without concealing it. I saw at once that she was utterly at home in that motley crowd. Indeed, the look she bestowed upon New York could not have been more natural had she been a native.

Now that she was in full view, her dark skin proved only that she had been exposed long (and carelessly) to the sun since her childhood. Like her radiant strength, it seemed part of her. If it had shocked me at first, it was only by contrast to the milk-white pelts of the town women—who looked daggers as she passed among them. . . . This, I knew, was no Malay princess, but a woman of my own race—albeit with a dash of foreign blood. A woman, in short, who had met the challenge of the tropics without fear and taken its savage hues as her own. I could only wonder if that brown tint ended at her arms and throat. It was easy to strip her mentally, to picture her sporting naked in the sun. . . .

I put the wanton image aside as she passed beneath our gangway. With no orders from my brain, I felt my body incline in a formal bow. It was a tribute to her beauty, nothing more: if she noticed, she did not raise her eyes. Burning as I was to address her, I did not speak. It seemed a poor moment to challenge the strange trio that shepherded her.

First came a huge, broad-shouldered Negro, black as the pit and handsome as a limb of Satan. He held a cudgel in one fist, a needless precaution, since the crowd parted to let him pass, much as the sea divides beneath a ship's prow. Burdened as he was with the lady's bandboxes, I could barely glimpse his face—but I recognized him as the helmsman of the *Star of Bengal*.

On the girl's right a jackal in sailor's garb fended off all comers with his sullen glare and a fist half closed on his cutlass. On her left a dwarf stumped on foreshortened legs—and, like the others, his outthrust jaw and beetle-browed scowl gave warning to all and sundry to stay clear. He, too, was armed with a sword, its scabbard slung at his shoulder blades. Grotesque though he was, he did not invite laughter: in sober truth, he seemed the most formidable of the three.

I have needed space to order my impressions. Actually, the group had quitted the waterfront in seconds, to follow a side street that led toward the center of New York.

"What d'you make of her, Dick?" Tom Hoyt asked. "An Indian ranee? Or the daughter of some Fiji king?"

"She's English. I'm sure of that much."

"*All* English—or part?"

"Does that matter?"

"Don't claim kinship too hastily," said Tom. "As you've observed, she's well guarded."

"Where would she be bound?"

"Judging by those bandboxes, to Mr. Pettingill's Inn, on Culpepper Lane. It's the finest ordinary in Manhattan—and our fair traveler is obviously accustomed to the best. Shall I book our own beds there?"

"By all means," I said. "And pay the asking price. I'll join you later."

My foot was on the gangway, making my first contact with the New World. Tom followed, at a more leisurely pace—still wearing his familiar, crooked grin.

"And where are *you* bound at present, Dick?"

"To McLane's emporium. It's still daylight—I may find Sir Luke there."

"If Metcalf were about," said Tom, "he'd have boarded us long ago. Let him seek us out tomorrow. Morning's time enough to begin taking orders."

"You've spoken my own mind there," I said. "Sir Luke's a mystery that can wait awhile. But I'm going to learn the lady's name within the hour. If possible, I'll even discover why she laughed at me."

"As you will," said Hoyt. "Meanwhile I'll make my own inquiries at the Inn. Just remember to walk warily at Mc-Lane's. And try to be at Mrs. Pettingill's early. Front Street is no place to stroll alone after sunset."

My experience with rogues of every stripe is an extensive one, and I have learned one fact early: your born scoundrel (regardless of the language he speaks) rarely looks the part. I had pictured Bob McLane as a dusty spider lording it in his cave. The actual roly-poly who greeted me might have stepped bodily from one of those constellations of cherubs that grace the ceilings of Italian palazzos. Nothing could have been less Scottish than his lisping greeting, the glass of nut-brown Madeira he poured me—and his eagerness to answer every question.

The lady who had just crossed Front Street, it seemed, had no secrets whatever. Her name was Senhorita Bonita Damao (McLane rolled the Portuguese on his tongue like wine). She was the daughter of a rich entrepreneur in Goa, and had just completed her education in the town of Boston. (For two whole years she had been tutored there in English, history, and the elements of mathematics: Senhor Damao had advanced ideas on the place of women in this brand-new century.) Now she was ready to go back to her father's establishment on the coast of India. She was taking the first available transport—in this case, the *Pilgrim Venture*.

McLane—rocking in the chair that was the focal point of his wide-windowed office, smiling down on the bustle of the waterfront—took my surprise in stride:

"The Company books lady passengers on its ships when they're vouched for," he said. "Sir Luke has no objections to giving Senhorita Damao passage, Mr. Douglas. Do you?"

"On the contrary," I said. "But why can't she return on the *Star of Bengal?*"

The Indiaman, said McLane, had been on a long cruise. She had brought house slaves to Havana, raw silk to Charleston Harbor, and a thousand casks of rum to New Bedford. The girl had boarded her at that port, having journeyed down from Boston. Tomorrow (when the last of the cargo had come ashore) the *Star of Bengal* would go to Jersey for careening, before returning to her home port of Lisbon. The brand-new *Pilgrim Venture* was said to be the East India Company's fastest ship. Since she was ready for sea—and since he was eager to see his daughter again, after her long absence—the merchant of Goa had arranged for Senhorita Damao's passage, via his New York agent.

"Were I your age, young man," said McLane, "I'd look

forward to such charming company on a four-month voyage. Or d'you feel it's bad luck to sail with a woman aboard?"

"Far from it, sir." Without quite knowing the reason, I was fighting disappointment: the exotic image of Bonita Damao that still lingered in my memory did not square with this matter-of-fact recital. If I pushed my inquiry a bit further, it was only to prove I had not been daydreaming in the Lower Bay.

"Why was there no captain on the poop deck of the *Star of Bengal?*"

McLane drew down his lips in a pious grimace of regret. "Her captain died at sea, Mr. Douglas—just after she cleared from Charleston. A man named Salazar—an able master. His first officer, Matthew Quill, was in command today. You were at close quarters at the time; he was probably giving orders from the shrouds."

The words put down my last faint spark of doubt. The shrouds *had* been alive with seamen while the *Star of Bengal* crowded on canvas: I could easily have lost sight of a first officer in that bustle. Nor was I surprised when McLane identified the fellow as one of the lady's three bodyguards (Quill, it seemed, was the hyenaman with a fist on his cutlass). The Negro was called Mozo, a freedman who had won steady promotion aboard the Indiaman. The dwarf—Majunga by name, a man of mixed bloods—had been Senhorita Damao's bodyguard since her childhood. During her stay in Boston he had slept across her doorsill. He would do so tonight at Mrs. Pettingill's, regardless of local taboos.

"A word of caution, Mr. Douglas," said McLane. "Make no sudden move when Majunga's nearby. It's wiser not even to address the lady until she speaks first. He's lightning-swift with a knife—and other weapons."

"Does he return with her to Goa?"

"Of course. I've already signed him as a supercargo aboard the *Venture*. Quill and Mozo will sign on too, as soon as I've cleared their papers here. Subject to Sir Luke's approval of course—and your own."

"Why should the crew list concern me?"

The factor smiled at me again, over steepled fingers. "Do I speak too hastily? I'm not privy to your orders—"

"So far, I have none."

"Surely you know you're to be master aboard the *Venture?*"

"I'm here with Dr. Thomas Hoyt to execute a secret mission," I said, swallowing my pleasure without too much effort. I was beginning to understand why I had spelled Greene so often in his own deck duties. "Naturally, I'm prepared to follow Sir Luke's wishes."

McLane was fingering a dossier he had just produced from his desk. "I have you down as captain here," he said. "Dr. Hoyt is listed as ship's surgeon. Aside from that, I can tell you little. Sir Luke keeps his counsel—even from me."

"May I see him before morning?"

"At the moment, he rests on a farm he owns in Harlem—a village to the north of us. I'll loan you a trap if you wish to call there."

"My friend is ordering rooms in town," I said. "Unless we're to sail with the tide, I see no reason for a journey to the backlands."

"Nor do I," said the factor. "Go on to Mrs. Pettingill's, by all means. With luck, you may join Senhorita Damao at table. Your landlady serves meals at all hours, since she caters to seafarers."

I knew I had succumbed to my propensity for blushing, and was grateful that the shadows of evening were invading the office windows. Tom Hoyt had warned me to reach Culpepper Lane before darkness fell—but I told myself I could fight off most comers, even though I had come ashore without side arms. Besides, I was reluctant to leave until I had learned more of this pink-faced cherub.

"May I see your wares before I go?" I asked. "You realize of course, that your fame has long since reached Scotland?"

"I'm proud of my reputation there," said McLane. "Follow me, Mr. Douglas. The light's a bit dim, but I'll show you what I can."

For the next half hour we roamed the storerooms of his vast establishment, where he proved the most knowledgeable of guides. Yet, try as I might, I could not pierce his armor as he displayed the prodigal abundance of his wares—most of which were already ticketed as sold, and waiting only to be transported to their buyers.

First, we visited rooms reserved for the silk trade alone, each of them heaped high with bolts of that precious stuff.

Next, we inspected arsenals of muskets and *pistolas* (McLane had outfitted wars in the Low Countries and in Spain, to say nothing of our own colonial disputes with our French enemies to the north). A whole floor was given over to displays of ladies' gowns and gewgaws (most of these, I gathered, had been bought at bargain rates from salvage sales) and to bolts of broadcloth, satins, and cloth of gold that would have made a London tailor's mouth water.

"You say these goods are from wrecked ships," I ventured. "Why are they undamaged?"

"My agents buy only the pick of the salvage, Mr. Douglas."

"How can you be sure these things weren't pirated?"

The factor's smile was bland as Devon cream. "I *can't* be sure—in every case. Still, if the bill of sale is stamped and in order, the seller's record is clean. That's all I'm concerned about."

"Which means you're willing to buy from privateers—not from outright pirates?"

"Privateer is a word that covers many sins," said McLane. "Naturally, in the unsettled state of world trade, cargoes may change hands often before they reach the market. Or—to put the matter in other terms—goods can be resold indefinitely, if the spirit of our Admiralty law is observed."

What the rogue said was quite true. England, fighting for her life as an island nation, had always taken a long view on privateers. It was common practice to attack merchant vessels of other countries (if those countries were belligerents) and to seize their cargoes outright: naturally, the practice was flagrantly abused in waters beyond the control of the so-called civilized powers. Most of the loot on display here, I was positive, had been pirated outright and resold under forged bills of lading . . . McLane was a past master at the light-fingered art of financing the gentlemen of fortune who kept his counters filled.

"Come into the next storeroom, Mr. Douglas," he said. "If you left a sweetheart in Glasgow, you'll find some bauble there to strike her fancy."

This was the finale of my tour—a high-ceiled chamber where ship's figureheads loomed like monstrous ghosts of battle on every wall. Here were gilded mermaids and Neptune's Tritons and dolphins and sea horses, high-breasted goddesses from antiquity, side by side with the owlish replicas of pious shipowners. These (I was sure) came from still other captured prizes, and now awaited resale to the frugal shipwrights of New England. Actually, the figureheads were but a flamboyant decoration to enhance the displays that were the factor's especial pride. (Later I would learn that the locked cupboards in each wall contained his account books, and the jewels and gold he was forced to market secretly, despite the present laxity of the New York governor.)

He showed me rugs from Anatolia and hammered silver from Byzantium, tables carved from teakwood, vases exotic with Oriental imagery, portieres from Baghdad, fans of ivory and sandalwood, shawls of peacock hues and crepe embroidered with pearls. In the end (numbed by this surfeit of contraband riches) I purchased a mandarin robe for Anne, a wondrous thing stiff with embroidered birds and a high golden collar. It was far too dear for my purse—yet I think he overcharged me but little. Knowing he was hand in glove with Sir Luke, it seemed a fair augury for my future.

As I gave my instructions for the robe's shipment to Glasgow, I could not but wonder if it would suit Anne's stern good looks—to say nothing of her father's belief that ostentation in dress is an invention of the devil. Still, the purchase served its purpose, in that it laid my conscience to rest. I was all too aware that my wanton thoughts had roamed far afield today. . . .

"Will you look further, Mr. Douglas? Or may I shut up shop?"

I glanced about me. Engrossed in my cataloguing of McLane's booty, I had not realized his staff had withdrawn.

"Do you lock up yourself, sir?"

"Always. It's a chore I'll trust to no one else."

I followed him in silence while he tested the bars on each window and made sure his iron shutters were bolted on the inside. This done, he escorted me through a kind of postern gate that gave to an alley bordering the harbor. This exit was closed with a special key, then double-locked with a hasp that protected the original keyhole. The factor executed these final moves with something like haste, and his good-by bow was stiffly formal.

"You'll excuse me if I hurry, Mr. Douglas? I've a meeting at the Governor's house—and it can't wait."

"Go by all means," I said. "I can find my way to Culpepper Lane."

"So you can," he said—and moved with almost comic haste toward the alley's mouth, where a rig and coachman were waiting. He was gone on the instant, with a great rattling of ironshod wheels on cobbles.

At the time, I saw nothing odd in the fact I had been deserted in this noisome cul-de-sac, with no exit but an archway that gave to the loading platform of the warehouse proper. At this late hour there was no stir of life among the boxes and bales that had been unloaded from the *Star of Bengal*. In a sense, I will confess I welcomed the solitude. I needed a chance to ponder—and McLane's glib air of frankness had raised more questions than it had answered.

Curiously enough, I felt no urge to hasten to Mrs. Pettingill's boarding establishment for another meeting with the girl who had stirred my fancies so profoundly. Sunset still lingered above the rooftops, reflected but faintly on the current-roiled surface of the harbor. While I weighed the problems that obscured my future I sat on a bollard and watched the powerful tug of that tide—in a river that was no river at all, but an arm of the ever restless sea.

In a few more days (if I could believe McLane) I would be spreading sail on that river as master of the *Pilgrim Venture*. Steeped as I was in melancholy, I could not even rejoice that the lovely Senhorita Damao was to be my shipmate. It was easier to surrender to the homesickness that always invaded my spirit in strange places—to dream I was already safely back in Glasgow, with a thousand English pounds in my wallet and Anne Sinclair my betrothed in fact as well as fancy.

After striking a spark from my tinderbox and smoking a pipe of Virginia shag, I managed to shake off my gloom. Evening had closed in on the alley while I sat there, but there was light enough to guide me among the bales to Front Street. Only when I moved into the deeper shadow of the arch was I conscious that I had outstayed my welcome. There was no mistaking the intent of the two figures who closed in to bar my further progress. Even without their truncheons I could guess they were footpads, with but one end in view.

"May I pass, gentlemen?" I said—if only to test their motives.

"Not without your purse," said one of them.

"And a bit of your hide, if you show fight," said the other.

My hand dropped to my sword before I recalled I was unarmed. The larger of the bullies was already tapping his persuader against his palm. Pretending to shrink back in terror, I focused my gaze on the truncheon—knowing full well he meant to distract me thus. From the corner of an eye I saw the second footpad rise on tiptoe and move to my left. Clearly he intended to strike from the rear while his companion held my attention riveted.

It was an ancient dodge, and I was ready before the trap closed. When my second enemy charged me from behind, I dropped to one knee to receive the rush. The man's club was raised to strike when I swiveled beneath it—tripping him neatly and catching him by the heels in the same lunge. Using his body as a club, I beat back the rush of the larger bully, who was now moving in to administer the deathblow his confederate had failed to deliver. The victim's head, colliding with my new assailant's midriff at the top of the swing, doubled him like a jackknife, with his wind spilled.

Before either could recover I was on my knees again—smashing a fist downward at the base of the smaller man's skull with enough force to stun him. Then, prying the blackjack from his fingers, I cracked the second bravo across the pate—hard enough to render him *hors de combat* without breaking bone. A blow above the ear of the other footpad finished what my fist had begun. Five seconds after joining battle I found myself in possession of the field—and got to my feet to make sure the rascals were otherwise unarmed. Then I turned again to the shadowed arch, to search out other assailants. I had not long to wait.

The enemy who now stood between me and safety was tall and wiry, with fanatic's eyes in a dead-white face and nervous hands. His close-cropped poll suggested that he was a man of quality minus his wig, though his clothes and boots seemed rough. Under his arm he carried a pair of naked cutlasses. Without a word, he flung one of the blades at me —then stood *en garde,* rising a bit on his toes, like a tiger about to spring.

"Defend yourself, sir," he said. "You'll get a fair fight."

It was the voice of a gentleman, and the order was given in the most courteous of tones. Yet this new threat chilled me far more than the crude attack of the footpads.

"D'you want my purse too?" I asked.

"Prove you can handle a cutlass," he said, "or you'll never learn." He charged me with that ultimatum, aiming a great, swinging blow that would have split head from body had it landed fairly. The ring of steel, when I lifted my blade to save my life, set the echoes flying in that confined space; a score of gulls, leaving their perches on the warehouse roof, circled wildly above us before spurting into the blue.

Not that I had much time to observe such details as our duel proceeded. Bewildered as I was, I could see no reason for his fury: I knew only that I would need all my strength and skill to hold him off. Now and again I shouted at him to desist—or, at least, to explain himself. But such demands seemed only to goad him on. Convinced that I was fighting a madman, I saved my breath thereafter.

He charged me from both sides (for a time, as though to prove his dexterity, he shifted his cutlass to his left hand). His repertoire of strokes could only be described as breathtaking. I am a master swordsman myself, with an iron wrist and nerves to match: I have fought my share of bravos afloat and ashore, but I will testify I have never met his match. When I forced the attack (as I felt I must), he took each of my blows in stride—only to leap aside as he wearied of the easy defense and renewed his own assault. . . . Indeed, as the fray proceeded (though I remained unwounded, as yet), I had the nightmarish conviction this was no mere alley brawl, but a classic exercise in some *salle d'armes*, with death the only prize.

Why, if he was chief of the two footpads, had he given me this chance to defend myself? Why had he half promised I could go free if I bested him? The questions gnawed at me with each clash of the blades—though I had but small hope of emerging from the fray alive. Already it seemed clear he had tossed me a cutlass as a kind of fiendish joke—and would dispatch me at will, when I had exhausted the stock of tricks that held him off.

Once I managed to break free of his slashing attack for a few seconds and worked toward the pier's end: with a running dive and the tide behind me, I might have escaped him

entirely. But he guessed my purpose—and, charging reck-
lessly across a stack of boxes, leaped down to the stringpiece and barred my path. In the shadowed archway the two
bullies had regained their wits and were squatting on their
haunches to watch the duel—which we now resumed with
redoubled fury. For a time I thought they would rush me,
ending matters in a three-to-one melee—but was not surprised
when they stayed clear, with no orders from my adversary.
It was all too evident he meant to finish the fight in his own
way.

Risking all in one effort, I charged him with a slashing
attack that risked my life a dozen times before I forced him
to give ground. For a few moments, at least, the initiative
was mine—and I saw his eyes change as he shifted (nimbly
but desperately) to protect his own head from a rain of
blows. Once, when he feinted a slip of the foot, I thought
I saw an opening and pressed on for the kill—only to be
forced to duck beneath a roundhouse swing of his blade as
he leaped aside and aimed for my neck. (I had seen that
ruse succeed too often: the counterblow, delivered with both
hands on a cutlass hilt, can split a man's neck as neatly as a
butcher's pole-ax.)

The bravos had cheered their master's stratagem. To my
astonishment, they applauded me no less lustily when I returned to the fray. Once again we traded ringing blows in
the alley mouth—but I felt that he was only playing with me,
now I had shot my bolt. If I continued to court death in the
moments that followed, it was only to force his final attack—
in the hope I could come to grips with him and inflict some
damage before he cut me down.

The duel ended as abruptly as it had begun. I had lifted
my arm for another parry: this time (as his steel rasped down
the length of mine) I felt our guard hooks lock. In another
second the weapon was wrested from my grasp.

I stood with both arms at my sides, watching helplessly
while it sailed through the air in a great, shining arc. One
of the bullies caught the blade before it fell to the cobbles—
and I wondered if he or his master would murder me. My
wonder deepened when my opponent tossed his cutlass to
the second footpad and stood regarding me with a fist on
either hip. When he smiled, his long, thin face seemed more
cruel than ever. Nor did my fears diminish when the grin

changed to a roar of mirth—and he approached me with his hand held out.

"Well fought, lad," he said.

I dashed the hand aside and doubled both my fists— ready, even in my exhaustion, to defend myself as best I could. The gesture only increased his mirth.

"Put down your fists," he said. "I'm a poor hand at *that* kind of brawling. Besides, you've proved you can use 'em."

"Does that mean I go free?" I demanded.

"If you like. I still hope you'll shake hands with me, now you've passed muster."

"Stand aside if you're a man of your word," I said. "I've had enough of this."

"Suit yourself," he said. "But it's taken me quite a while to find you—and I'm convinced you're just the fellow I need."

For another instant (as he continued to bar my path) I toyed with the urge to smash a fist into that grin. But it was all too clear that I owed my life to this lunatic's forbearance. I could hardly risk enraging him.

"What d'you want of me?" I asked.

He held out his hand a second time. "Need you ask, Mr. Douglas, now you've crossed a sea to meet me?"

"In God's name, who are you?"

"Your employer, if you'll still have me. I'm Sir Luke Metcalf."

CHAPTER 3

Sir Luke Metcalf

SIR LUKE'S New York domicile was a fine brick house on Bowling Green—which is a pleasant oval park not too far from the southern tip of Manhattan. (McLane's story of a farm in Harlem, he told me, was a deliberate fiction.)

Once he had led me to his paneled study (and installed me there, with a jug of rum at my elbow to amuse me while he changed), I was hardly startled to find that one of my two attackers in the alley was his wine steward, the other his butler. Both served as his bodyguards, since they were also employees of the Company. As such, they were accustomed to a variety of strange duties: cornering me as I tarried at the warehouse had been but part of the day's work. . . . So much he told me in our short walk from McLane's—so much, and no more.

Sir Luke Metcalf, as I had already gathered, was a man of many parts. He had enjoyed his role of bravo. En route to his mansion it had amused him no less to change to a man of great affairs—who chose, as it were, to talk around those affairs, leaving me in the dark as to his main objective. Now, sipping his excellent rum while I awaited his return from the washhouse, I could still wonder if I was dreaming—though my aching muscles were warrant enough that our fight had been real.

Nor could I doubt, even now, that he would have cut me down without compunction, had I been found wanting. Metcalf had won his post in the East India Company with brute force as well as guile. Now we were met at last, I knew it would be fatal to oppose his will. I could not fight back a second time. Having signed the Company's articles in London, I was already subject to his orders.

Thinking back on his long and not too savory career, I found it but natural he should be in charge here—since he was a master wolf who could howl with any pack, a kingpin in England's endless mercantile intrigues who could fight England's enemies with their own weapons. Small wonder he had been cursed in many tongues as a tyrant without peers. Or called a shameless adventurer by men he had sent to the wall—and worse by the women he had used and discarded.

In a sense, I reflected, our lives had run parallel, to a point.

I had cut down no competitors en route to my first captain's berth. Nor had I seduced more than my share of wenches. Yet, like Metcalf, I was the son of a seafarer—and had taken to salt water as easily as a petrel to its nest. Like him, I had risen in the Company from able seaman to bosun to mate. At that milestone our paths had parted. I had been content with my first master's license, more than willing to finish my law studies between voyages. When Anne Sinclair had entered my orbit, I had vowed to bid the sea and its manifold temptations a long, sad farewell the moment we could marry. Sir Luke had followed stormier courses.

It was he (if I could believe Company gossip) who had fomented the Sultans' War in Arabia—with the result that our sea lanes had been cleared of pirate dhows for years on end, while the corsairs fought ashore. It was he who had smashed his rivals in the Company one by one—until the posts of his choosing were firmly in his grasp. I could not doubt that some of his rivals had died at his orders, if not at his hand. Others had been driven to bankruptcy or suicide. Still others, like the legendary Jonathan Carter, had turned pirate in Madagascar, to fight him to the death.

All in all, he had earned his place in the knightage by means no less forthright than Sir Henry Morgan himself had used. If the choice were mine, I would have demanded a less sinister mentor when I reported for duty in London and asked for the most rewarding (and, by that token, the most dangerous) task on the Company's books. I will confess my spirits had plummeted when I was told to report to Metcalf in New York. Nor can I pretend my fears were at rest, now we had crossed literal swords—despite the show of good humor he had displayed when he bested me.

When he returned, my host was bandbox-clean, in a canary-yellow coat of the finest velvet, with silk stockings and breeches to match, and a short clubbed wig. When he welcomed me to his house a second time, the flourish of his long aristocrat's hand would have graced a king's anteroom. I kept my own mask in place, feigning an urbanity I did not possess. Despite the elegance of the room and the fine furbelows of its owner, I could not escape the conviction that this was the home of a distinguished bird of prey.

"You'll forgive me, I hope, Mr. Douglas," he said, pausing to admire his image in a cheval glass that stood against the wall. "In my calling we must use masquerades to suit our purpose. This is the popinjay garb I wear in society. My costume at McLane's was more comfortable."

I spoke the thought that had been in my mind from the start. "Why didn't you introduce yourself at once? It would have been far simpler."

"Would you have fought so well had you known it was but a fencing match—and not *guerre à outrance?*"

"Forgive my stupidity, Sir Luke," I murmured, "but why so elaborate a ruse in my honor?"

"The men you mistook for footpads meant business. So did I. Had you surrendered your purse without a fight, I'd have had no part of you. Nor would I be offering you a place under my command if you'd fought me a whit less ruggedly. The moment our blades crossed, you knew I'd win. Yet you dueled to the end, with every trick you had, and asked no quarter. I can use that brand of courage, Mr. Douglas." He dropped into a facing armchair and poured himself a tot of rum. "How much did McLane tell you?"

"Only that I'm to command the *Pilgrim Venture* on a voyage to Madras."

"No more than that?"

"He said you'd give me the rest."

"I'm glad he stopped there—the man's tongue has a way of running on. The London office told you our other ports of call?"

"They said we'd victual at the Canaries, then proceed to the Cape."

"Can you handle a ship in the Atlantic trades?"

"Captain Greene thought so," I said modestly.

His hand slapped my knee. "And so do I—now. I've great faith in Jeremy Greene's brains. For a time I considered using him on this voyage. But he hasn't your knowledge of the Monsoon Sea." He paused and studied me narrowly: I knew he was gauging the effect of his compliment. "Fort Dauphin's our first landfall after Cape Town. How well d'you know that roadstead?"

"Well enough—though I've only called there to fill my water casks."

"Finish the voyage for me," he said. "I'll stop you if you err."

"From Madagascar we proceed to Goa, and thence to Madras. There'll be cargo for both ports—"

"Correction, Mr. Douglas. *We* proceed to Madras. At Fort Dauphin you and Dr. Hoyt will jump ship."

"I'm afraid I don't follow, sir."

"You will in a moment. That, I needn't add, is a detail I have not confided to Bob McLane. Nor does he know I'll be aboard the *Venture*—under a disguise, of course." Metcalf paused again, and shot me another of those gimlet glances. "Are you beginning to follow me now?"

"Not too well."

"What d'you know of the Madagascar pirates?"

"Only that they're a thorn in the Company's side."

"You haven't visited the island since they took over?"

"When I last sailed in those waters, they were safe as the North Sea—if you carried enough cannon to frighten off the dhows. I hear things are quite different, now the heirs of Morgan have changed their base."

"You state the case too mildly," said Metcalf. "So far as the Company's concerned, conditions there are intolerable. I'll go further: if these buccaneer nests aren't burned out soon, we'll cease to show a profit."

"You astound me, sir," I said. Actually, I had heard the same story in London—but I was eager for his point of view.

"As you know, our charter was rescinded two years ago, for political reasons. We continue to function in the Orient— simply because there's no other power that can maintain order there, including the British Crown. Eventually, I'm sure, our charter will be renewed by the King—if we can really drive the French from India and keep our sea lanes open. I'm not sure which goal is the more important. Pro tem, I'm leaving the French to future planners. It's my task to smash the Madagascar pirates—simply because I'm familiar with their dodges."

He was on his feet, lifting his fist again and again to drive home a point. Sensing that he was addressing an invisible audience (the Company Board of Governors, perhaps, or a grateful monarch), I did my best to offer the attention he deserved.

"D'you know of the *Speedwell*, Mr. Douglas?" he asked, whirling upon me.

"I was at Clydeside when she was building for the Scotland Company," I told him. "I'm sure I'd remember her hull today."

"She's vanished without a trace on her first trading voyage to the Orient. A year later we sent out one of our own vessels, the *Speedy Return*, to search for her—and she, too, disappeared off Cape Sainte Marie. We've reason to believe that both ships were taken by the outlaws. Possibly they've been rebuilt and used as corsairs."

"What of their crews?"

"Wiped out, to the last man Jack. Gentlemen of fortune take few prisoners."

Again I said nothing: the coldness of his recital discouraged speech. The scandal of the *Speedwell's* disappearance—to say nothing of the rescue vessel—was small change in Company gossip. In sober truth, they were but two among many losses. These days even when our Indiamen sailed under escort they dared not skirt Madagascar en route to the Cape of Good Hope. Instead, they sailed far to the east of the island—a ruinously expensive delay that often meant weeks in the doldrums. Despite the precaution, the convoy captain expected to lose one or more ships to the buccaneers, who were past masters at picking off stragglers in the open sea, often without exchanging a shot with their heavily armed escorts. On the rare occasions when a convoy risked the Madagascar run, the enemy swarmed out en masse with every gunport blazing—and chose his prizes almost at will.

As Sir Luke had said, it was an intolerable situation. Within a space of years it had made the East India Company the butt of scathing criticism, both at home and abroad. Granted, the ancient profession of piracy also flourished on the western coast of Africa, where infidel dhows plied the slave trade and hunted down any unprotected merchantman sailing from the Thames to the Cape. The same was true of the Indian Ocean (which I have called the Monsoon Sea, as is the fashion among seamen). The Grand Mogul owed most of his wealth to his pirate fleet while pretending to be our ally—and the corsairs of Malabar, on the very flank of India, had harassed our vessels for a half century. These, however, were but minor annoyances. Once we had put gun decks on our merchant vessels, they could be driven off, in most cases, with but minor damage.

Madagascar was an enemy stronghold of a different sort. So long as it remained a bastion for outlaws (whose sworn purpose was to bleed the East India Company white) the future of the Company was in jeopardy. The British Crown, harassed by its wars on the Continent, could not muster a force powerful enough to storm that bastion: this was a tour of duty only the Company itself could discharge.

I came back to what Metcalf was telling me with a slight

effort. Determined though I was to be a perfect audience of one, I had let my thoughts wander.

"Our first task," he said, "is to pin down the thief who took the *Speedwell*. Once we've tracked him—as I just remarked—we'll discover the *Speedy Return* in the same anchorage. The recovery of those two vessels will do much to restore our prestige in London."

"You tell me we're to touch at Fort Dauphin," I put in. "Does that mean we're luring the thief into battle?"

"Far from it. When you've taken the *Pilgrim Venture* on her trial run, you'll find there's no finer ship in our service. She's gunned like a man-of-war, though she's listed as a merchantman. She'll show her heels to any corsair afloat—or outfight any who come within range. And she'll sail past Madagascar unmolested, for the best of reasons. The enemy knows she's coming—and he'll hold his fire."

"How can you be sure?"

"It's common knowledge in Cape Town that she's about to make her maiden voyage. Red Carter isn't the sort of buccaneer who fights—when the odds are against him." Metcalf fixed me with another of those piercing glances. "You've heard of Red Carter, of course?"

"Who hasn't, sir? To be frank, I never believed he was human."

"You'll find he's real enough. Twenty years ago I drove him from the Company—after he'd robbed us of a million pounds, as our chief factor in Madras. Since then, as you know, he's turned freebooter and robbed us openly."

Once more I was careful not to interrupt. The story of Jonathan Carter (called Red Carter by every seaman in the Orient, thanks to the beard that was part of his legend) was a classic in the annals of the Company. As the account ran, the discovery of Carter's monstrous embezzlements had been Luke Metcalf's first coup when he was but a minor official in his own right. When Carter had been hounded into exile, Metcalf had assumed his post—and its perquisites. . . . It was said that Carter had fled Madras with only hours to spare, that he had doubled on his tracks to elude the Company bailiffs and vanished into the darkness of Africa.

Over the years (it was here the legend really began) I had heard fearful tales of a flame-bearded pirate king who had set up his domain among the aborigines—first in East

Africa, then in Madagascar. Bit by bit (or so the story went) he had consolidated that domain—and had offered asylum to all seamen who would obey his orders. Later the depredations against Company shipping began in earnest: losses rose sharply when Morgan's former henchmen descended in force on the island. (Some said the two camps had fought for supremacy, with Red Carter the victor. Others insisted that the Morgan men had merely joined Carter *en bloc*, as it were, adding their skills to his own.)

Searching Sir Luke's face as I considered these facts, I found small comfort in his scowl. Yet I forced myself to speak boldly, convinced that now was the time to spread our cards.

"Can you prove Carter still lives?" I demanded.

"That's why you're in my employ," he said. "I'm sending you to Madagascar to find him."

I had always prided myself on my *sang-froid*—but that soft-voiced challenge sent me rolling on my beam ends. Metcalf's wolf grin only chilled me further.

"Don't look so unstrung, Mr. Douglas," he told me. "I've already said that you and Dr. Hoyt will jump ship at Fort Dauphin. Surely you half guessed the reason."

"You've also said I'm to captain the *Pilgrim Venture*. How can a master desert his own vessel?"

"When you desert, you'll no longer be master. Company orders will be waiting at the Cape, putting another captain in charge and reducing you to mate. You'll have the best of reasons for taking your leave." Again the hand fell heavily on my knee. "Pay attention, lad! Your eyes are wavering: don't tell me you're afraid?"

"Just bewildered, sir. Pray go on."

"When we're off Cape Sainte Marie, you and Hoyt will purloin a longboat and go ashore. At Fort Dauphin you'll make discreet inquiries about Carter's whereabouts: I've an agent there who'll help you all he can. If need be, you can hire native guides and scout the coast. Once you've made contact with the buccaneers, the rest should be simple. You'll enter Carter's kingdom damning the East India Company and thirsting for revenge. His force is made up of renegades. If you tell him a straight story, he'll enlist two more."

"Suppose he refuses the bait?"

"Then you and Hoyt must beat up to Madras as best you

can. All I ask of you is a map of his roadstead—and some idea of the strength he can muster. Later we'll try to lure him into open battle. If not, I'll storm his stronghold."

"In the *Pilgrim Venture?*"

"She'll be the flagship of an armada. It's assembling in Madras now—ready to sail south, once I've named its destination." With that announcement he settled in his chair and waited for me to speak. If I hesitated, it was only to search for a bargaining point. Both of us knew how firmly his mad scheme had trapped me.

"One item in this business merits discussion," I said. "How do Tom Hoyt and I manage to stay alive?"

"That's your affair, not mine. Obviously the game's up if your true motives are discovered. Gentlemen of fortune have their own way of dealing with spies."

"Surely there's an easier way to prove Red Carter still lives."

"I'm convinced he's alive, Mr. Douglas. Just as I believe it's my destiny to destroy him and all his works. But I must still pin down his whereabouts."

"Let's assume he exists then," I said. "And let's agree he'll take us into his service. We'll be watched carefully until we've proved ourselves. How can we send you information?"

"That's another dilemma you can solve on the spot. Naturally, you must take the blood oath and voyage a bit with the corsairs. That's all to the good. Before I make my own move, I'll want a complete estimate of their methods."

"You'd have us turn pirate to achieve your purpose?" I asked incredulously.

"I'd do as much myself if my face weren't known to Carter."

"What if we find we can scout his headquarters without joining him?"

"Follow that course, by all means, if it gets results: you'll have ample funds to bribe the local headmen and hire spies of your own. But I fear you'll get nowhere unless you become part of the brotherhood."

"If money's no object," I said, "it's my opinion we're being underpaid."

"Spoken like a true Scot, Mr. Douglas. I expected that."

"My life's worth more than a thousand pounds," I said.

"So is Tom Hoyt's. I'm asking two thousand for myself—and half as much for him."

The brilliant eyes did not flicker. "You're a hard bargainer, lad."

"Company masters have earned as much when they've gone shares on a cargo."

"Very well, we'll rephrase our agreement. Two thousand on the barrelhead if your mission's a success—if Carter's empire is wiped out. Not a farthing if you fail."

I saw I had been outmaneuvered, and surrendered with a shrug. "Is there a time limit?"

"Of course not. I realize your difficulties fully. For my part, I've a hundred other matters to settle in Madras. After all, I've waited nearly two decades to even my score with Jonathan Carter. I can wait a bit longer."

"A year—if need be?"

"A year—or five. I've lived much in the East. Patience, as they practice it there, is a virtue too little known among the English."

"What if I decide to make a career of piracy?"

"That's another risk I'll have to take. Tom Hoyt is at least a half scoundrel: for all I know, you're two cherries on the same stalk. In that event I'll find other means to come to grips with Carter. Two more freebooters will hardly swing the balance against me."

He held out his hand as he spoke. For no valid reason, I suddenly remembered a visit to a fakir's tent in Cairo, and the cobra he offered for my touch. The snake had been rendered harmless, its fangs drawn and its poison sac removed. Sir Luke, I feared, was another breed of viper.

"I've a few questions more," I said.

"Ask them, by all means."

"Is it wise to confide so much in McLane?"

"All he's sure of is that I'm sending another well-gunned merchantman to Madras—with you in command. I told him as much six months ago—to make sure the news reached Madagascar in good time. It'll do your cause no harm, if Carter hears your name before he meets you in the flesh."

"Does that mean Carter's hand in glove with McLane?"

Metcalf's smile was knife-thin. "Of course. Like every New York factor, Bob McLane has friends in all the pirate camps. It's vital to his prosperity. I don't begrudge him his success—as long as he takes *my* orders too."

"You've no fear he'll betray you to Carter?"

"For all I know, McLane could have sent both the *Speedwell* and the *Speedy Return* into Carter's hands. He knows this voyage is my special project—so he'll hardly take the same risk with the *Pilgrim Venture*. This time, he'll tell Carter the simple truth—that we're a match for any corsair he can pit against us."

"Wouldn't it be wiser to sail from London—with seamen on the Company rolls?"

"I think not, Mr. Douglas. If we let McLane outfit us we can hold him accountable later. And we can be sure whatever word has gone to Carter will be accepted as gospel. If we signed our crew in London, he might suspect a trick."

"Is that why we're taking passengers?"

"Precisely. Myself, for one, masquerading as an invalid making a sea voyage for his health. Senhorita Bonita Damao, for another—to prove the *Venture's* safe."

I got to my feet, aware I must not outstay my welcome. A picture of Bonita Damao rose to my mind—and I permitted myself an inward smile as I admitted my true reason for accepting Sir Luke's outrageous offer. My life would be in the balance once I set foot in Madagascar. Meanwhile a three- or four-month voyage awaited me, most of it as master of my own quarter-deck. . . . Come what may, I told myself, it should be time enough to win her favor.

CHAPTER 4

Bonita Damao

WHEN I arrived at Mrs. Pettingill's for a belated dinner, Senhorita Damao was not in evidence. Tom Hoyt (dozing over brandy and water in the ordinary) informed me that she had taken her repast in her room, with only the dwarf in attendance. I confirmed this bit of news while lighting myself upstairs to my bed. Majunga was lying across the girl's doorsill, exactly as McLane had predicted. From a distance he seemed asleep—but he roused instantly when I took a step toward the portal, and I saw a knife flash in the candle flame.

I made no attempt to challenge his guardianship, nor did I seek the lady's acquaintance in the days that followed: there would be opportunities to spare aboard the *Pilgrim Venture*—and we were booked to sail just one week after my arrival in New York. Masts had long since been stepped, and rigging strung: McLane, in his capacity as chandler, had fitted us with a suit of canvas, and packed extra sail in the lockers. A gunsmith, working from an iron foundry on the Hudson, had installed the last of the armament on the carronades. . . . Inspecting these items in the Jersey shipyard was a chore I relished: I was in love with my ship from our first contact, for she was a sea witch who belied her austere name, and her long, clean lines seemed designed for a century more graceful than ours.

Despite her airy lightness in the water, the *Pilgrim Venture* was built for war. Aside from her rows of gunports, there were swivel mounts at bow and stern. The rudder chains were housed in copper casings to protect them from mischief; spare masts and yards were nested amidships, ready to be stepped into place in the event of a crippling hit. Fo'c'sle and afterhouse were laid in almost flush with the deck, and roofed with iron plates. A special storeroom beneath the captain's cabin contained guns enough to arm a crew twice our size, and enough powder and shot to mount an invasion. I blessed Sir Luke's providence each time I stepped aboard.

Three days after my first inspection, when her stays still gleamed with fresh tar and the white-and-gold paint on her flanks was hardly dry, the ship was towed to an anchorage below Staten Island, then warped into one of McLane's slips with the tide. Here stevedores labored in shifts to complete her commissioning—which now included the stocking of the lazarette with the basic stores that would take us to the Canaries. At that port of call we would provision with fruit enough to combat scurvy on the run to Cape Town, and sufficient *boucan* (or dried beef) to supplement our regular diet of bacon, rum, and salt biscuit. Last to come aboard, after the crew had slung their hammocks, was a crate of fowls and two calves, to provide the fresh meat essential to any ship if hands are to give their best on the first leg of a voyage.

Overseeing these details, hurrying from shipyard to chandler's barn, I caught only fleeting glimpses of our lady passenger. Our paths crossed in the town as she flitted from shop to shop to purchase her own necessities: I saw her once in McLane's showroom, chaffering over a bolt of silk —and, apparently, getting the best of the bargain. Majunga was always a step behind her, one hand resting on the naked blade that gleamed at his belt. Paying the fellow no heed, I gave her a bow, with a look that did no more than brush her eyes in passing.

By now, of course, I felt sure she knew my identity—and realized we must speak in time, if not as friends, at least as shipmates. But she showed no awareness of my presence, nor did she acknowledge my salute. I would have liked her less had she returned those greetings, or granted me the bounty of a smile. Her poise was a thing I could respect. The triumph would be all the greater (or so I promised myself) when that wall of reserve was breached at last.

Besides Senhorita Damao there were four other passengers. One was a broad-beamed Dutch landowner, returning to his home on the Cape—a dour *mynheer* who kept much to himself. The others were Metcalf and a brace of minor Spanish officials, ending a stint in Manhattan and taking up new posts in the Canaries. Like most members of their race, they were icily aloof, visiting the ship only to make sure their luggage was safely stowed, and wrapping themselves in a cloak of mystery that, to the Latin, is a second skin.

As for Metcalf, he was happily engaged in acting out a mystery of his own. The shutters had gone up on the house on Bowling Green (a formal announcement appeared in the *Gazette* stating that he had returned to England on Company business). Meanwhile a note reached me by courier, explaining he had retired to a patroon's estate on the Hudson to prepare a new identity. On the eve of our sailing he arrived at the pier in a bath chair, swathed in shawls despite the heat, his eyes masked in dark spectacles, his jowls hidden in a lazy man's beard. A valet nurse, who answered to the name of Jackdaw, was in attendance—a hard-bitten fellow who, I guessed, was another of his bodyguards.

Sir Luke was down on the passenger list as Horace James,

a gentleman of property stricken during a tour of his colonial holdings. His doctor, we were told, had prescribed a voyage to India to cure his agues. He had engaged one of the two best cabins aboard, with a sliding panel that opened to my own. Senhorita Damao's quarters were across the wardroom—a large and airy cabin with a second door that led to the quarter-deck itself.

Recruiting a crew had been no problem, thanks to Bob McLane's waterfront connections: New York was teeming with sailormen, and there were prime hands to spare. I accepted Matt Quill as my first officer, after a secret conference with Metcalf—the fellow was a first-rate seaman, and I felt I could overlook his rather sullen manners. There was no question that Mozo would be our first helmsman, after our first trial run off Sandy Hook, since he handled the *Venture* as easily as though she were an extension of his superbly muscled body.

My second officer was a man named Lawson, an amiable fellow whose red nose suggested a fondness for the bottle, though he seemed more than capable when sober. Knowing he could be tapered off when at sea, I engaged him on my own initiative, when McLane was out on other business. Our bosun was a battle-scarred Dutch Malay who answered to the name of Hans (thanks to a bastard origin, he had no surname). A veteran of the Indian Ocean, he could also be trusted to handle a watch in easy weather.

If I mention these preparations in some detail, it is only because of their bearing on future events. For the present, I was truly pleased with my crew—and positive that the *Pilgrim Venture* would prove as happy as she was well founded. . . . When we left McLane's slip at last, on a bright morning in July, with an outgoing tide to speed our passage and a spanking summer breeze on our quarter, I was among the most contented of mortals. It was only when we were standing out to sea that I recalled it was considered bad luck to begin a voyage in ideal weather. Most mariners prefer to go from storm to clearing skies, on the theory that a bad start means fair sailing ahead. . . .

Be that as it may, our first long leg was a miracle of smooth navigation. (My logs are long since vanished, but I am sure they were models of brevity.) For a maiden voyage, with a knocked-together crew, the *Venture* handled wonderfully well: the men, eager for their first glimpse of the green hills of Las Palmas and the grogshops of Teneriffe, worked with a will to chalk up a record run to the Canaries. Even a squall off Cape Spartel (which spoiled that chance) did not dampen our spirits since it demonstrated our ability to ride out a blow with only routine shortening of sail.

Our Atlantic crossing was devoid of other incident. As befitted my status, I presided at the officers' table—though our meals were anything but gay, with Matt Quill hunched wordlessly above his plate and the two Spanish *pékins* hissing at one another in their singsong Castilian. The Dutchman (who spoke no language but his own) wolfed his food without even an attempt at conversation.

Sir Luke took all his meals in his cabin, as was expected of an invalid. When we fetched the trades, it was his custom to lie in the sun for hours on end, studying the tomes he had brought aboard—which dealt (if memory serves) with the history of the world and the future of man. Privately, I am sure, he regretted this choice of disguises. A voyage is cramping enough at best for a mere passenger—and though he gave me orders aplenty in the privacy of his cabin he could hardly touch a halyard without revealing his true identity. After our first weeks at sea he could at least pretend that his "cure" was complete and resume normal activity. Day and night he paced out a measured five miles on the decks—or ascended to the mizzen crow's nest, where he swept the sea in a vain search for a landfall.

Not even our cabin boy, I am sure, was more eager to reach the Canaries than Metcalf. There was a burning font in the man, a rage to seize life and mold it to his will that could only fret against the restraints of a ship's deck he did not command. As time wore on, he fell into the habit of endless chess games with his valet—and howling fits of temper when he lost. Another custom I could not condone was his tippling with my second mate when the latter was off watch. More than once Mr. Lawson reported for duty more drunk than sober. By the time we had dropped anchor at Teneriffe, I had seriously considered replacing him—and relented only when he promised to better his ways.

As for Senhorita Damao, we had only fugitive meetings, for all our enforced intimacy. Majunga prepared her meals on a brazier, save for tea and other staples, which he fetched from the galley. Twice a day she took her own constitutional on the deck, wrapped to the eyes in a snow-white *djellabla*. At such times I did not venture to invade her apparent wish for privacy.

The few questions I asked Quill were turned off with a shrug. He had served Senhor Damao long and faithfully (if I could believe his papers), but his knowledge of Damao's daughter seemed slight. Mozo communicated with me only in Spanish: I could hardly quiz him on the same subject when his devotion to the girl was so obviously doglike. As for the dwarf, I had received only reptilian hisses in return for my overtures of friendship.

Such was the situation aboard when we lifted the Canaries at last and moored in the pleasant roadstead of Teneriffe. Bonita Damao made no move to go ashore—and her cabin was still closed when we put to sea again. It was only when we had dropped the last of the islands astern (with a battlement of thunderheads on the northern horizon and the sea oily with the threat of storm) that I heard a sound I had awaited since New York. It was a faint rasp of a lifting crossbar, a sign that the door from her cabin to my quarter-deck was swinging wide at last.

I was standing my own watch that evening, with Mozo in his hammock and Hans at the wheel. Studying the worsening weather, I had been about to call the Negro to the spokes. I will confess that all worries of the sort deserted me when the girl stepped on deck—as calmly as though she had belonged there always.

"If the captain permits—?"

Her English, I noted, was flawless—and she appeared sure of her welcome. I had rehearsed that welcome a hundred times: now that she was really here, I spoke it from memory, even as I cursed the huskiness of my voice. Thanks to that voluminous Arab burnous, this was the first glimpse I had had of her face in more than eleven weeks. No woman on this earth (I told myself) had the right to be so darkly lovely —and so supremely confident.

"Come out, by all means, senhorita," I said. "The honor is long overdue."

"Your manners do you credit, Captain Douglas," she said. "I hope you'll find me worthy of your forbearance."

She did not speak again for a moment. Instead, with a

slight inclination of her head, she moved to the weather rail to study the storm in the making. Hans, I saw, had touched his forelock as she passed: only the sorriest lout could have failed to respond to that grace in motion. . . . I drew in my breath sharply: my best strategy, it seemed, was a waiting game.

This afternoon, her hair was twisted into a tight braid, and she was wearing the pea jacket I remembered from the *Star of Bengal*. Bulky though the garment was, it suited the moment. Beneath it I had a glimpse of a silken robe and flat-heeled slippers of Moroccan leather that clung firmly to the deck—which had begun to cant a bit in the freshening wind. Oddly enough (after the first shock of her appearance), I did not find her presence strange. In a space of seconds we had become shipmates, facing the threat of heavy weather.

"You're sure I'm not intruding, Captain?"

Spindrift had begun to come aboard. I moved forward to protect her—and paused when I realized she was enjoying the buffet of the wind.

"On the contrary," I said. "I'd have invited you here long since—had I not feared you'd think *me* the intruder."

"Most masters say it's unlucky to have women aboard," she murmured. "Since I'm a stranger to you, I felt I should keep to myself until you outgrew that notion."

Sensing a hint of mockery behind her politeness, I stood my ground. "Few women can grace a quarter-deck, I'll grant you," I told her. "Especially with bad weather making. Somehow I don't think you're the kind who frightens easily."

"Your prescience does you credit," she said. "The fact is, I've plotted a course through typhoons in the Monsoon Sea, and learned my lesson from them."

"Don't tell me you're a navigator, senhorita."

"I hold no license," she told me. "But my father has instructed me in the science—more than enough to pass the tests."

"May I ask why?"

"Because I wanted it," she said, with her eyes on the gathering storm. "Because he felt it was part of my education."

"McLane said your father was a Goa merchant. Is he a sailor too?"

"In his day he's handled ships in all weather, Mr. Douglas.

Since he has no son, he passed on his knowledge to me. Not that I've had much chance to use it." As she spoke, she spread both feet wider, adjusting instantly to a sudden tilt of the deck.

"You've good sea legs," I ventured.

"And good hands for a wheel," she said. "Will you believe I could hold course tonight—as easily as your helmsman?"

Her eyes turned to Hans, even as her flashing smile dared me to contradict her. The Malay loomed against the angry sky, the great corded muscles of his back and arms straining hard as he held the rudder steady. Bonita Damao laughed aloud as she felt my eyes shift from those all-male tendons to her own slender frame.

"Test me, Captain," she said. "I came by my skill honestly."

She held out an arm as she spoke, freeing it from the pea jacket and drawing the sleeve of her gown shoulder-high. There was no trace of coquetry in the offer. Crossing to the rail, I let my fingers close on her biceps. What she had said was true. Under that golden skin the muscle was like steel, rippling with tensile strength even in repose.

"My legs are just as strong," she said. "Test them as well, please. I won't have you think me a liar."

As though conspiring in her favor, the wind eased the hem of her robe, then lifted it knee-high. Bonita finished what Boreas had begun, folding her skirts back until a brown thigh was bared for my inspection. Had we been boys together, matching our strength as new-found comrades, she could not have made the offer more simply.

"You are blushing," she said. "Is it true, then, that women are supposed to walk without legs? In Boston, I never heard 'em mentioned; I'd hoped for greater candor at sea."

Using both hands this time, I circled her limb with my fingers, at a discreet distance above the knee. Slender as she was, I found that fingers and thumbs could almost meet—until the muscles beneath them tensed. She laughed again as my hands were sprung aside—as easily as though hidden springs had exploded beneath the skin.

"See, Captain? I *have* held ships on course in a typhoon." She dropped her gown again and thrust both arms into the protection of the jacket. "Do you find it unseemly that a woman can have the strength of a man?"

I swallowed hard as I shook my head in vigorous denial, then pretended to take another squint at the weather while I waited for my pulses to subside. I had expected sloe-eyed flirtation from Senhorita Damao, perhaps a teasing sarcasm that passed for wit, at times, among your high-born ladies. Complete honesty from a woman was a novelty in my book. So far, I could not deny I found it entrancing—even as common sense warned me she had lifted her robe to prove a point, not to lead me on.

"I appreciate your candor," I said, feeling I must give tongue to my confusion. "I hope you'll see why I find it unsettling."

"Few women would forgive my father for such Spartan training," she said. "You must admit he made amends when he gave me my schooling in Boston."

"You've been two years away from him?"

"Two years I thought would never end," she said. "Still, I've been taught to behave as a lady should. And I *can* behave, Mr. Douglas—though I find it trying at times."

"Is your mother living?"

"I scarcely knew my mother. Are you suggesting that she would never have raised me as a hoyden?"

"I meant nothing by the question," I assured her. "You can't fault me if I'm curious."

"Your behavior's beyond reproach, Captain," she told me. "I've no wish to wrap myself in enigmas. Would you like my life story—while we wait for the gale to strike?"

A step below the quarter-deck, in the angle formed by the low-roofed afterhouse and the starboard rail, a bench was lashed to the planking—a captain's chair where I was accustomed to take my ease during watches. Sheltered from the wind, it commanded a view of the whole ship, even as it afforded privacy to the occupant. As though by common consent, we moved to this vantage point. The bench was a snug fit for two: now we were out of the weather, I could feel my senses falter, for an instant, while I breathed in the clean, salt aroma that lingered in her hair. . . . This (I told myself again) was no woman of the world ogling for my favors. This was a Lilith from the dawn of creation and unconscious of her lure.

"Where is your bodyguard?" I asked. "Will he approve this meeting?"

"For shame, Mr. Douglas. I came on deck today to tell you who I am—not for a flirtation. That's an art they don't teach in Boston."

"The fellow has already murdered me with his eyes," I said. "I've a right to ask his whereabouts."

"Majunga is my slave," she said quietly. "He takes my orders. At this moment he's below. He'll remain there, under pain of death."

"And you've come topside to tell me everything?"

"I'm here to be your friend, Captain. If friendship is possible between us."

"We can try," I said.

"If I tell you my story, will you return the compliment? I'll confess I'm curious too."

"Try me first," I said. "I've nothing to conceal."

To this day I cannot define the impulse that forced me to open my heart to her so readily. Perhaps it was the excitement of this first meeting—which had turned out so differently from my fancies. Be that as it may, I told her of my humble origins, of my steady rise in the Company, of my plan to find a berth ashore, as an Admiralty lawyer. With an effort, I paused on that note—with the flat statement that this would be my final voyage. In a sense, I was glad my lips must remain sealed on our mission to Madagascar.

"Will you be happpy ashore?" she asked. "I doubt it."

"I doubt it myself, on occasion," I told her truthfully. "Still, a man must settle down."

"With the sweetheart of your choice?"

"There's but one. And her father vows I must turn landsman if I'm to wed her."

"So your story has a neat ending—and a happy one."

"If I survive my last voyage," I said.

Senhorita Damao gave me an odd, searching glance. I would remember it later. "Why should you have doubts on that score?"

"Sailors never take life for granted," I told her. "Navigating the Monsoon Sea in these times is no schoolboy lark, even with the cannon we mount. You would have done well to return to Goa as you came—aboard an Indiaman in convoy. Had it been within my province, in fact, I'd have refused you passage, senhorita."

"You may call me Bonita, since you've been so frank," she

said. "And I shall call you Richard, with your permission. At least, when we are alone. Before others we'll do well to observe the formalities. *They* needn't know we've twin natures."

"How so, Bonita?" I asked—feeling the breath catch in my throat as I spoke her name aloud.

"I fear no man living," she said. "Including the pirates of Madagascar. Nor do you, Richard. Am I right?"

"I've fought gentlemen of fortune with their own weapons ere now," I said. "I don't fear 'em—but I've a healthy respect for their prowess."

"You're sailing past their stronghold because you enjoy running gauntlets," she persisted. "Deny it if you can."

"It's a man's place to defy his enemies," I said. "I'd prefer to spare you the risk."

"I've paid for a fast passage to India," she said. "And I'm trusting you to bring me there. Meanwhile I'll worry about the risks."

"It's my turn to listen," I said. "I'll venture your story is more colorful than mine."

"You're wrong on that count, Richard. Nothing could be more drab than my life at Goa—save for the time I've been at sea."

She spoke of her own past then—in an easy, slightly wearied tone that held me spellbound, though the incidents she related, for the most part, were both proper and prosaic. Life at her father's manse, I gathered, was a mirage of boredom for a girl forced to obey an iron-bound social code that had changed but little since the days of the great Navigator.

As she told it, she had yet to breathe free air ashore. At Goa (since her mother's death) she had presided over her father's formal dinners. When he was absent on business, she took charge at his countinghouse, where she had learned to keep his books and see that his bills of lading were accurate. But she had lived only for the sloop she kept in a cove nearby, the next voyage her father had promised her—and the discovery (as she grew older) that she could handle a wheel with the best of his quartermasters.

The years she had spent in Boston, I gathered, were part of a grand design. Now that he was getting on in years, Senhor Damao was scheming out ways to put his fortune into her hands, along with trading monopolies that grew richer year by year. Under her country's laws she could not make contracts in her own name—so he had already arranged a marriage of convenience. Formal papers would be signed on her return to Goa: the groom was a cater-cousin, also called Damao. The name, said Bonita, was held in high esteem in Lisbon. She was quite resigned to the fact that she must perpetuate it—if only to conserve the family business.

"Have you seen your future husband?"

"Only a miniature. But he'll come out to India next year for the wedding. My father won't hear of a marriage by proxy."

I could not gainsay such serene acceptance, since it was the way of the world when a family estate lay in the balance. Still, I felt a pang of disillusion as I wished her every happiness.

"I hardly expect to be happy, Richard," she said. "One seldom marries for happiness. At times there's a small pleasure in being a woman in a man's world. Especially a woman like myself, whose only true love is the sea. Remember this is my last voyage too."

"Perhaps your husband will turn sailor."

"There's little chance. He's never been on shipboard."

She left me on that, going again to the weather rail. The wind, having its way with her, untwisted the great ebon braid of her hair and whipped it madly about her shoulders. When she spoke, her voice came to me in snatches.

"Perhaps I've said too much, Richard. But I needed to talk with someone. At sea one always takes one's troubles to the captain."

Moving to join her, I could not be sure whether the moisture on her cheeks was spray or tears. Somehow I could not picture her weeping for self-pity.

"May I say I'm moved by your confidence?" I asked— and risked covering her hand with my own.

She took her hand away, not too quickly. When her laughter rang out, I knew she would never weep over her life story, no matter what its ending.

"In time, I trust, we'll both learn to make peace with the future," she said. "It isn't your fault I'm in a rebel mood. Shall I tell you the real reason I came topside today?"

"To make friends with me, I hope."

"That was the first reason, Richard. The second was to enjoy the storm. I needed this kind of wind in my hair again. Nothing else can clear my brain."

"Not even a good listener?"

"It's true you've been an excellent confidant, Captain Douglas," she said, with a glance at the helmsman. "My cure would be complete if I could take the wheel when the watch changes."

"I fear that's out of the question."

Her eyes flashed. For the first time, I sensed the tumult within her, controlled though it was.

"D'you doubt my competence, Mr. Douglas?"

"Not for a moment. It's a matter of discipline. The owner of the *Venture* would have my head."

She gave me a slit-eyed glance, her eyes still hot with the same disciplined rage. "The owner's well down the horizon. How would he know?"

"He'd read my logs at the voyage's end," I said. It had been a narrow squeak: in another moment I might have blurted out the true identity of the pseudo invalid below.

"Spoken like a true East Indiaman," she said. "I'd heard you were famous for honest logs."

"Admit it would make strange reading if I confessed I'd surrendered my wheel to a lady passenger."

"It would make strange reading indeed, Captain. Yet even stranger things have happened since Noah put to sea."

"Perhaps later, when the seas go down," I hazarded.

"It's poor sport, handling a ship in a favoring breeze," she said—and moved toward her cabin door. One foot was on the sill when she turned back. "May I say two things before I go in, Mr. Douglas?"

"I'm still a willing listener."

"In your place I'd sail a few points closer to the wind. And I'd stow those topsails before you lose 'em."

She was gone with those bits of advice—and I needed but a glance at the sea to realize how sound they were. Engrossed as I'd been with her story, I had all but committed a sin unpardonable in a sea captain—failing to watch my ship and the way she handled in a rapidly rising storm.

Barking an order to Hans, using my best bellow to send the watch scampering aloft to shorten sail, I could still hear the fall of the crossbar just inside that cabin door. Our first meeting (which had begun on so high a note) had ended as gloomily as the dying day—simply because she could no longer remain on my deck as an equal.

CHAPTER 5

How We Rode Out the Storm

AT SUNSET we were running before a gale, our yards bare save for a brace of staysails. The seas were mountainous now, the air a lash of spindrift. For a space lightning had crackled all around us and our spars had bloomed with the green Saint Elmo's fire that is supposed to presage disaster for all mariners who behold it. . . . As darkness fell, however, the storm blew the heavens clean and I could set a reasonable course by the stars. Even in that blow the *Venture* answered her helm like a thoroughbred—and, since the bad weather was driving us ever southward, we had run far ahead of our day's log when the evening watch was changed.

With Quill on deck and Mozo at the wheel, I risked a visit to the wardroom for the hasty supper I had ordered. All signs pointed to a hard night: it seemed wise to fortify myself while I could.

I had half hoped Bonita would honor us with her presence —but her cabin door was closed and Majunga, as always, sat with folded arms on the sill. The Dutchman, our steward told me, was also barricaded in his quarters, armed with a crock of gin to fight off seasickness. A babble of voices came from Sir Luke's cabin: with a flush of anger, I realized he was drinking with Tom Hoyt and my second officer. Metcalf was a fretful sailor when forced to remain below. In heavy weather he followed the age-old custom of gentlemen and drank himself insensible as the night advanced.

I charged into his cabin, determined to assert my authority—and choked down my wrath when I observed that Mr. Lawson was reasonably sober. True, there was a glass in his hand—but I could hardly deny him his after-dinner tot. Sir Luke welcomed me with a nod and held out the jug. I shook off the invitation and thumbed the mate into the wardroom.

"You're wanted on deck," I said. "Quill can't handle the watch alone in this weather."

"Aye, aye, sir. I was just going up."

A lurch of the vessel threw us together, and I caught the reek of rum on his breath. But he righted himself at once and moved toward the deck with rocklike solidity. I let him go without reproof. At another time I might have sent him to quarters—but he was needed too badly. Mr. Lawson had been born to the sea: his papers stated he had sailed twice around the globe. How could I guess we were meeting for the last time?

Sir Luke was shouting for my company, and I returned unwillingly to the cabin. Swimming in a blue fog of tobacco smoke, the room could have passed for a submarine grotto. The illusion was heightened by the almost constant slam of waves against our hull. Jackdaw (the ever present valet) was hovering with a freshly opened jug. He left us posthaste when his master pointed to the door.

"Will this gale end by morning, Captain?" asked Sir Luke. There was a testy edge to his voice, as though the elements had conspired to plague him.

"I've every hope of outrunning it, Mr. James," I said. (From our first day aboard I had been careful to use his pseudonym, even when we were alone.)

"See that you do," he said thickly. "I've had no cause so far to doubt your seamanship. I'd like to leave a favorable report in Cape Town."

I closed the door carefully, realizing he was too far gone in rum to think clearly. Forgetting (for the moment) that he was traveling incognito, he had reverted to his own identity—or, rather, to the favorite role of Company tyrant. On my side, I had half forgotten his plan to demote me at the Cape. Tom Hoyt (throned like a sultan in a bunk, with his head swathed in a wet towel) threw me a wink when he noted my anger.

"Don't take our distinguished passenger too literally, Dick," he said. "If you ask me, he's jealous. Or are you denying you spent an agreeable hour today with the senhorita?"

Metcalf had swayed to his feet. Tonight, in a singlet and

tasseled nightcap, he was a caged Lucifer, growling for a victim.

"Tell me this, Douglas," he sneered. "Are you planning to renege on your bargain?'"

"By no means," I snapped. "Are you?"

"What's that mean?"

"At the moment, sir, I'm not quite sure. Perhaps you'll explain your own remark."

"Are you implying I'm afraid—because I'm forced to give you carte blanche and lurk in this cabin?"

"I don't blame you for disliking a hole-in-corner life," I said. "But this is my ship—and she'll sail by my rules. From tonight there'll be no sots aboard beside yourself. I'm including my mates in that, and my doctor." I snatched the jug from Tom and dragged him from the bunk. "To your cabin," I said sternly. "Get what sleep you can. We may have broken bones tonight—or broken heads. I'll want you sober when you care for 'em."

Neither of us spoke when Tom shambled out with a hangdog air that did not deceive me for a moment. Actually, I had no doubts as to his competence, drunk or sober—but I did not regret the precise definition of my authority. It was only when I faced Metcalf alone in that airless cabin (and read the madman's hate in his eyes) that I realized I had made myself a lifelong enemy.

"So you're master of the *Venture*," he said icily. "I acknowledge it. What comes next?"

"I've spoken my mind," I told him. "The matter's ended so far as I'm concerned."

"I heard you cooing with that Portuguese wench," he snarled. "Have you forgotten my cabin's next to yours?"

"I said nothing unseemly, Sir Luke."

"How can I be sure you'll even call at the Cape, now you're love-sick? For all I know, you'll set a course for Goa and make yourself her paramour—"

My fist clenched—but I remembered myself in time. Tonight, with all his evil brought to the surface by too much drink, I could see Metcalf for what he was—a martinet who accepted no opinion but his own, a destroyer who was happy only in the act of killing. In the past such talents had served the Company well. Tonight, having no logical target, he had lashed out at me—without rhyme or reason, like a cornered serpent.

"Perhaps you'll decide to eat those words tomorrow," I said. "Until you do, I'll have no part of your company." The defiance took me out with dignity, though my fingers were still curling for his throat when I went on deck.

I saw at once that I had been unwise to leave my post. The wind had freshened mightily in the last half hour, and was now clawing at our spars with hurricane force. Between that wailing, I could hear the sucking breath of the pumps: Quill had wisely ordered the bilges emptied, lest we strain our timbers later. One of the staysails had gone while I was below. Before I could grope my way forward, the other snapped free and winged into the night like a prehistoric bird. With only a jib to hold us on course, the *Pilgrim Venture* had begun to roll heavily.

It was a backbreaking task to set new sails, but we managed it before we came broadside to one of those towering combers. During our race with disaster I felt the wind slacken, and guessed that we had begun to run toward the eye of the storm, the calm vortex round which the tempest spun. With fresh sheets to steady her, the *Venture* was a living ship again. Dropping from the shrouds, where I had helped to lash the last eyelet to the yards, I found time to join Quill in the lee of the fo'c'sle, where I took his report.

"She's a darlin' ship, sir. We'll ride this out."

"Where's Mr. Lawson?"

"He went overside, Cap'n. Ten minutes ago."

"What are you saying, man?"

"We took a wave amidships. He was gone when the ship rode away."

"Why didn't you send for me?"

The fellow shook his head with the maddening, doglike calm I hated. "God help me, sir, *I* almost went with him. When I knew he was overboard, it was too late to toss a line. He'd gone under."

"You might have come about."

"With that gale abaft, sir? We'd have broached to."

The mate was right, of course. Even the *Venture* would have foundered had she come broadside in that sea. In any event, there was no time for further questions. A wave (one of those proverbial seventh combers) had just curled above

the afterhouse, to fall with thunderous impact on our stern.
With that crash, I heard one of our sails rip clean away—
and caught Mozo's shout of pain above the keening of the
storm.

Thanks to its lashings, the wheel held steady, even though
the Negro had been flung across the deck by the smashing
impact of that sea. Quill and I anchored his legs just as the
suck of the wave was dragging him overside. The mate was
on his feet at once, throwing his full weight on the spokes
before the wildly kicking rudder could snap its chains. So
far as I could tell in that uncertain light, Mozo had broken
no bones in the fall—but he was bleeding badly from a gash
in the upper thigh. Using my belt as a lashing, I staunched
the worst of the flow before I shouted for help.

"Can you hold her steady, Mr. Quill?"

"Easy, Cap'n—now we're running into the eye."

I looked up at the dance of the masts against the stars.
As the mate had said, we would enter the dead-calm center
of the gale in a few more moments. The respite would be
brief: since she would drift there, the *Pilgrim Venture*
would soon cross the circular path of the storm—where we
could do no more than hold a course again. Meanwhile
(with the loss of my second mate heavy on my conscience)
I felt I could risk leaving the deck for a while to help save
Mozo's life. I had seen such wounds before. Judging by the
copious, spurting bleeding, I felt sure that a great trunk
artery of the leg had been severed.

With two sailors at the Negro's massive shoulders and my
own hands anchored at his legs, it was an easy task to carry
him below. I was glad to observe that he was still unconscious after his brush with death. Our chances of saving him
were far better if that mass of bone and sinew remained
inert until Tom Hoyt had finished his work.

The companionway was barred against the storm. It
seemed strangely quiet in the wardroom, despite the shudder of the portholes with each pound of the waves and the
screech of a chair that glided from bulkhead to bulkhead
with each long roll. Once we had spread-eagled Mozo on
the carpet, it was a simple matter to cut away his clothing
and determine the extent of the wound. The gash, as I had
expected, was an ugly one: to make matters worse, it was
plugged with a six-inch splinter. My makeshift tourniquet

had bitten cruelly into the victim's flesh. Even so, there was a thin ooze of blood at the lips of the wound.

I had sent a seaman to fetch Tom Hoyt from his bunk, and looked up impatiently when a shadow fell between me and the light. But it was Bonita who stood beside me—a disheveled, wide-eyed Bonita who had obviously roused from slumber and paused only to fling a robe about her. Her cabin door stood wide—and I saw that the dwarf was bustling about inside. Evidently it was he who had awakened her.

"Will he live, Richard?"

"I think so—if Dr. Hoyt can reach the artery."

"Mozo was my father's favorite bondsman," she said quietly. "We must do what we can for him."

I could hear Tom stirring across the way—and cursed his fuddled state beneath my breath. "Trust us, Bonita," I said, "He's my best helmsman—we'll save him if we can."

"Take him to my cabin," she said. "The light is better there."

She had already tossed one arm over her shoulder: when I had performed a similar office, it took but a moment to transfer the Negro from wardroom to cabin, where we stretched him full length on the wide bunk. Mozo had begun to come drowsily awake now: he smiled when he realized he was in Bonita's presence. Majunga came forward at her nod, with a mound of white powder on a spoon. Bending closer, the girl whispered a few words to the Negro in a language I did not understand. The faint grin broadened as the man's lips parted to receive the contents of the spoon.

Tom had come in during this interchange: when I looked up, he was arranging his instruments on a towel. "I thought this was a one-man job," he said. "Do I have assistants?"

"Majunga gave him a drug to ease the pain," said Bonita. "It should make your task easier, Dr. Hoyt."

"Be that as it may," said Tom, "I'll need four pairs of arms to anchor him." He turned to give the order. "May I ask the name of the posset?"

"It comes from India," said the girl. "Majunga's father taught him to grind the roots from which it's made. They say it is chewed by the mongoose before he attacks the cobra."

"Mandragora, most likely," said Hoyt, with a yawn. Yet

he seemed entirely alert, for all those drooping eyelids: he was studying the patient narrowly as he stepped back to allow four brawny sailors to anchor the legs and arms. *"Give me to drink mandragora,"* he intoned. *"That I might sleep out this great gap of time my Antony is away—"* He yawned again. "What did the blood look like, Dick—before you tied it off?"

"Bright red, and pulsing."

"It's an artery then. Probably the *arteria femoris*, or a branch thereof." It was Tom's custom to speak in this orotund fashion when he operated.

"Does that mean amputation?" asked Bonita.

The surgeon seemed not to have heard. He was examining Mozo's foot, running long fingers down its length, like a musician testing some stringed instrument.

"Release the tourniquet, please."

When I loosened the belt, the blood welled noticeably around the cruel obstruction of the splinter: even to an untrained eye its pulsing character was obvious. Hoyt, with a glance at the wound, continued to tap Mozo's foot.

"Tighten, if you please," he said crisply. With the words, he shed his air of fuddled repose like an outworn garment. He was all surgeon now, dedicated to the task ahead. I had witnessed the miracle before—and never ceased to marvel at it.

"Can you save the leg?" I asked.

"Most doctors would not be so daring," he said. "But I'll try. I'll need at least a quart of wine or rum. Will you fetch it, senhorita?" He smiled at Bonita's involuntary look of alarm. "Not for *me* this time. Wine was recommended by Hippocrates for washing wounds."

The preparations for surgery were soon made. Forceps were set out in a row where they could be easily reached. Scalpels were ready—laid a bit to one side, where nothing would strike them or dull the edges. So were the familiar suture needles, with their whipcord thread, and the oddly shaped scissors these scientific butchers used. Hoyt, tearing napkins into strips, nodded his approval as Bonita returned with a jug of wine.

"We're ready, senhorita," he said. "I suggest you leave us. This will be rather gory, I'm afraid."

"Mozo has served me well, Doctor. I'm not squeamish about blood."

"As you wish. Stand across from me, Dick—and take orders for a while." Again he studied the feebly thrashing patient, who had begun to steady, bit by bit, under the compulsion of eight strong hands. "Keep those anchors, men. I'm going to take out the splinter so we can measure the damage."

He was already at work, gently loosening the six-inch plug of wood until he could lift it from the wound. Thanks to the tourniquet, there was little increase in the flow of blood when it was completely removed. A few deep strokes of a scalpel enlarged the opening still further, exposing a whitish, glistening layer in its depths.

"The fascial aponeurosis," said Hoyt. "Observe the reddish bulge beneath. We call it the *musculus quadriceps femoris*. The femoral artery itself will be in its compartment on the medial side."

He was reversing his knife now, using its blunt handle to separate the resoundingly named muscles. Already, to my untrained eyes, he seemed to be working fearfully deep. When the separation was complete, he thrust a forcep into the tissues and closed my fingers on the handle.

"Hold this and press upward, please. It will help me to see what I'm doing."

The maneuver was repeated on the other side of the wound—and I found myself staring into its depths, at the bluish tear the splinter had made. Hoyt was clearing the area of blood, and humming a wordless tune.

"The main channel is unsevered. I thought as much, from the pulsation in the foot."

Bonita spoke calmly from the shadows. "Does that mean you needn't amputate?"

"Not unless complications ensue." The surgeon was using his free hand to loosen the tourniquet. Blood spurted upward like a fountain: I needed all my control to keep the forceps in place as Hoyt took them, one by one, forcing them to bite even deeper. Magically the red fountain subsided immediately.

"I've secured the damaged vessel above the injury," he said quietly. "We will now move to the lower end and control the backflow. The worst is over. Hold steady, Dick, while I ligate."

Whipcord was looped round a forceps and tied in a loose knot, where the red flow had subsided to a trickle. I could feel the iron strength of Hoyt's finger against the instrument: in another moment the loop had been thrust home and tied off. Two extra strands were set above the first to secure the ligature. The same process, repeated at the lower end, established the location of the backflow, and tied off this portion of the artery in turn.

"The wine, senhorita, if you please."

Strips of linen were held at the mouth of the bottle and soaked in the amber fluid. Hoyt laid them carefully across the wound, without squeezing out the excess. "Vinous spirits have many uses," he said. "This one, unfortunately, has been largely forgotten."

When he had strapped a bandage over his work, the surgeon stepped back from the bunk and washed his blood-stained hands.

"Those stitches are neat, though I shouldn't say it," he remarked. "Milady's maid could not have done better."

As always, I found myself regarding Tom Hoyt with new respect. He looked ten years younger, at peace with himself and the world. Each man to his trade, I thought. Yours is a ship in a gale; his, the healing knife.

"Will he recover?"

"He'll be good as new in a week's time. Wounds of this sort heal cleanly at sea; don't ask me why." Tom dried his hands on a towel Majunga offered, his eyes shining with that special pride. "As bleeders go, that one wasn't too difficult. By the way, what *was* the drug the senhorita gave him?"

I turned to question Bonita—and found she had quitted the cabin while I was helping with the bandaging. Judging by the way she had stood by during the surgery, I could not believe she was queasy now. The dwarf only shrugged when I asked her whereabouts: I was still unsure if he could follow a conversation in English.

"Perhaps she's gone topside, Dick," said Hoyt. "I'd send her back if I were you."

Bemused with the scalpel's work, I had half forgotten my duties aboard. Once again I noted that the wind was keening its song in our rigging, that the *Pilgrim Venture* was running before the blast like a wary bird. Evidently we had spun out of the storm's eye while Tom was finishing.

"The dwarf will watch him until morning," said Hoyt. "You can leave with a clear conscience, Captain. You've been a most able assistant."

Knowing just where I would find Bonita, I paused a moment more in the wardroom to make sure the portholes were snug against the storm. Sir Luke's door was banging wildly, and I closed it on my way to the deck. Our distinguished passenger, I saw, was snoring in his bunk with an empty bottle cradled in his arm. Even in stupor there was something fearsome in that craggy profile, a hint of buried hatreds which only blood could slake.

I cursed him silently as I followed the companionway to the quarter-deck. The man's sixth sense had been accurate enough: I would have given much to cancel our contract. How could I go ashore at Madagascar now—when every instinct I possessed was urging me to sail on to Goa and explore Bonita Damao's secret to its depths?

I shook off the picture impatiently. The roar of the gale, clearing my head of such dangerous woolgathering, warned me that I had more urgent problems to settle tonight. Waiting between waves, in the shelter of a lashed-down tarpaulin, I gained the quarter-deck stair in a bound, determined to relieve Quill at the wheel.

To my amazement, I heard the mate's voice at once, booming an order amidships. Hans (the only sailor I would have trusted as a helmsman in such weather) was helping to secure a new sail. The mystery explained itself when I heard Bonita's voice above me.

"Steady as she goes, Captain Douglas!"

I was beside her in a dozen strides—yet some power I could not define held me rooted to the deck, unable to snatch the wheel from her hands. I needed only a glance at the vessel's quivering length to see she was handling perfectly, that Bonita was close enough to the wind to hold our course. Had we changed places, I would have done no differently: while my trance lasted, I could not stir—charmed as I was by her wild, proud silhouette against the stars. For that moment, she was a figurehead come alive. The thin silken robe, molded to her body by wind and spray, made no secret of her beauty—from the lifting of her breasts to the long, tapering legs braced to master the following seas.

"Forgive me, Captain," she said, with her eyes on the

plunging bowsprit. "As you see, Quill was needed forward. Don't blame him for yielding the wheel. He's sailed with my father—and knows what I can do."

Hans, high in the rigging, had just finished testing the new sheet—and shouted to her in Dutch that the canvas would hold. Bonita ordered him to the deck in the same language. I shook off the last of my moony wonder and stepped forward to possess myself of the wheel. The eerie illusion that she—and not I—commanded the *Pilgrim Venture* was too much to endure.

"Does my seamanship pass muster, Richard?" she asked. Her voice was more teasing than rueful: I needed no second glance at her eyes (I could see their sparkle, even by starlight) to realize that a few moments of ship-handling had brought her vibrantly alive.

"I'm aware of your skills, Senhorita Damao," I said. "But this is still my deck, and I'm giving the orders. And I'll tell you more—Quill's confined to quarters tomorrow for yielding his place. I need him too badly tonight."

Bonita accepted the rebuke calmly. "Mozo will live," she said. "I could see Dr. Hoyt knew his business. That's why I slipped out—I felt I could be far more useful topside."

"You won't be needed now," I said shortly. "You can go below and put on dry clothes."

"Don't send me away, please. Let me ride out the storm here."

"Must I remind you that you're soaked to the skin?"

"There's nothing I like more, Richard—" She took a step forward just as another of those mountain-high combers smashed down on the afterhouse roof and creamed greedily across the deck. For an instant, before the ship rode free, we were waist-deep in that boiling surge. She clung to the wheel spokes (there was no other anchor) and laughed as the threat receded. Thanks to her added weight on the rudder, the *Pilgrim Venture* shook off the inundation without even slowing her driving pace.

"Well, Captain?" she said triumphantly, with her arms still locked in mine. "Can you deny you need an extra hand?"

There was no further question of her right to remain. It was I who set our course (making no attempt to fight the storm, but running with its fury until the wind had blown itself out). But it was she who helped to hold the kicking rudder steady. And it was Bonita who (hours later) was the first to interpret the message of the dawn, written in red above a mangrove forest in Africa, a scant five miles beyond our larboard bow.

"The weather's moving inland, Richard. We'll have smooth sailing when the watch changes."

Her reading of the sky was accurate enough. In full daylight the gale-tortured sea subsided to gentle rollers and our wind gauge steadied into the northwest quadrant. With a lee shore, our most pressing need was sea room. After I had sent the new watch to spread main and topsails again, our danger was behind us. Had the blow lasted another hour, we might have been smashed beyond repair in the sullen maze of mangrove. Now, with all sails taut and a glassy sea beneath our cutwater, we made westing until we were out of sight of land and firmly on our course.

"You're a sailor, Captain Douglas," said Bonita. "I guessed as much when we left New York Harbor. This morning I'm sure of it."

"I've survived worse blows," I told her. "So, I gather, have you."

"I told you that yesterday," she said. "I'm glad you believe me now."

"We needed two men at the wheel," I said. "Otherwise we'd have broached to a dozen times."

"So I was as useful as a man," she murmured. "I suppose that's the ultimate in compliments."

I took the wheel away, forcing her to unlock her arms from mine. This time she yielded gracefully enough.

"The fact remains you're a woman," I said.

"Don't hold it against me, Richard."

"I can't have you giving orders from my quarter-deck. Not if I'm to retain command. Quill must be punished for permitting it—even for a moment."

"You're right, of course," she said.

I studied her carefully as she moved toward her cabin door. Yesterday, when we had told our life stories on this same deck, I had felt she was without guile. I was not half so pleased by her apparent yielding this morning—though there was no mistaking the note of contrition.

"I'll enter your tour of duty in my log," I told her. "You'll get full credit for helping to save the *Pilgrim Venture*. But

I'm forced to report Quill's breach of discipline too. In those circumstances I can hardly invite you to visit the deck again."

"You're quite right, Captain Douglas. I accept the rebuke."

She had hesitated, with one foot on her doorsill. Through the half-open portal I saw Mozo had been moved to the sick bay which Tom had established in the two empty cabins behind the afterhouse. There had been other casualties of the storm last night—a broken leg bone, two broken arms, and a fractured skull. These men lay groaning in their hammocks now: I could only hope they stood a chance of recovery before we reached the Monsoon Sea. Once we crossed the equator, Sir Luke had given orders for a daily run of the carronades to test our gun crews. Shorthanded as we were, the off-watch would be forced to double in brass as it were, and serve as cannoneers. It was, therefore, doubly important that our sick bay be cleared in record time.

I considered discussing these matters with Bonita—who was clearly seeking an excuse to linger—and decided against it. Until I understood this strange girl better, I told myelf, I had confided quite enough.

"You can be useful in another way, if you will," I said. "What do you know of nursing?"

"My father maintains a sailors' hospital at Goa," she told me calmly. "I've worked there often."

"Will you be Dr. Hoyt's assistant? He has more than he can handle now: we're bound to have scurvy cases before we clear the tropics. Can you handle those as well?"

"Of course, Captain. Is this a form of penance?"

"Call it that, if you wish," I said. "It's also a rare boon for my crew."

"I'll be glad to serve."

"You've been on deck a long time," I said. "Shouldn't you go off watch for a while and rest?"

Her chin lifted: I saw she was laughing, and could not decide if chagrin or defiance had prompted her mirth.

"I'm stronger than you think, Richard," she told me—and went into her cabin with her pride unshaken. Once again I had been left with the last word—and the conviction that I had scored the emptiest of victories.

CHAPTER 6

Picnic at Blomfontein

QUILL accepted his punishment (three days in quarters, on hardtack) with a shrug and a crooked grin that seemed part of the fellow's features. Nor did he offer a reason for giving up the deck, beyond a stubborn insistence that Senhorita Damao could manage a wheel better than any sailor aboard. Far from endangering our safety, he added, he had made sure we would hold course while he was engaged in imperative business forward. When I suggested (in a towering rage) that he should have summoned me, he merely shrugged again and refused to defend himself further.

Had Quill been less than a first officer, I would have hit back in earnest: most masters would have considered twenty lashes and a keel-hauling a minimum punishment. The fact remained that the girl *had* managed the ship like a veteran— and it was common knowledge in the fo'c'sle that she had remained on the quarter-deck until dawn as my assistant helmsman. In these circumstances I was willing to accept a *fait accompli,* pray for fair weather to the tip of Africa, and hope that Bonita would take to her nursing duties as well as she had to ship handling.

My fears on that score were soon laid to rest. From her first visit to the sick bay, she was a true angel of mercy—one who met that polyglot, rough-gained crew on equal terms and spoke its several languages perfectly. Naturally, it was an added bond that many of the men had sailed on her father's vessels. Several, I discovered, had been her shipmates on other voyages, when Senhor Damao had permitted her to stand watches at his side.

Mozo, as we had expected, was up and about within a week: long before our first gunnery practice he was able to handle the wheel again. The others, for the most part, were not so fortunate. The man with the broken skull died in his hammock. Both the arm fractures healed within a month—but the broken leg went into gangrene and was buried at sea the day we crossed the equator. This, together with the drowning of Mr. Lawson during the storm, left us a bit short-handed—and yet, thanks to favoring winds, we held to our log.

As I had feared, scurvy struck during our last weeks in tropic waters—and once again Bonita was an invaluable assistant as Tom Hoyt battled that loathsome malady with the meager medications at his disposal. I have been told it is caused by the lack of certain foods, and that such items as the Irish potato and fruits (especially the lime) are sovereign specifics. Since our potato bin had gone to mold in the drenching dampness and our supply of fruits was limited, we counted ourselves lucky to lose no more than six hands. I have since learned we might have saved even them by feeding them raw onions, pounded to a pulp, but our supply was none too large and we did not know of their alleged effectiveness in the raw state.

As for Sir Luke, his spirits improved with each day's sailing—particularly when I was able to assure him (on the basis of existing logs) that we would fetch the Cape less than four months after leaving New York. He had even mumbled an apology of a sort for his fit of choler the night the storm struck. Now and again I caught an anxious gleam in his eye when Bonita passed his cabin door on some nursing errand or paused amidships to chat between watches. But common sense had now assured him I must fulfill my part of our bargain, since my whole future depended on its success.

We rehearsed our plan of action again and again, whenever we had a moment alone. During my hours off watch we pored over charts of the Madagascar coast, from Fort Dauphin to its northernmost capes, until I could have recited each known anchorage from memory. Sometimes, when he could steal a half hour from his sick bay, Tom Hoyt joined in these councils of war. But it was evident Sir Luke set small value on the doctor's intelligence, and intended that I should be the leader of this mission to the enemy's stronghold.

"Assuming, of course, we can make contact," I said. "It's always possible our man will have none of us."

"My agent at Fort Dauphin thinks otherwise," said Metcalf, with the gleam of battle in his eye. Already he had plotted his assault on Red Carter's anchorage to the last salvo.

"I still question the wisdom of jumping ship there," I said—if only to tease him into a fresh outburst.

"Haven't I told you that Captain Spenser is coming aboard at the Cape?" he demanded—and his rage was no less violent for being pitched in a whisper. "Aren't you actor enough to pretend you're furious at the Company for reducing you to second mate?"

"What valid reason can you give for the demotion?"

"The entry in your log, which shows you permitted a female passenger to take the wheel," he said testily. "Most owners would consider it reason enough for beaching you."

I accepted the rebuke in silence. When I consider subsequent events, after Captain Spenser took over my duties, it had its ironic side—but once again I am outdistancing my story.

We made our first landfall after the storm on a bright October day—in these southerly latitudes, a time of full spring. I could rejoice that Bonita was below at the time, since my navigation was not quite perfect after all. Because of a natural desire not to ground the *Pilgrim Venture* in shallow water, I had overshot the markings on the chart. Instead, I raised a headland called Falso, somewhat to the east of the actual Cape of Good Hope—a rugged hook of land, enclosing what mariners of this region call False Bay.

As a consequence, we were forced to come about and sail a bit to the northwest to reach the settlement itself, taking good care to avoid the well-marked shoal that has wrecked many a ship venturing for the first time into these waters. . . . Making my last entries in the log, I was aware that Sir Luke (or rather his Cape Town agents) would use this blunder as an added reason for supplanting me—but I was past caring.

By noon we were able to draw a bead on the true Cape, with a clear view of the whitewashed houses of the town and the elevation behind them called the Tableland—or, sometimes, Table Mountain—a rocky *massif* like a huge, truncated sugar loaf. Today it was streaming with pennons of cloud. These fleecy banners were the harbingers of a stiff offshore breeze—but so sweetly did the *Pilgrim Venture* respond to her helm we were able to negotiate the entrance to the fine deep-water harbor without signaling for a pilot.

I selected an anchorage halfway between two hills that framed the town itself (lesser eminences below Table Mountain, known locally as the Lion and the Rump). Having every confidence in our crews after the regular drills at sea, I called for a nine-gun salvo, in honor of the Dutch fort that guarded the harbor mouth. We received a frugal seven-gun response as our hook went down in six fathoms of crystal water a mile offshore. (It was my last official order as captain, though the secret was mine so far.)

Besides the guard ship (which directed the comings and goings of all nations in this great roadstead) there were several coastal galiots and many merchant vessels already at anchor. Night was falling while we secured our mooring and stowed our canvas, mindful of the occasional southerly gales that sweep this roadstead at all seasons. Knowing that this was a peaceful port, and well policed by the Dutch, I gave permission for shore leave in the morning, keeping only the routine harbor watch aboard and letting Quill arrange its orderly rotation.

The announcement was received with cheers, since it was accompanied by a cask of grog, which the mate broached amidships, to celebrate the completion of our run. I accepted the plaudits as my due—and could not help but wonder how the crew would take the news that I had been replaced by a new skipper for the drive through the Monsoon Sea.

In the morning my first act was to clear our sick bay. There was a well-equipped hospital ashore, and I asked Tom Hoyt to take his patients there in the hope their recovery would be speeded. Sir Luke had commandeered the first longboat: at dawn he had gone ashore with his valet and his boxes. As he was well known in these parts (and wished, at all hazards, to keep his incognito) he planned to shun the town during our layover, and would visit with friends on an upcountry farm. They could be relied on to preserve his secret.

After Tom had taken our sick ashore, I strode the quarterdeck for the last time, watching the crew go shouting to their leave as fast as boats were available. It was my duty to report to the captain of the port to clear our papers. Then (as I was painfully aware) I would be referred to the local countinghouse of the East India Company, where I would be asked forthwith to resign my command. I was in no hurry to submit to this indignity. Though I realized that it was an essential element in Sir Luke's spider-web scheming, the demotion would smart no less keenly.

It was nearly noon when Bonita emerged from the after-house and took her place in a longboat, with Mozo and Majunga in attendance. (Quill, as befitted his rank, would remain aboard today as the master's deputy.) I bowed formally, from the height of the quarter-deck, and received a cool nod in return: since the night of the storm the girl had obeyed my request to the letter and stayed clear of my domain. It was only when I saw her step ashore that I ordered the captain's gig broken out from its davits. Today I had no wish that our paths should cross—not, at least, until I had concluded my chores.

The settlement at Cape Town had increased in size since my last visit. Well built, well planned (and, of course, tidily Dutch), it now comprised more than a hundred houses and a square white church. Farms and other small settlements extended far inland from Table Mountain. As I crossed one of the geometric green parks, I saw a troop of soldiers drilling—and learned it was a volunteer force about to leave for Europe to combat the French king in his bootless effort to secure the Spanish succession for his heirs. In this instance the Dutch were England's allies—as they had been through most of our wars.

So far, the rough breath of Mars had disturbed this spot but little: remembering the bustling prosperity of New York (which had once been New Amsterdam) I could not help wondering how long the British Crown would leave it in peace, since it was so obviously a way station on the English march to empire. However, with more pressing matters on my mind, I had little time to ponder the inevitable fate of the small nation vis-à-vis a greater power. For today, at least, it was enough to know we were in friendly hands.

Five minutes after my call at the port captain's office I was on my way to the *entrepôt* of the East India Company, a dry-as-dust corner of a huge warehouse—where a dry-as-dust clerk handed me my orders, still stamped with the imprint of the packet ship that had brought them from London. As of today I had been reduced in rank on the listings. Captain Peter Spenser, a veteran of the Indian Ocean, would take the *Pilgrim Venture* to Goa and Madras. As befitted my demotion, I was ordered to move amidships as his second mate.

I protested the orders violently, of course (Sir Luke had agreed that a temper tantrum was mandatory). Pounding the desk, I insisted the dispatch was a forgery and refused to be bound by it. The clerk (who was evidently used to such scenes) took my railing without a flicker. Nor did he show the slightest alarm when I threatened to thrash him personally, as the unwitting instrument of my disgrace.

"You'll find Cape Town is well policed, Mr. Douglas," he said. "I'd hate to put you in irons as a brawler."

"Give me one reason for this, man! You know it's an outrage."

"Does God give reasons for his thunderbolts? The Company's like your Creator: it's accountable to no man for its acts. Not even to the King."

"I've no recourse then?"

"None whatever. Captain Spenser goes aboard this afternoon to take command. Your shore leave ends at sundown, by his order. Either you'll report for duty at that time or sleep on the beach. In the latter event you'll go on the Company's black list. I need hardly add you'll get no other berth —here or elsewhere."

What he said was only too true. Thanks to its towering position in the world of commerce, the British East India Company had a working agreement with the Dutch concern of the same name, and other mercantile establishments in Europe and America. Once an officer fell out of favor with the central office in London he was in sore straits: the black list meant that he had the choice of quiet starvation or enlisting with the corsairs. In my case (and the fine hand of Sir Luke was evident here) I had merely been used as a pawn in a larger game—and would continue to move, with wooden conformity, as the player chose. Until I deserted at Fort Danphin, and stepped ashore with Tom Hoyt beside me, I must play my part.

"Well, Mr. Douglas?" said the clerk. "Are you still taking orders?"

"I'll let you know by sundown," I shouted—and stormed out of the office with what I hoped was a convincing air of fury. So great was my pride in my performance that I just escaped colliding with Senhorita Damao, who had emerged from the arcade of a hostel across the way.

"What's amiss today, Captain?" she asked.

"Don't give me a title I no longer hold," I said.

"It's true, then? You've been relieved of your command?"

"Is it common gossip about town? I might have guessed."

"Mozo brought me the news an hour ago," she said. Drawing an arm through mine, she led me into the grateful shade of the arcade, and did not speak again until we had moved out of earshot of the loungers at the hostel entrance. Her eyes sought mine anxiously as we walked on: I could feel her distress was genuine. Yet, oddly enough, she seemed elated by the fact I no longer commanded the *Pilgrim Venture*. It was almost as though my demotion were a bond between us—though to save me I could not see why.

"What reason did they give, Richard?" she asked eagerly when we stood alone at the arcade's end in the shadow of a great purple spray of trumpet flowers.

"It isn't their habit to supply reasons," I said. (Sir Luke had given me permission to voice my bitterness to her—or to any other passenger or crewman who might question me. After all, a picture of near-mutinous anger would explain my ship-jumping later.)

"Could it be my fault?" Bonita asked. "What of the entry in your log admitting I took the wheel?"

"Is that the gossip too?"

"I'm afraid so."

"Set your mind at rest," I said. "There's no way to stop tongues from wagging—but the facts are otherwise. The order of demotion came straight from London, by packet. Evidently they decided to remove me from command after the *Pilgrim Venture* left New York. Of course they'll use the logs to defend their action if I sue for redress. But there's no chance of that—"

"They must have had some cause, Richard."

"One doesn't argue with a Company order," I said. "One obeys it—or seeks out greener fields."

"You'll return to the ship then, as a second mate?"

"Until I've made up my mind about the future."

"Do you have other plans?"

I gave her a long, intent look—and decided to play the game out. "Don't let me bore you with my troubles," I said. "I've always had a knack for survival. It won't desert me now."

"When must you go back to the ship?" she asked quickly.

"Not before sundown."

"I've the whole day free," she told me, with the same breathless air of haste. "Perhaps there's some way I can help solve your problem."

I glanced down the arcade, where the loungers still regarded us curiously. "We can't go on talking here."

"How well do you know Cape Town?" she asked.

"Well enough to realize there's no privacy inside it."

"We'll have none aboard the *Venture,*" she said. "This could be our only chance."

"For what?"

"To decide your future. What else?"

"How could you help me, Bonita?"

"How can I answer until you've spoken your mind?"

Again I had the odd sense that I was but a marionette on strings, at the mercy of an unseen puppetmaster. One thing was certain: caught up as I was in Sir Luke's game, I would be forced to quit the world of Bonita Damao before another fortnight passed. How could I accept her assistance, even if she had tangible help to offer? Yet while reason warned me against involvement, the temptation was too strong to resist. After all, this bright day in Africa might be the last I could spend with her on earth.

"Do you know the Blomfontein?" I asked.

"Of course. It's the stream that flows into the sea beyond Table Mountain."

"There's a grove of pepper trees just below the *kloof,*" I said. "It'll do for a rendezvous."

Her eyes met mine, quietly, calmly. "How soon can we meet?"

"Hire a rig at the Leather Star livery," I said. "Have Mozo drive you there. I'll join you with a picnic hamper from the inn. At Blomfontein we can talk to our hearts' content."

"Dare we go that far, Richard?"

"Until sundown I'm my own master," I told her. "From what I've seen, *you've* courage enough."

In the end (after we had engaged an ancient dog cart at the one public stable the town boasted) we rode to Blomfontein without an escort. Mozo and Majunga accompanied us to the western edge of the settlement, where Bonita dismissed them—bidding them both to take such pleasure as they could find in the grogshops until it was time to return to the *Venture*.

Mozo had become my fast friend after his accident: he accepted the command with the most docile of grins. The dwarf, growling in his throat like a balked hound, watched us go with a visible baring of his fangs. When the dog cart rattled downhill and began its descent to the shore of Cape Town Bay, he was still resting on his heels in the shadow of the last outbuilding, marking our progress with his eyes. Though it was too far to be sure, I imagined his fist was still knotted on his knife handle.

"It must be comforting to have such loyal bodyguards," I said. "Should you dismiss them so quickly?"

"They were my father's notion, not mine," said Bonita. "I've told you already that I fear no man."

The road we followed was called that only by courtesy: actually, it was little more than a rutted wagon track cut in the springy turf of the meadows that lay between Table Mountain and the sea. I had followed that track before, when I had paused at the Cape in mid-voyage for a precious day ashore. At Blomfontein (which, in reality, was not a fountain but a cataract that spilled down one of those ravines the Dutch call *kloofs*) I had dozed in the green shadow of the pepper trees, or swum in the surf that creamed the beach below. Usually I came alone, to rest and build dream castles for tomorrow: when I brought shipmates to cheat the solitude I regretted it. . . . Today I was sure Bonita's company would make my savage Eden complete.

She was wearing a sprigged-muslin gown, and a wide straw hat she had purchased in the town. The effect was an odd one, mingling the rustic and the urbane: the jeweled sandals on her feet, and the graceful brown ankles innocent of stockings, suggested a princess on a lark—or an odalisque, escaped from a seraglio beyond the dreams of Saladin. Holding our two shaggy ponies to an easy gait, I studied her from the corners of my eyes and saw she was relishing our outing as completely as myself.

When I spoke, my attack was deliberate—picking her last remark from mid-air, so to speak.

"Perhaps you'd fear me, Bonita—if you knew me."

"I do know you, Richard, better than you think. Shall I prove it?"

"By all means. But I warn you I'll defend myself."

"You're a rarity among mortals," she said. "So far, at least, you've been your own master. Until today you've shaped life to suit your fancy. If you let the *Venture* sail without a second mate, I'd scarcely blame you."

"Then we've still twin natures," I reminded her. "You've lived as you like, I gather?"

"I've tried, Richard. It's a privilege for a woman."

"Perhaps you've abused that privilege today," I said. "Your watchdogs are in Cape Town. For the next four hours you're at my mercy."

She did not resent the impudence. Instead, she tucked an arm through mine as a jounce of the dog cart threw us closer. "For the last time," she said, with twinkling eyes, "I can defend myself against all comers."

"Don't be too sure, Bonita."

"Face me with a cutlass, and I'll prove it."

"Did your father's course in seamanship include fencing lessons?"

"Of course. I was brought up as the son he never had."

"Did you bring your steel to this picnic?"

"No, more's the pity," she said, with a lift of her brows I found enchanting. "At the moment, my cutlass hangs in Goa. I'd enjoy a bit of swordplay before we lunch."

The dog cart was mounting a slope of the meadow—and it was well she drew into her own corner as the bouncing wheels steadied. For the last mile of our journey I devoted myself to my driving: I was still pondering the contradictions in her when the cart rolled into the grove of pepper trees.

As always, Blomfontein was a welcome vale of coolness in the blaze of afternoon. While I hobbled the ponies and turned them out to graze, Bonita carried the picnic hamper (as though by instinct) to my favorite spot, a strip of green-sward halfway between waterfall and beach. The day was flawless, the sea calm beyond the reefs. It was a moment when past and future seemed one. In the profound stillness (broken only by the gentle surf and the pulse of the stream) it was easy to pretend we were the only beings in the world.

I had led the ponies to a corner of the meadow where the grass was thickest. Returning to our picnic site, I found no trace of my companion, save for the jeweled sandals, which she had placed side by side on the hamper. Then I heard her call my name, and realized she had taken the path that spiraled down to the beach. Guessing she had gone wading before our repast, I kicked off my boots and followed. A moment later, as I turned a corner in the path, I found that a thorn tree had served as her clothes rack, since it held both her hat and her sprigged-muslin dress.

Modesty rooted me to the spot until she shouted my name again.

"The water's lovely, Richard. Won't you join me?"

Apparently she had worn nothing beneath that muslin gown. At least I stumbled on no more discarded clothing in my descent to the beach, at a gait that tried hard to be sedate even though it resembled a run. She was sporting in the shallows when I glimpsed her first—wading waist-deep and lifting the sea in her cupped hands to shower it on shoulders and breasts. I was just in time to watch her dive into a pool that opened to the deep water inside the reef. Long before she struck out toward the spout of surf on the bar, I observed she was an expert swimmer.

"Afraid of the water, Mr. Douglas?" she taunted.

Knowing she had stripped to her pelt as naturally as any child of nature, I realized this was no occasion for false modesty. I was out of my own clothes in a trice, entering the cove in a long, raking dive and swimming strongly in her wake. For a while we bobbed side by side in the backwash of the surf, letting an occasional wave break over us, or coasting halfway to shore with the larger rollers. While this game lasted, I kept a discreet screen of water between us. Even that barrier was broken when the girl began a game of touch tag that carried us from bar to river, and upstream to the stinging buffet of the waterfall.

During this flight and pursuit I was careful to keep my eyes to myself—though it was impossible to escape breath-taking glimpses as she bore down upon me, proving (to my chagrin) that she was the better swimmer. Long after I had tired in my efforts to elude her, she was eager for more of the same sport. It was only when I cried quarter at last (and floated by myself for an instant at the meeting place of sea and river) that she desisted with a teasing laugh and began to glide slowly toward the beach.

A saint on his pedestal would have turned to watch her emerge from the sea like the nut-brown Aphrodite she re-sembled—and I was feeling anything but saintly at the moment. Like all perfect things, her naked loveliness is beyond describing, but my heart still faints at the memory . . . One thing was apparent as I let my eyes feast upon her at last: from high, taut breasts to rippling thighs her skin was of an identical golden hue (my guess at our first meeting had been quite accurate). In the same breath, watching her move to the meadow above the beach and stretch there full length, I saw she was unconscious of her nakedness and the tempta-tions it stirred in me—as blissfully unaware of my devouring glance a though she had been sunning here alone.

What life had she led in Goa that permitted her to sally forth like Eve in the blaze of noon? What manner of man was Senhor Damao—who could train her to handle tiller and cutlass like a man yet fail to warn her of the lusts male flesh is heir to? The questions rose angrily in my brain while I fought a losing battle with my own hungers. For a space the devil had his way, and I began to swim toward shore. While that impulse lasted, I felt I must possess her or lose my sanity.

My feet touched bottom, and I lingered a moment in the surge of the sea. I saw she was lazing in her nest of green like a sleepy kitten while she waited for the sun's rays to dry her. Less than a dozen feet divided us: before she could stir from that trustful repose, I could be upon her in a bound and have my way. . . . Once I had changed this girl-child to a woman (my instinct shouted out the truth, above the hammer blows of my heart) she would be all mine. It was against nature to stay my hand, now the virgin fruit was ripe for plucking.

Yet even now, while the beast within moved my laggard feet toward shore, I knew I would not go beyond the beach. The chains that bound me (though invisible) were stronger than mere lust: I could never violate her innocence. Standing there, still waist-deep in the sea, I faced the truth: I was in love with Bonita Damao. I had loved her from our first meeting. Because I loved her, I could never return to the pale affections of Anne Sinclair—and, since there was no present alternative in view, I must renounce Bonita as well.

Because of my love I could not betray her trust today—even if it meant losing her. Later (with the perils of Madagascar behind me) I might find a way to seek her out, even to press my suit, if it was not too late. . . . Today I would tell her the truth. Enough, at any rate, to make the break complete. There was no other way to retire from this situation with honor.

"Aren't you coming out, Richard?"

My senses cleared. I saw she was standing above me on the bank, shading her eyes from the blinding white light reflected from the water. I forced myself to answer naturally.

"I'll swim a moment longer. If you like, you can set out our picnic."

"Don't be too long," she called back, with the same cheerful poise. "I'm ravenous."

"So am I, Bonita," I shouted—glad to put some of my passion into words, though she would never divine their true meaning. When I looked again, she had vanished into the shade of the pepper trees.

I made myself swim to the reef and back (it winded me for fair) then paced the beach a while, until the sun had dried my own pelt. Finally, when I was decently dressed, I moved up the path with a quaking heart. I was fearful my self-control would snap if the muslin gown still hung from the thorn tree—but both dress and hat had vanished. In another moment, I glimpsed Bonita, moving demurely from cart to picnic ground, and realized she was fully clothed.

My moment of testing was behind me: unlike Saint Anthony, I had renounced the lures of the flesh. The victory brought me no sense of triumph. It is a lesson all men learn to their sorrow—but nothing is so galling as the memory of a temptation resisted.

"Do you swim like this often?"

"Ever since I was six years old," she said. "My father's house adjoins the sea. We have our own beach—and acres of garden behind it."

Bonita's eyes were dancing as she held out one of the glasses I had brought from the inn. I refilled it with wine, and gave it to her without comment. The blood had leaped in my veins when her fingers touched mine. I knew she was unaware of the torture she had caused me—yet I could still curse the knight-errant's role I was playing. I had proved myself a truant animal indeed in this crisis. Until our paths divided, as they must, my desire for her would be intolerable as hunger.

"No wonder you swim so well," I said lamely—and turned to gather up the picnic plates and restore them to the hamper. Our lunch had been excellent—a fresh-roasted fowl, a fruit basket spilling over with guava and nectarine, and the finest of Dutch cheeses. The wine, a famous Spanish vintage, had gone down my throat untasted: in my stormy mood it might have been water.

"I trust you've enjoyed this day as much as I," said Bonita.

"It's a time I'll not forget," I answered, truthfully enough.

"Have these hours at Blomfontein helped to solve your problem, Richard?"

It was the opening I had awaited—but I was careful not to seize it too eagerly. "To my mind," I said, "it's time the Company and I dissolved our contract."

"After your years of service?"

"I've captained their vessels for many voyages," I said, with what I hoped was a believable savage note. "I've saved their cargoes from the Malabar pirates, and outwitted the Moguls. Yes, and fought off the corsairs from Madagascar on a dozen runs to the Cape. If this is their reward for loyalty, I'll sing another tune hereafter."

Bonita was looking at me with real concern. "This morning you said you'd return to the *Venture*. Have you changed you mind?"

"Not at all. I'll need transport to carry out my plan. I'm not sure I can confide it."

"I'm good at secrets, Richard."

"See you keep this one," I warned her. "I mean to go ashore, once we're off Madagascar. If we call at Fort Dauphin, I may jump ship there. Or steal a longboat and set my course for Cape Sainte Marie. I'll take Tom Hoyt with me, if he'll come. Otherwise I'll go alone."

"To join the buccaneers?"

"Yes, Bonita—to turn gentleman of fortune."

I had expected her to recoil at the words. Instead, she leaned forward and took my hands in hers.

"Is this your revenge on the East India Company?"

"I won't be the first deposed captain to join the renegades."

"Whose flag will you fight under?"

"Red Carter's, if he'll take me," I said. "Is there any better?"

Again she drew in her breath, as though my remark had pleased rather than startled her. "Somehow I never thought you'd go this far," she murmured.

"Don't pretend you approve," I told her. "I felt you should see me as I am."

"I'm honored by your frankness," she said. I could not yet understand why she seemed almost happy at my decision.

"You grasp my reasons?"

"Of course, Richard. A man has a right to revenge."

"Will you think of me in Goa?"

"Constantly," she said—and her hands were still warm in mine.

"Perhaps I've no right to ask this much," I said. "But I'll hope to visit you there—when I'm rich enough to quit the brotherhood."

"Try me, Richard," she said. "You'll find we've a tolerance that's lacking in Glasgow."

"Of course you'll be wedded to your cousin by then," I said. "He'll probably show me the door."

"I might put off the wedding," she said demurely, "if I've another suitor in prospect."

It was a forthright statement, with no hint of mockery. Startled though I was, I found I could reply in kind. "Does that mean you'd *wait*—for me?"

"What else could I mean? Must you pretend to be stupid?"

Still refusing to release her hands, I leaned forward to look deep into her eyes. She returned the look without flinching, her lips curving in a half-smile.

"Hasn't this baiting gone far enough, Bonita?"

"I meant every word," she said. "Did you?"

"Will you let me prove myself someday?"

"You'll have a chance to prove yourself," she said. "That much I'll promise you."

"I'll hold you to that vow," I said—still wondering if I had dreamed the last words.

"Naturally, I must be wooed before I'm won," she said in the same calm tone. Her lips were still smiling, but the eyes above them were grave enough. "I think you can do both—once you break free of your pious mold."

Granting her a degree of independence I had not thought possible in a mere female, I could not believe she would dare to bait me this far and hope to escape me unhurt. I put one question more, if only to test that conviction.

"D'you know what you've just promised me, Bonita?"

The eyes that had been so tranquil blazed with temper. "You said you'd prove yourself when you had the chance. Don't play with me, Richard."

"I want you, with all my heart and soul," I said. "But I'll speak no words of love until I'm worthy. Which means, in this case, that I must first settle my score with the Company."

"That I can understand perfectly."

"There's hope for me then?"

"More than hope," she told me—and I was certain she was teasing, now I had told her all I could. "Meanwhile let's pray my father keeps that cater-cousin of mine in Lisbon."

She was already on her feet. When I rose and stood beside her, I could feel her sway toward me. I knew I could have taken her in my arms then, that I had touched her maiden heart at last with the oldest of goads. Like a hundred girls before her, Bonita Damao had been unmoved by Richard Douglas the knight-errant. The Richard Douglas who was about to swagger hilt-free into the buccaneers' world was quite another matter. . . . I had meant to break off our relationship today, once and for all. Now, like the great booby I was, I had merely strengthened the bond.

I remembered my vow in time, as my arms moved to claim her. We did not kiss after all. Instead, I took her hand and pressed it to my lips before I helped her into the dog cart.

CHAPTER 7

Action at Cape Sainte Marie

CAPTAIN SPENSER was all I had feared—a martinet of the old school, with a sneering mouth and the ability to make a man's hackles rise with each word he uttered. When I reported as his second mate, I was berated roundly for being absent when he was piped aboard. When I explained that my orders specified shore leave, I was given forty-eight hours in quarters for answering back, and kept there on a starvation diet until we cleared Cape Town Harbor.

It was a dreary time (with only an occasional visit from Tom to cheat my loneliness). Expecting treatment of this sort, I was not too surprised: I had guessed that Spenser knew Sir Luke's true identity, and was taking orders direct from the Company bigwig. At least I could be sure that no obstacles would intervene when my moment arrived for jumping ship.

Now that my testing was upon me, I was strangely calm. I was even glad of those solitary days on bread and water, since I needed a chance to brood over my future. With the picnic at Blomfontein behind me, I could see that I had behaved badly. I had had no right to tell Bonita of my plans. It had been an even more glaring fault to open my heart to her—to say nothing of the impossible promises I had made. Women (as I had learned by extensive trial and error) are docile only if they are handled roughly—and I was aware that I had mooned over her that afternoon like a love-sick calf. Yet even as I admitted my errors, part of my mind rejoiced. Come what may, I told myself, she knows your true feelings. Someday she may realize why you acted as you did under the pepper trees. She may even learn why you left her—when you yearned with all your soul to remain.

Bonita kept to her cabin on our first week out of Cape Town. I was thankful for her absence, since it gave her no

chance to witness Spenser's slave-driving when I returned
to stand my watches. Not that the man's hard discipline
passed the bounds of decorum (save for a single instance,
when he sent me aloft in a squall, with three daring members of my watch, to save a topsail). But there was no miss-
ing his intention to break my spirit—to prove, for all his
crew to see, that I had fallen from grace and must swallow
my humiliation to the last drop.

At the Cape we had taken on six new hands, to replace
those we had lost on the Atlantic voyage. They had been
Spenser's choices. I was forced to admit they were excellent
seamen, though they clashed frequently with the older salts
aboard, for no reason I could discern. Rain squalls and nag-
ging head winds did nothing to lift our spirits. The *Pilgrim
Venture* had been a happy ship while I trod the quarter-
deck. (I can say this with no false modesty, now I know
the true reason.) With Peter Spenser in command, she was
but another slogging merchantman, reaching northward for
quick profits rather than glory.

As for Sir Luke, he had kept out of sight completely on
this leg of our voyage. Save for the visits of the doctor (who
was dosing him for his liver, according to shipboard gossip)
his door remained closed at all times. In my new status I
knew better than to disturb his isolation—since I was but a
second officer, I must await his summons. Nor did I blame
him for taking cover, now we were sailing into waters the
corsairs ruled. His day would come when my mission was
over—when I had determined Red Carter's strength. The
impending run up the Mozambique Channel was a dare
cast into Carter's teeth. Had Carter known his ancient enemy
was aboard this well-armed vessel, he might have picked up
that challenge.

Or so I reflected while I paced out an afternoon watch—
ten days' sail from the shadow of Table Mountain, with the
ship rolling lazily in a dead calm. A scant three leagues to
the north a blue-black smudge at the horizon's rim could
only be Cape Sainte Marie, the southernmost tip of Madagascar.

At the captain's command I had put out three of our
longboats to kedge us on our way; the crews were still cursing at their oars, their backs drenched in sweat and their
spirits drooping. With the stealthy pounce of darkness, I

called the hands aboard and ordered a jury anchor dropped off the larboard bow. This clumsy contrivance (it was really no more than a square of balsa logs balanced on water casks) would cut down our drift in the darkness. It could be loosed in an instant if we raised a wind.

Spenser was topside now, glaring at me as he always did while I helped the last man over the side. I had watched him stump from afterhouse to quarter-deck, and guessed he had come from Sir Luke's cabin. Prepared as I was for his next order, I felt the goose flesh rise along my arms as he barked it.

"I'll take over, Mr. Douglas. You're wanted below."

"By whom, sir?"

"By the doctor. You'll find him in Mr. James' cabin."

I hesitated an instant at the companionway, wondering if I should risk thanking him for the message—if only to show I knew (quite as well as he) that we were about to part company. Discretion prevailed, as I saw there were other ears about. The chill had left my blood when I knocked on Sir Luke's door. To my surprise, I could even feel resigned to the thought that I would be dropping into one of those longboats by morning (with only Tom Hoyt as an ally) to fetch Cape Sainte Marie as best I could.

Sir Luke lay in his bunk, with a vinegar-soaked cloth across his eyes as a defense against the cloying heat. One hand gripped a cutlass; he was slashing the air at intervals, as though dismembering an invisible enemy. Tom Hoyt sat well out of harm's way, his eyes sleepy, his mouth drawn down in a familiar quirk. Spenser was a bluenose, and our grog had been under lock and key since he took command.

"You sent for me?" I said to no one in particular.

"Come in, Mr. Douglas," said Sir Luke, without opening his eyes. "The doctor has a message that may interest you."

The words, as I knew, were mere lagniappe, to give me time to close and bar the door. With the portal shut, Metcalf bounced to his feet.

"You take off tonight, lad," he said. "Tom agrees you won't get a better chance."

"It's a ten-mile scull to land," I said. "Can't Spenser fetch us closer?"

"Spenser's an old woman with a case of hives," said Sir Luke. "Already he's itching to put the island behind us. Believe me, he can't drop you soon enough."

"May I say the feeling's mutual, sir?"

Metcalf whirled the cutlass about my head so closely I felt my hair rise.

"You've held your temper, Mr. Douglas. I don't blame you for damning this subterfuge—but we could take no chances on your motives."

"Will Spenser leave the longboats in the water?"

"He should, curse him: it'd make your departure seem more natural. Unfortunately, he's too finicky a seaman for that. He knows this calm will last till morning—but he says it's too great a risk even if he must kedge again tomorrow."

"Tom and I can't lower away without rousing the watch."

"There'll be no need. He's brought the largest boat under the stern and moored her to the rudder post. She'll float directly below this cabin, on a painter. All you need do is drop down the rudder chains when you go on watch at midnight."

I looked through his porthole at the longboat, already bobbing in the windless swell. She was a stout vessel: in addition to her paired sweeps there was a mast beneath the thwarts, and a fair-sized triangle of sail. Even without a breeze we could be in the shadow of Capt Sainte Marie by dawn, with Fort Dauphin a few hours to the east. If a wind should rise sooner, we could set foot on Madagascar by sunrise.

"So I'm a bear with a sore ear, deserting my post," I said. "My shipmates may well believe the story. So, I hope, will Red Carter. How do we explain Tom's departure?"

"Tom is your friend," said Sir Luke. "He won't let you take this risk alone."

"Don't fret over *me*," said Hoyt. "The gentlemen of the coast can always use another surgeon."

"Don't fret over anything," Sir Luke put in, with another slash of the cutlass. "You're a stranded buccaneer as of tomorrow—ready to show your prowess. Chin up, man—it's a part you can play easily."

"Consider the deed done," I answered crossly. "Just don't lecture me further. I've had enough of lectures."

"Remember my agent's name in Fort Dauphin?"

"Like my own."

"Prove it!"

"Emile Potin," I said. "Tall as a whooping crane—and

looks like one. Has a thatch hut at the south end of the roadstead, and four native wives. He trucks vegetables for ships that call at the harbor. He also has a foot in the corsair's camp, and will arrange a meeting with Carter. For a price he'll even supply a coasting pinnace. Have I left out anything?"

Sir Luke took a scabbard from beneath the bunk and sheathed his hanger before he tossed it into my arms. "You've forgotten nothing, lad. Just get back your courage, and the battle's won."

"If we'd had time," I said, "I'd call you out for that."

"Your will to live then," he said in a gentler tone. "Get your sleep before the watch changes. I'll lecture you no more."

Tom Hoyt followed me as I stormed across the wardroom and into the tiny cabin we had shared since my demotion. Again a door was closed carefully and the crossbar dropped. Tossing himself into the upper berth, my doctor friend kicked open the only porthole the room boasted.

"Don't mind Sir Luke's barking," he said in the low tones we used when we were alone. "For over three months he's been caged—and knows he can't break out. If you ask me, he'll be glad to shed our company."

"Now you mention it," I said, "why did he risk the voyage?"

"To put us ashore—and prod us enough so we'll do his work perfectly."

"I gave my word to go ashore," I said. "He has no right to doubt me."

"Be honest, Dick," said my friend, with a yawn. "Wouldn't you sail straight for Goa if you were a free agent?"

I had told Tom enough of my impasse with Bonita to explain my state of mind—but even now I could not help coloring under his lazy-lidded stare. "The question's point-less, with Metcalf's brand on me," I said. "He knows I won't fail him. So do you."

"Have it your way," said Hoyt. His voice was blurred by his yawns: already he seemed half asleep. "Just stop your fuming and get what rest you can. You'll need fresh muscle if we're to cross ten miles of open sea."

A snore punctuated the words, and I knew I should follow his example, but I could not. I even toyed with the idea of going to Bonita's cabin to say good-by to her, but put the idea from me. We had said good-by at Blomfontein: what could I tell her tonight that I had forgotten then? Once, I opened the cabin door a crack and stared across the wardroom—if only to assure myself that the dwarf was squatting on her doorsill. If she slept behind that doorsill (and how could I think otherwise?), I prayed that she might dream of me before morning.

Eventually I put my treadmill thoughts behind me and flung myself into my own bunk, positive that repose would elude me tonight. I must have dropped off instantly, for all my brooding: it seemed only a drugged moment before Hans was shaking my mattress to remind me of my next watch.

The four-hour tour of duty that straddles midnight has its own rewards when the sea is quiet. Tonight both ship and ocean were motionless when I came on deck. The sailor at the forward lookout, like the helmsman, seemed carved in stone against a waning moon. Spenser, who had been smoking a pipe on the captain's bench, heaved to his feet at my approach. Even in the misty light I could not escape the stab of contempt in his eyes. It was quite like the man to stay at his post, though he knew well enough that his first officer had the deck.

"All's well, Mr. Douglas," said Quill from the shadow of the afterhouse. "Boats in chocks, and no promise of a breeze."

"Carry on, sir," I said—and took the place Spenser had vacated. For an instant I hoped he would flare at me, so I might flare back. Instead, he contented himself with a snort before he moved toward the wardroom, with the mate a correct step behind.

When I had made sure I had the deck, I inspected the wheel, lashed it down, and sent the helmsman to his hammock. (An order of this sort was contrary to Company rules, but it was essential that I clear the area before Tom Hoyt joined me.) Feigning to light a pipe of my own, I went to the taffrail to knock out the ashes—and assured myself that the forgotten longboat still nuzzled the rudderpost; it was secured there by a length of cable tied to the hasp of Sir Luke's porthole. Checking my watch by the light of the binnacle, I saw that it was still barely ten. Mist was rising fast from the black mirror of the sea, but there was still a sliver of moon far down the sky. Until midnight I could do nothing but wait.

Hoyt and I had agreed that he would come on deck about eleven, ostensibly to smoke a pipe with me; he would bring cutlasses, pistols, and other gear we would need for our journey. To pass the time, I made a double circle of the decks, pausing to chat with each man on watch, testing the halyards to make sure we could break out sail at the first whisper of a wind, and tugging hard at our jury anchor, which held the *Venture's* bowsprit as snugly as though she were resting in her New York slip.

Hoyt was not on deck when I returned from my second round, though the hands of my timepiece hung a little past eleven. Even with his iron nerves, it was hard to believe he had overslept his rendezvous. I was on the point of going below to rouse him when I heard the slap of a bare foot in the companionway. Matt Quill came yawning into view, clad only in his drawers and carrying a nightcap wadded in his hand.

I watched him curiously as he fumbled his way amidships, said something to the man on watch there—then turned (still with that odd air of sleep-walking) to ascend the quarter-deck. Sniffing the air for a telltale sign of rum, I could half believe that he had found the key to Spenser's locker.

"Wake up, Mr. Quill," I said. "You aren't due until four. Did you *under*sleep tonight?"

"No, Mr. Douglas," he said, with another cavernous yawn. "It's just time you went below."

"Have you lost your mind, man? I've a good two hours left."

"Sorry," he said. "You haven't ten seconds."

We were eye to eye when he spoke: the wadded nightcap had dropped to the deck, to reveal the short-nosed *pistola* beneath it. The muzzle of the gun was already hard against my chest.

"Don't you move, sir," he said. "Not till I give the word. And don't let out a peep. You're dead on either count."

"What's this mean?"

"You might call it mutiny," he said. "Only there's little left to mutiny against." He glanced down the deck, nodded at the motionless men on watch, then moved behind me, pressing the *pistola* into the small of my back. "March, if you please," he said in the same gentle whisper. "You won't be hurt if you'll follow orders."

We crossed the wardroom without another word. At my cabin door I lifted the hasp on his nod. Tom Hoyt lay on his bunk, trussed up like a fowl ready for the oven, his jaws locked on a prodigious gag. He gave me a wink as I entered, and seemed unhurt.

"You may untie him at your leisure, Mr. Douglas," said Quill. "Howl all you like: I'm about to rouse the captain, so noise will no longer matter." He took up my cutlass, whipped out the steel, and tossed the scabbard at my feet. Then, with a brisk salute, he left the cabin, locking the door from the outside.

I opened my mouth to bellow, and thought better of that childish impulse. A devil's tumult had begun overhead: a patter of feet, followed by a salvo of small-arms fire that ended with a single high-pitched scream. Across the way, in Sir Luke's cabin, there was a sound of furniture overturning, the crash of a wardrobe door. From afar off I heard the voice of Jack Ketchell, the second bosun, ordering a search of the bilges—and another rush of footsteps down the gundeck. . . . Remembering that uproar, I am sure that the various sounds assailed my ears at once. While I continued to stare down at Tom, they seemed to invade the cabin one by one, like the echoes of a distant battle I could picture only in snatches.

The last sound to reach me (since it was the nearest) seemed the most fearsome—the deadly war of steel on steel, just outside our door. Judging by the exchange of oaths, Captain Spenser was fighting for his life, with Quill as his assailant. I flung my weight against the door, knowing in advance that the portal was far too massive to burst from its hinges. The clash of cutlasses had gone ringing down the companionway when I gave up the futile effort and began to loosen Tom's bonds.

He sat up calmly enough, rubbing wrists and ankles where the ropes had bitten deep. When I cut away the gag, he spat just once, like an angry tomcat, before he rose and peered through our porthole.

"A clean break, as I expected," he said. "Having that long-boat handy saved Sir Luke's life."

"Keep your voice down, Tom!"

"All bets are off, my friend," he said, with that same maddening calm. "As well as all subterfuge. Who d'you think they're hunting out there, from crow's-nest to keel-son?"

"Stop talking riddles, man! What's happened?"

"Didn't Quill explain?"

"Only that it was mutiny, of a sort."

"Let's put that more precisely, Dick. We've been pirated by our own crew."

Thinking of Bonita (a bit belatedly), I flung myself at the door a second time. Tom's fist, closing on my coattails, discouraged a third attempt.

"Don't fret over the girl," he said. "She's part of it."

"Stop talking nonsense, Tom. What have they done with her?"

"Your tongue's a bit twisted. Ask what they've done to *us*—and you'll put the matter fairly."

I sat on the bed and rocked my head between my hands to steady a whirling brain. Clearly we could accomplish nothing by force while the door remained barred: I could not even be sure our own skins were safe—now it was evident crewmen loyal to Spenser were being wiped out all over the *Pilgrim Venture*. . . . Still, a picture of sorts was emerging from the welter of confusion—a picture I dared not give a name.

"So we've been pirated by our own sailors," I said. "Can we blame McLane for that?"

"Who else? He signed 'em on in New York."

"All but Mr. Lawson," I admitted. "And we lost him off the Canaries." I lifted my head and gave Tom a searching glance. Granted, he had had time to ponder while he lay trussed in his bunk. I could still envy his calm acceptance of our *bouleversement*.

"How much did Quill tell you?" I asked.

"Enough to convince me that the take-over was planned long ago." Again he glanced at the open porthole. "All but the longboat, of course. As I just remarked, it saved Sir Luke's bacon, with only minutes to spare—"

I listened with boiling impatience while he told me what

little he knew of the mutiny. Quill had entered our cabin almost an hour ago, and supervised his binding at pistol point. While this was proceeding, the first mate had revealed just enough to whet Tom's imagination, without spelling out the plot *in toto*. . . . Quill's plan, I gathered, was to seize absolute command—first by dispatching the seamen our new captain had brought aboard, then by cutting down the captain himself. Judging by the ominous quiet that now prevailed, these aims had been accomplished.

"What of Sir Luke?" I asked. "Did they plan his murder, too?"

"Wake up, Dick," said Tom a trifle impatiently. "Can you name a single Indiaman they've more reason to hate?"

The picture was a trifle clearer now. McLane, or course, was the original villain in the piece. Not only had he recruited a crew ready to take Quill's orders—he had revealed the true identity of the bogus invalid who had called himself Horace James. Ever since we had left New York, it seemed, Sir Luke had lived under a literal sword of Damocles. When the sword fell at last, it had missed his neck by inches. The gentlemen of the coast had plotted their revenge with care. It had suited their purpose to let the ship revictual at the Cape and take extra shot and powder aboard. Choosing their own moment to strike, they had waited until we were in the very shadow of their stronghold. . . . A thought crossed my mind, and I cut through Tom's whispered monologue to utter it.

"Are these fellows under Red Carter's flag?"

"Your guess is as good as mine, Dick. Obviously Quill is taking orders from someone higher up. He's not capable of this sort of an operation on his own account."

"At least you're sure the objective was twofold—to capture the *Pilgrim Venture,* and to cut down Sir Luke."

"Exactly. They carried off the first part brilliantly. The second misfired."

While Tom was bound and gagged, I learned later, a guard had been placed on Sir Luke's door, which was locked from the inside. The lock had been sprung at Quill's orders and the buccaneers had stormed in, only to find that their quarry had flown. The frantic search of the ship was still proceeding, if I could judge by an occasional door-slam.

"Sir Luke's a light sleeper, as you know," Tom said, with

a chuckle. "He must have awakened when he heard voices—
and realized he must run for his life. Or is *row* a better
word?"

I thrust my head through our porthole and let my eyes
rove down the rudder chains. The painter still hung from
the knob of the stern window, but there was no other sign
of the longboat. The mist that had covered the sea with the
waning of the moon was thicker now, though it was beginning to lift as a ghostly breeze riffled the water. With an
hour's leeway, and rowing with the demons of hell behind
him, Sir Luke could be nearing coastal waters by now. The
breeze (which was still too fitful to give the *Venture* sea-
weigh) would be a godsend to a vessel as light as our longboat. Once he had spread his triangle of canvas, and set
a course, he could reach Fort Dauphin by dawn.

"You're sure he went that way, Tom?"

"How else? They've scoured the whole ship and found no
trace of him. Doesn't that prove he got away clean?"

"And his valet?"

"Jackdaw? I heard his voice in the cabin. They must have
escaped together."

I tossed up my hands. Somehow the fact Metcalf had
made good his escape filled me with a consuming anger.
Not that I wished his death (though I guessed, even there,
that his soul held more evil than good). Nor did I blame
him for saving his skin when it was impossible to intercede
in *our* behalf. I could not help feeling we had been abandoned to our fate. . . . My eyes turned toward the locked
cabin door as a shuffle of footsteps passed through the wardroom. A moment before, I was raging for my liberty, burning with the need to explain this mystery. Now (fighting a
dread I could not put into words) I was grateful to cling
to such shelter as the cabin offered.

"Don't look so crestfallen, Dick," said Tom. He seemed
almost cheerful now. "You might call Sir Luke's escape the
one bright spot in our story—save for the fact we're still
alive."

"Don't rejoice too soon," I said. "I'm not sure either of
us will see another day."

"Use your head, lad," he said. "The fact we *are* alive
proves they don't suspect us—so far."

"What does that mean?"

"A great deal. Quill could have spitted me when he burst in here. All he did was hog-tie me to keep me out of harm's way. He could have dispatched you on deck—yet he escorted you below. Doesn't that mean they want us to keep kicking?"

"Have it your way," I said dourly, recalling the mate's odd air of deference even when the *pistola* nuzzled my back-bone. "I still say our case is desperate enough."

"Look on the bright side, Dick: think of the time we've saved tonight."

"Will you stop talking nonsense, you dunderhead?"

"You're the dunderhead, lad. We planned to go ashore tomorrow and seek out the gentlemen of fortune. Now the gentlemen have come to us—to say nothing of the lady."

Tom had spoken in his usual whisper—but the words echoed through my brain as they stung my laggard wits alive. In that flash of perception the pattern of tonight's events came clear—including the part I would soon be play-ing. The knowledge we must give a flawless performance in this drama of life and death (that a single dropped cue or misread line could spell our doom) did not faze me un-duly. After all, we had been well rehearsed—and would have, it seemed, a friendly audience.

"Are you sure Bonita Damao's one of them?"

"Answer that for yourself," said Tom.

Once the query was voiced, there was but one possible response. I remembered her laughter aboard the *Star of Bengal* when she had just missed scraping our paint in the Narrows. I saw Bonita again on Front Street, with Quill as her worshipful escort. I recalled her prowess at the wheel in the Canaries, her boast that she could match a man at swordplay, her golden-brown nakedness on the sands at Blomfontein. All these things had seemed alien to the daugh-ter of a Portuguese merchant. They fitted a pirate princess like a second skin.

"She's outwitted us nicely, it seems," I remarked, not too bitterly.

"I'd say she played the game fairly," answered Tom. "As-suming, of course, that she swallowed your story and expects us both to take the oath of brotherhood. Beginning now, we must play by her rules."

"Meaning we must join all the way—or toss in our hands?"

"And our lives," said Tom. He broke off as the sound of

a heavy splash came through the port. It was followed by a second, then another—until I had counted six in all. I thrust my head out one more time, only to have my worst suspicion confirmed: the six loyal seamen had just gone to briny graves.

Two had already plummeted to the depths, leaving only a rack of bubbles to mark their passing. Three more, floating face down, seemed oddly inhuman as they bobbed in the ground swell. As I watched, the sixth (sighing the air from collapsed lungs) disappeared from view. I drew back just as the first of several jib-shaped fins converged on that impromptu graveyard: in another moment, I knew, the sea abaft would be a crimson froth.

"See that you keep her trust," said Tom. "Remember, this game's for rather high stakes."

There was no time for more: both of us had heard the key in the lock. Tom thrust out his hand and clasped mine briefly. Then we turned to meet whatever fate might offer.

The opening door revealed a bright-lighted wardroom and the wildest disorder. Expecting to face Matt Quill, I was startled to find the Negro on the threshold. Mozo's grin, and the fact he was unarmed, did much to lessen my dread.

"You may come out, señores," he said. "The ship is all ours."

"What does this mean?" I thundered. Regardless of that grin, it seemed sound tactics to bluster. "I'm not used to *pistolas* at my back. Nor does Dr. Hoyt take kindly to a gag."

"A thousand pardons—but it was captain's orders."

"Not Captain Spenser's, I gather," said Tom.

The Negro's massive shoulders shook with laughter. This time there was no mistaking his change of attitude. Before tonight he had seemed only a handy deckman, ready to bow and scrape on order. Now he was an obvious officer: as such he addressed us both as an equal.

"Captain Spenser is no longer among the living, *Señor Médico*," he told Tom. "Nor is Matt Quill. Tonight we've had *two* changes of command."

"Can we go topside now?" I asked.

"But of course, my friend. The new captain expects you on the quarter-deck. If you'll go up now, she'll tell you everything."

CHAPTER 8

Captain Carter

THE first sound I heard topside was the slap of canvas, as the *Pilgrim Venture,* rolling under the lazy puffs of wind, just failed to put herself in motion. Save for that one mournful noise, the ship was oddly quiet, though the barefoot crew, moving like busy cats on deck and in the rigging, seemed to be everywhere. Habit dies hard: I caught myself barking an order just in time when I realized both watches had turned out. A closer look told me that the men had never been better disciplined. Each sailor had a task to perform, and he was doing it well.

Hans (the Dutch bosun) and Jack Ketchell were in charge amidships, making sure the planks were swabbed clean: the loyal hands, I gathered, had fought bravely and well before they were cut down. I will not pretend our scuppers ran with blood—but there were reminders enough that lives had been sold dearly here. . . . Two bodies still lay side by side on a hatch—and Tom Hoyt (as befitted his calling) moved forward to examine them.

"Spenser *and* Quill," he said. "What does this mean?"

The captain had been made decent, with a British standard wrapped about him in lieu of a shroud; as we stood by, a sailor came up with a bolt of black cloth, which he tossed over the fallen mate. This, I saw, was the pirate flag—the so-called Jolly Roger, with a death's-head rampant and crossed bones beneath. Quill (I thought numbly) would go to his rest in the proper winding sheet.

"How did he die, Mozo?" I asked.

The Negro paused, with a foot on the quarter-deck ladder. "Captain Spenser was a good hand with a cutlass," he said. "I feared Quill had met his match—but he was in command. They had no choice but to cross steel."

"Is this, too, a pirate custom?"

"But of course, Señor Douglas." Mozo spoke as calmly as though I had questioned a point of etiquette in some fencing room. "When we take a prize, the master is always given a chance to defend himself."

Tom dropped the last of the two shrouds. "Quill lost rather badly, it seems."

"*Exactamente,* Dr. Hoyt. We'd already offered to put Captain Spenser and the others ashore—but they said they'd fight the ship rather than surrender it." The Negro turned to the still figure of Spenser and clicked his heels in a respectful salute. "He was a hard man, and a righteous one. When he'd bested Mr. Quill, the others were disposed of and he bore grave wounds. He fell on his sword, rather than yield, when his wounds would not let him fight again."

"Were you ready to take him on?" I asked curiously.

"Not I, *amigo mio*—our next-in-command." The Negro lifted his massive shoulders in a shrug. "It's as well Spenser died by his own hand. No man born of woman has crossed swords with a Carter and lived."

"Did you say *Carter?*"

Mozo smiled at each of us in turn. "I am forgetting myself, gentlemen. She told me to fetch you straight to the quarter-deck." He sprang up the ladder in a bound, then stood aside so that Tom and I might follow. "*Hola, señorita!* I have brought them both."

What had gone before had prepared me in some measure—but I felt my senses reel when Bonita strode into view. She was all in black: boots of cordovan leather, black tights of the finest China silk, a leather jerkin that half covered her thighs and was secured by a broad leather belt from which a cutlass hung. Her hair was gathered in a sailor's kerchief, and a broad-brimmed sombrero was set jauntily above it. It was a costume of sorts, but she might have worn it always —and she could have passed easily for a wiry, eager boy.

"Join me, please," she said. "And try not to look so startled." There was something almost carefree in the way she welcomed us to her deck, settled on the captain's seat, and —throwing one knee across the other—smiled into our blank faces. Looking back on the moment, I am sure it was her *sang-froid* that troubled me the most.

"Who *are* you?" I demanded in a choked whisper. The

question was as inane as my hushed tone—now I knew Bonita Damao was a pseudonym.

"I'm Red Carter's daughter," she said calmly. "Didn't Mozo tell you?"

Red Carter's daughter. The words were a gale, whipping the last cloud from my seasick brain. The capture of the ship (to say nothing of Sir Luke himself) had been of first importance to that gentleman of fortune. So important, he had sent his daughter aboard with the conspirators.

"No one told me Red Carter had living offspring," I said. Again, I had spoken like a hobbledehoy.

"It's a well-kept secret, Richard," she said. "Forgive me if I couldn't share it until now."

Tom's eye caught mine, with a wordless message. I pulled myself together, aware of the game we must play if we meant to save our skins. "I gather tonight's business was successful," I murmured. "May I offer congratulations, Captain Carter?"

"I'll endorse that, Captain," said Tom.

"Call me Bonnie when we're together," she said, with a flashing smile that included us both. "The name is *still* Bonita—after my mother. My father and his captains call me Bonnie, in the English fashion. Until you're one of us, it must be Captain Carter before the crew. As you see, I'm in command here, now Quill is gone—and will be until we drop anchor in Ringo Bay."

"Is that your father's stronghold?" Tom asked boldly.

"Yes, Dr. Hoyt. I doubt if you'll find it on the Admiralty charts of Madagascar."

We stood aside as Mozo climbed the ladder once again, with a wounded shipmate slung over one shoulder, and strode into the sick bay. Tom moved after them, with what I gathered was a certain relief: I was glad to observe that my doctor friend was as flabbergasted as I, despite his outer air of insouciance.

"May I go to work, Captain?" he paused to ask.

Bonnie had given the wounded man a concerned glance. Now she nodded Tom a permission to follow. "Go, by all means," she said. "Enrique isn't seriously hurt. You'll find a few other fleabites you can patch: those new hands fought like terriers before they were bested."

"Did you lose many men?" I asked.

"Just two, save for Quill."

Once more she had spoken quite casually: such coolness, in other circumstances, would have been appalling. Here (like her easy assumption of command, like the garb that suited her so well) the dismissal of my question seemed proper enough. If I could believe the stories of Red Carter's long war with the East India Company, life was a weed in his cosmos. Bonnie was Red Carter's daughter in every way—knowing what I did of her, I could accept that premise. Why should she behave otherwise?

She did not speak for a moment after Tom had left us. Instead she moved to the rail to study the clouds forming above the fiery edge of dawn. It was a sure sign a breeze was in the making.

I felt she was permitting me to collect myself—and could only hope to be a worthy opponent in the duel of wits to come. True, our new master had welcomed me as an apprentice in her trade—with Tom Hoyt as my confederate. Our behavior so far had been an earnest of our intentions. We had yet to prove those intentions with deeds, except for Tom's offer to care for her wounded.

"Give yourself time, Richard," she said, with her eyes still on the horizon. "Accept me for what I am. You'll find me quite real."

"You're real enough now, Bonnie," I said, stumbling a bit as I used her English name for the first time. "I won't deny it's set me on my heels—meeting you on this deck instead of a man."

"D'you find me so poor a substitute?"

"On the contrary," I murmured, all too aware I was feeling my way. "You can still pardon my astonishment, I trust."

"Why should you be astonished? In the storm I proved I could handle a wheel. I can plot a course and command a boarding crew. Yes, and match cutlasses with anyone—though I couldn't prove it tonight." She gestured to the hatch amidships, and the two bodies that lay there. "After Spenser had bested Quill, he killed himself rather than face me. It's a pity a brave man should die needlessly: I'd have spared his life, once I'd convinced him I was the better swordsman."

My eye moved to the hanger that swung at her supple thigh. The steel was part of her, an extension of a coiled, resilient power I had only begun to measure. . . . I could picture her giving Spenser blow for blow, reveling in the skill that drove him from attack to defense, and shouting her triumph (as lustily as any of her crew) when she forced him to surrender.

"Forgive me if I've yet to get my bearings," I told her. "But was *Quill* in command when tonight's mutiny began?"

"Yes, Richard. He was my father's right-hand man."

"And you were his first officer, so to speak?"

She nodded solemnly. "I've yet to be trusted with a command: that will come when we return to Ringo Bay. Quill crossed half the world to fetch me—in the *Star of Bengal*."

"Did he command the Indiaman as well?"

"Of course—with one of my father's crews."

"Was the *Star of Bengal* a corsair?"

"By no means. She's an honest merchantman, flying the flag of Portugal. Goa is her home port. We need many ships to transport our cargoes."

"I gather Bob McLane's in your employ."

"We've made that Scotsman a Croesus, thanks to the plunder he's marketed. Naturally, he does our bidding."

So my suspicions in New York had been accurate. Smelling out Sir Luke's plans, McLane had put Carter's men aboard the *Pilgrim Venture*—save for the drunken second mate I had lost off the Canaries. Letting us sail her to the Cape (and into the Monsoon Sea itself), they had simply chosen their moment to take over.

"Have you used this scheme before?" I ventured.

"Twice," said Bonnie, with the same easy smile. "Two years ago McLane helped us take the *Speedy Return,* of the old Scotland Company. Last year we took her sister ship, the *Speedwell*. So far, we've managed to cover the old spider's tracks." She took a long-legged stride toward me and laid a soothing hand on my shoulder. "Try not to look so puzzled, Richard. It's a rough trade you're signing for: there's but one way to ply it—a clean sweep, all the way."

I swallowed hard and managed a travesty of a conspirator's grin. "Did you hope for a clean sweep tonight?"

"What else? The ship's ours. You and the doctor are about to join the brotherhood. We'll chalk up another prize once we've ferreted out our passenger."

"If you mean Horace James—"

Moving to answer a call from amidships, she only half noted my last words. One of the sailors had just emerged from the hold to announce that the ship had been scouted to the bilges, with no sign of the quarry.

"Try the sail lockers, you chowderhead!" The order was a whiplash, sending the man diving for cover.

"Is it Mr. James you're seeking, Bonnie?"

"So he calls himself," she told me, her voice still hot. "His real name is Sir Luke Metcalf."

"I'm afraid I don't follow," I lied—hoping the lie would ring true.

"He took that *nom de guerre* when he came aboard. Metcalf wouldn't dare sail into Madagascar waters under his real name."

"Never mind his name," I said—glad that I could offer some proof of my new allegiance. "And you can call off the search. Your man and his valet jumped ship some time ago, by longboat."

"Damnation, Richard! What are you saying?"

Her disbelief persisted until I had led her to the rail and pointed to the painter that still hung from the stern window. When she was convinced that Metcalf and Jackdaw had indeed made good their escape, she turned icy-calm—contenting herself with a single barked order that brought Hans to the foot of the quarter-deck ladder.

The Dutchman went white as she questioned him regarding the disposition of the longboats. He had been off watch when they were brought aboard: the second bosun, a Frenchman named Dumont, had been in charge of that operation—and, by an unlucky chance. Dumont was one of the buccaneers who had lost his life in the mutiny. . . . I could understand the lapse well enough. The Frenchman was a competent seaman—but he had been wearied by the day's kedging. Too weary, no doubt, to pause and count the boats in their chocks after Spenser had ordered them in. Instead, he had taken to his hammock the moment he went below.

Fearing that Hans might still be punished, I spoke up—knowing it might cost me my own head. "If Captain Carter pleases—"

Bonnie broke off her tongue-lashing and turned slowly

toward me. She was master of the ship now, in every sense. It was hard to believe she was still a woman, so absolute was the command that blazed from those fury-bright eyes.

"Yes, Mr. Douglas?"

"*I* brought the longboat under the rudder. Dr. Hoyt and I meant to use it later, to leave the ship. As I told you at the Cape, that was our original plan."

It was a risky statement—since Spenser, not I, had moved the longboat in the dusk. I waited breathless while she pondered it—lest some seaman on that watch bring out the fact and demolish my story forthwith. But no man spoke when Bonnie shrugged off the interruption.

"Dumont's no less guilty," she said. "It was his task to report on the boats. *Quill* thought they were all in chocks: he told me as much." She turned again on Hans, with her rage in control. "Perdition take Dumont! He's beyond punishment—and luckier than he knows. As for you, Hans, you'd have done well to stay on deck."

"I was off watch, Captain Carter," said the bosun, in his slow, methodical Dutch. "Spenser might have wondered, if I'd remained topside."

"You could have invented a reason. Consider yourself lucky my father isn't aboard: he'd give you twenty lashes for this." She stamped toward the cabin door, recalling my presence just in time. "Come with me, Mr. Douglas," she said—in a tone that still held traces of choler. "I must estimate last night's drift before I set our course. As you can see, a breeze is on its way."

I hesitated for a moment before following her into the captain's quarters, watching the crew from the corners of my eyes to spy out any latent sign of hostility at this mark of favor. So far as I could judge, I had been accepted as a comrade: the discovery that my play-acting had been adequate did little to restore my peace of mind.

Bonnie sat over a map in Spenser's sanctum, as naturally as though she had dwelt there from the start of our voyage. Mozo (who was clearly second-in-command) waited beside her for orders. As I entered, I heard the sound of a hatchet forward, severing the rope that had bound us to our jury anchor. The sails were filling at last, after the long, windless night.

"We have time to talk now, Richard," she said when the Negro had left us. "Mozo is taking what's left of this watch, and I'll relieve him at eight. Ask me what you like. I'll answer fully—when I can. Some things must still be kept from you—until you take the oath. Only my father can administer it."

"I'm sure he'll have use for Tom Hoyt," I told her, as steadily as I could. "Let's hope he'll want me too."

"You'll be one of us soon enough," she said. "Leave that to me." She gave my arm a comradely pat as she spoke, and untied the bandanna that bound her hair. With her tumbled black locks framing her face, and the jerkin unbuttoned to disclose the soft white shirt beneath, she was the girl I remembered. Enough, at any rate, for me to feel almost easy in her presence. . . . Man is a stubborn animal (as I will be the first to admit), and I was well aware that there was pique in my present emotional turmoil as well as terror. Granted, I was still in mortal fear of my life. But I was also not at all pleased that a woman could supplant me on my own ship. Spenser had been bad enough: this was intolerable.

"What'll you have first, Richard?" she asked. "My father's story—or mine? The latter, I can assure you, is dull enough."

"I'll be the judge of that," I answered. "Tell me both, in your own way."

As I had expected, it was a tale told in snatches—interrupted by visits from Hans or Ketchell, to settle disputed points—or by Mozo, to verify his course from the chart. She broke off the narrative again to share breakfast with me—a hasty affair of hardtack and coffee (a beverage much favored in these parts). Finally we were called on deck to stand at attention while the bodies of Quill and Spenser were consigned to the deep. We were running northeast then, ahead of a stiff breeze, and the dark-finned scavengers had been dropped astern. I would discover later that it was customary to bury captains thus when we were under way—if possible, with a following sea. Since both had gone overside with round shot at their feet, they were carried straight to Fiddler's Green—with unravaged bodies, if not with unsullied souls. . . .

"Tell me about Spenser," said Bonnie when we had settled

again in the cabin. "In your opinion, did he know Sir Luke's true name?"

"I'd guess as much," I said. "They were both Company bigwigs."

"Then he deserved death after all—if he was on that scoundrel's side. Do we agree?"

"Of course, Bonnie."

"I've convinced you that Metcalf is an evil man?"

"You've gone a long way," I said. "Tell me the rest."

She banged a hard young fist on the chart table. "He hasn't escaped us yet, you know."

"The longboat has a sail," I reminded her. "He must be fetching Fort Dauphin."

"We'll drop anchor there ourselves by sundown if the wind holds," said Bonnie. "He'll find it a poor place to hide."

"What if he goes elsewhere?"

"There's no other port this side of the Cape. And I've a fair idea who'll give him asylum."

I thought of Potin, the Company's agent, who had made himself a fixture in that barren roadstead—and took care to keep a checkrein on my knowledge.

"Surely Metcalf will know better than to linger," I said. "If he can get passage north—"

"That's what I mean to prevent," said Bonnie. "He doesn't know this, of course—but the agent on whom he relies is one of my father's men. Tomorrow, I think, we'll have an unpleasant surprise in store for Sir Luke."

"What's your plan, to hang him from the yard-arm?"

"Metcalf's fate is my father's concern, not mine," she said. "*My* task is to deliver him to Ringo Bay in a state of health. We've a great deal to settle with Sir Luke—as you must have gathered."

"Only a smattering. I'd still like to hear the details."

Her attack on the past emerged thus, in bits and pieces: and *attack* is the right word, for she told her tale (and her father's) in a kind of white heat that defies capture on paper. If I set it down from the beginning, in a more orderly fashion, it is only for the sake of brevity. At the time (as we drove on toward Madagascar, ahead of that roaring breeze), I had the sense of peering into a seething hell of passion few mortals have known. Not that Bonnie shared her father's fury completely. Nor was she aware of every reason for his hatred of his ancient enemy. But there was no doubt that she backed him wholly.

The tale has its start in the heyday of the East India Company's first great victories in the Orient. It was also the heyday of Jonathan Carter, then a merchant princeling with the might of Britain behind him and a brilliant future ahead. Even then his flaming beard defied his clean-shaven peers. Red Carter (he had welcomed the nickname from the beginning) was too busy for barbers—and too sure of his own star to trouble with such things as conformity. When he had crossed a forbidden boundary to marry the daughter of a merchant in Portuguese Goa (a girl who was said to have a ranee's blood in her veins), tongues had wagged at every Company outstation. It was even said that Carter had sold out to the Company's rivals—but his star continued rising.

Two years after his marriage, when he returned from a successful foray against the Malabar pirates, he had been given a district of his own to manage. A year later (when he had concluded a peace treaty with two warring sultans) he had been awarded another. At the time, there seemed no limit to his ambitions. He sailed in his private dhow; he owned his own palace in Madras, and palaces no less splendid in the provinces he governed in the Company's name. A troop of Gurkhas served as his personal cavalry—and there were servants by the score to care for his wife and two small children. (The first-born was a girl, named after her dark-eyed, olive-skinned mother. The second was Red Carter's son and heir—a blue-eyed boy who seemed even more English than his father, and was marked to take over the father's mantle when scarce out of his cradle.)

Such was the man's enviable status when the blow fell—with all Sir Luke Metcalf's cunning behind it.

Metcalf was then a Company factotum whose rank was only a trifle below Carter's. One of his principal occupations (or so Bonnie insisted) was investigation in the Company's behalf. When it suited his purpose, he was not above planting evidence of all sorts. As Bonnie told it, the charge he brought against her father was a barefaced lie—including the doctored ledgers he produced to support his case.

Fact and fable have a way of blending when the dust of oblivion settles on the record. Whether Jonathan Carter was innocent or not, his Company record closed with a verdict of guilty. Sir Luke's findings were upheld—first in the court at Madras and later in England. It was alleged that Carter had mulcted the Company of huge sums—from collections in his districts, from tribute exacted among the Malabar corsairs, from fines paid by the very sultans he had brought under the Company banner. It was even stated that most of these gains had been sent into Goa, through family connections of Carter's wife.

The scandal had been whispered through Madras when Carter was adventuring in the backlands. He returned to find his wife prostrated, his creditors clamoring for the settlement of their bills. Like many a merchant prince before him, Carter's finances were overextended: at the moment, he found it impossible to settle his accounts. . . . When a writ was issued for his arrest by Company police, he challenged Metcalf to combat, only to learn that his wily accuser had just sailed for England.

Within a month Carter's fortune had dwindled and his personal bodyguard had fled. Only a few stalwarts (Mozo the slave, the hard-bitten Quill) remained to protect him from the bailiffs who came to demand his surrender. Carter's reply had been in character. First, he had cut down the man who served the writ: the others had been driven off at sword's point. That same night, he had taken his wife and children out of India forever—using his dhow as a means of transport, and damning his enemies as he sailed down the Madras roadstead with guns blazing.

Company men-of-war had pursued him when he set a course for Africa—but he had outsailed them with ease. That same year, he had established himself on the African coast with a picked band of brothers as the avowed scourge of all he had helped to create. His wife, broken by what she considered his disgrace, did not survive the voyage. His infant son died of blackwater fever soon after the landing.

Faute de mieux, from that moment Red Carter had raised his daughter as a boy.

"As you see," said Bonnie, "the story I made up was mostly true. Only the names were changed. I grew up on a bay in Madagascar, not in Goa. We *do* have a house on salt water—though it's really a fortress castle. We have a mile of beach and gardens, all our own. And I *was* trained to hold a wheel, the moment I could see above the spokes."

Carter was tried again, *in absentia,* by his London employers—and this time he was damned outright as an enemy of society. He was now an avowed corsair, dedicated to the capture of every Company ship that ventured into his bailiwick. And yet, curiously enough, these facts had increased his reputation. To the common man Red Carter's exploits as a firebrand of Empire had been a glorious legend: he now began to take on the aura of a tropical Robin Hood, whose heroic dimensions were enhanced by time and distance. . . . Sir Luke's charges were never disproved: Carter no longer had friends in court. But it was said that revenge against a successful rival had been Metcalf's motive, rather than honest exposure. It was also said that Sir Luke had been prudent to leave Madras before Carter sent his challenge—else he could never have survived their duel.

I will add nothing here of the rise of Jonathan Carter as the pirate king of Madagascar. The story of that reign has been told elsewhere—and its finale (of which I was an eyewitness) will be related in its proper place. For the record, he abandoned his depots on the African mainland within two years—crossing the Mozambique Channel to build a new stronghold at one of the many uncharted bays on the island. The French had all but abandoned their tenuous hold on Madagascar—and Carter's empire had prospered from the first.

Many of his comrades in the Company turned renegade to join him. Thanks to the information they brought, he was *au courant* in both London and India—and thus able to plunder the Madras convoys at will. As his needs dictated, he increased his fleet by the outright capture of such vessels as the *Speedwell* and the *Speedy Return* (and now, the *Pilgrim Venture*).

Bonnie had made her first voyage, as an apprentice, at the tender age of fifteen—with Quill as first officer, Mozo a second mate, and Red Carter himself on the quarter-deck. The pattern had repeated until she was eighteen—when her father had seen he could educate her no further in his chosen trade. Wary of London (where he had too many enemies), he had sent her to the New World town of Boston to complete her schooling. . . . As this narrative has already suggested, she sailed from Goa with a forged passport that identified her as Senhorita Bonita Damao, the daughter of a wealthy factor there. (The actual Senhor Damao, who was Carter's secret agent in Goa, had been glad to supply his employer's daughter with a pseudonym.)

Two years later (just before our paths crossed) the *Star of Bengal* had called at the Massachusetts port of New Bedford to take Senhorita Damao aboard. Quill was in command, with Mozo and the dwarf Majunga as his lieutenants: he was also to serve as the ringleader of the mutineers when they took over the *Venture*, with his lady passenger as second-in-command. In New York it had been a simple matter to fill out the crew list with sailormen in Carter's employ. This had been McLane's greatest gamble—but he had been promised a fabulous commission if the scheme was successful, and greed had overcome caution. . . .

"It's evident that McLane's days are numbered," I said. "He'll learn at last that no man can serve two masters. When Sir Luke reaches Madras—"

"He hasn't escaped us yet," Bonnie said—and her eyes flashed fire as she spoke.

I saw that I had spoken hastily, and covered myself as best I could. "You still hope to corner him at Fort Dauphin?"

"I do indeed."

"As you've told it," I remarked, "Metcalf's escape is the only flaw in today's action. You must admit he's had a long head start."

Bonnie glanced through the open cabin door at our booming towers of canvas.

"Give Mozo this following wind for the next two hours, and he'll be standing off Fort Dauphin."

"Can we enter the roadstead?"

"When we fly my father's banner, we can enter any port this side of Cape Town. If Sir Luke is still ashore, we'll hound him down. I've ways of tracking him, as you'll see."

"Is this another of your secrets?"

"Of course not, Richard. I refer to a Frenchman who lives at the Fort—a man called Emile Potin. For the past year he's been posing as an agent of the East India Company. In reality, as I've told you, he's my father's spy."

I felt my heart sink as the import of that statement sank home. "So you have a McLane in Madagascar too?"

"Precisely. The Frenchman knows that Sir Luke is bound for these waters: he'll be on the *qui vive*. If Metcalf comes to him for help, he'll clap him in irons and await our orders."

My blood had almost congealed—but I managed to return her smile as she rolled up her chart and tossed her calipers aside. "Your father thinks of everything, it seems," I murmured. It was ominously true, God knows: I could speak the words with conviction. In this solemn chess game Carter had been a move ahead of Metcalf from the start—and, I suspected now, several moves ahead of me.

"If you like," said Bonnie, "you may go in tomorrow and capture Sir Luke. We'll call it your first shore duty under our command."

CHAPTER 9

The Blood Oath

AT NOON we lost our following wind abruptly—and, for the next six hours, rolled scuppers down in another of those oily doldrums so characteristic of the waters off Madagascar. When the wind rose with the sunset, we could do no better than sail off and on until morning. Even had we fetched the harbor of Fort Dauphin, we would have been forced to stand offshore. These waters are treacherous with coral outcrop—and I commended Bonnie Carter's prudence, rage though she did at the unforseen delay.

She gave me few idle moments to ponder my changed status. First, at her command, I conducted her on a stem-to-stern inspection of the *Pilgrim Venture,* including an exact cataloguing of our arsenal and a careful check of the bounteous stores we had taken aboard at the Cape. These included a dozen pipes of wine Sir Luke had intended for his own cellar in Madras and a prodigious quantity of bright-hued calicoes and other stuff used for trade in the Orient. All in all, it seemed, the vessel and her cargo were a rich prize indeed. Had Metcalf been included in the capture, the double tot of rum that went to all hands at sundown would have been drunk to celebrate one of the most brilliant *coups* in Red Carter's history.

As things stood, I could hardly blame Bonnie for her growing impatience as we set a triangular course just out of sight of land and swept the sea from both our crow's-nests at moonrise in the vain hope that Sir Luke had been delayed as well as our own ship. Knowing him to be a consummate seaman, I felt sure we had seen the last of the longboat. Sailing close to land and skimming among the reefs as easily as a homing swallow, he could have nursed every scrap of wind—and, though the harbor of Fort Dauphin was a good twenty leagues from our position at the time of the mutiny, he should have reached it at sundown.

As later events showed, my guess was all too accurate. Fate can turn on small matters: had our following wind lasted through the day, I am sure we would have gained our objective with time to spare, trapping him red-handed in his latest perfidy. But once again I run ahead of my own story. . . .

Tom Hoyt and I had time for only a few whispered words as we turned in after a long day. My friend the doctor had been busy every moment in the surgery: the "fleabite" wounds that Bonnie's stalwarts had dismissed so casually had needed their quota of stitches. Tom was justly proud of his first stint as a pirates' surgeon.

"Give me a little time, Dick," he said. "I'll be a worthy member of the team. Or is trio a better word?"

"Don't make the mistake of dubbing *me* the captain's right-hand man," I said crossly. "I've passed my first catechism, it seems—but I'm still very much on trial."

"You'll last, my friend. Just keep your head, and don't let Scotch morality trip you. I'm sure you'll prove invaluable."

"How can I play a part my conscience won't endorse?"

"Most of us go through life on just that basis," said Tom. "With the right friends, and enough grog, we find it tolerable. So will you—once you grow used to your part."

"I'm not sure I'm able."

"You'll handle your steel nimbly, Dick: I'll guarantee that. In a week's time you'll be a first-rate buccaneer. *That* isn't the rub—and you might as well avow it."

"What are you trying to tell me?"

"Only this—what really sticks in your craw is being ranked by a woman. Even a woman you love."

"Don't call me a greater booby than I am," I told him. "Yesterday I thought I'd seen the last of Bonnie Carter. Now I find we're still shipmates—and learn she's the devil's daughter to boot. How can a man love a vixen?"

"For the best of reasons," said Tom. "At the Cape, I gather, you planned to seduce the lass—and failed, for what reason I don't know. Now she's beyond seduction, you want her all the more. It's only human nature."

"Have it your way," I admitted. "But for a cynic you do seem on the romantic side."

So far, I had not been assigned to a watch. Until the all-important interview with Red Carter, I gathered I would have no fixed duties aboard the *Pilgrim Venture*.

Next morning (I admit it to my shame) I slept through the bosun's pipes—and did not come topside until we had sailed between the headlands of Fort Dauphin and anchored near the ruined French bastion that gave the roadstead its name. (The fact that Tom Hoyt was still snoring like a navvy when I left our cabin did little to console me. Like all men who have made their peace with destiny, my friend the doctor did not concern himself overmuch with the problems of tomorrow.)

Bonnie was on deck. She was in the act of accepting a lighted calabash from a great, kinky-headed blackamoor who was stark-naked save for a tuft of ostrich plumes that rose from his rump like a second tail. This, I realized, was the local chief (or dean, as they are named in this strange country). A cluster of outrigger canoes, hugging the sides of the vessel, told me how our caller had arrived. A dozen of his fellows were roaming the decks—chattering at the sailors and trading melons and other garden truck for such gewgaws as our crew could produce.

A wave of the new captain's hand invited me to join her just as she was in the act of blowing forth a great cloud of smoke from the calabash—or peace pipe, as it is sometimes known. Mozo took a puff in turn, as did the chieftain. Then, bowing to us all with natural good manners, he snapped the pipe on his knee and tossed the fragments overside. This ceremonial act signified that the amity now existing between his tribe and Red Carter (unlike the ruined calabash) would remain unbroken.

"D'you speak the Malagasy tongue, Mr. Douglas?" asked Bonnie. "If not, this fellow knows a little French. I'd like you to hear his report."

In the past I had touched at Madagascar often enough to pick up the Malagasy dialect—which is a kind of *lingua franca* for that whole vast island. "I understand the jabber well enough, Captain," I said. "Though I speak it poorly."

The dean told his tale in a high singsong, rolling his eyes prodigiously as he talked. His domain, I saw, had changed but little since my last visit. A score of huts still clung to the beach, like ragged children clutching the skirts of mother sea. (These coastal folk are fish-eaters, having turned their backs on the rain forests that close their horizon on the landward side.) Save for melon patches, and a kind of stunted corn the Dutch call *mealies,* there was no sign of cultivation. Only one change had occurred in the years between. Besides the crumbled walls of the fort a row of palings enclosed the yard of a high-stilted house. It seemed built entirely of discarded ship's timbers, save for its palm-thatch roof. This, obviously, was the abode of Emile Potin, the Company agent who also took orders from Carter.

As we had surmised, Metcalf's longboat had come in with the tide (it was still moored in a basin adjoining the Frenchman's stockade). Sir Luke and his valet had gone straight to the agent's house: so far as the dean knew, they had been closeted there ever since. . . . Potin and these aborigines had little truck with one another—though he had taken no less than four black squaws to console his loneliness and paid for his residence with periodic bribes. For the rest, he kept strictly to his walled domain—and the society of his half-caste offspring, who were now numerous.

The dean's story, I realized, was a twice-told tale. Both Mozo and Bonnie nodded in unison while he made his points. When he had finished, he stepped back with a second courteous bow, as though awaiting our captain's pleasure.

"Will you bring Metcalf aboard, Mr. Douglas?" she asked.

"As you wish," I replied steadily. "Unless it's too important an arrest to delegate."

Her eyes glowed with the sudden fire I was beginning to

know so well. "You're right about its importance," she said. "However, this is one villain I'd prefer not to face in person. If our paths crossed on land, I'd be tempted to cut him down—an act my father would scarce forgive." She looked at me narrowly, and I realized she was testing my mettle. "You can take help if you like. I'm aware our man's a slippery customer."

"Send Mozo with me, if he can be spared," I said. "We'll collar him between us."

In the end (since Tom Hoyt came yawning on deck just as we were lowering away) three of us converged on the Frenchman's stockade—each armed with *pistolas* or cutlass, and each uncertain of his next move. Though Mozo was now first mate, I was the leader of this shore patrol—Bonnie Carter's eyes were upon me, though she continued her ritual parley with the dean.

This, as she had said, was my first mission in her father's behalf, and I could scarce afford to bungle it. I will confess a queasy moment when I stood at the stockade gate and sprang the hasp with my blade. Clearly I was expected to seize Metcalf and bring him to the ship—delivering him (at best) to the rough justice of a pirates' court-martial. What if he showed fight and forced me to fight back? Or (what was even worse) exposed both Tom and me to the enemy?

My fears soon proved groundless, for Potin's house was empty. From the moment we crossed the yard, it was evident that whatever birds had roosted here had flown to other parts. The Frenchman's aloofness from the native village, I gathered, had proved useful: it had certainly permitted him to decamp without their knowledge. Nor could I doubt that Sir Luke had been an honored guest here. A note (scrawled on a sheet of foolscap and pinned to the wall) was the first object to catch my eye in those empty rooms.

Since it tells much in few words, I have kept the note among my papers. It is before me as I write—and it brings back that house in all its forlorn squalor:

Carter:
This (as we say in the Prize-Ring) is your Round. Take no comfort in't, if I choose to skedaddle, like a whipp'd Cur.
I go straight to Madras, taking your Janizary with me.

Happily for himself, he has learned there is still Gold in Company Coffers. Enough, at any rate, to purchase his Allegiance.

This Missive will serve notice that your former Servant has suppli'd me with a complete Chart of your stronghold on Ringo Bay. When the Monsoon Wind's in my favor, I'll take pleasure in calling there, to settle our ancient Feud, once & for all.

Metcalf

The moment I had skimmed through this missive, I sent Mozo racing to the beach with the news. Bonnie accepted it calmly enough when she came ashore. After we had explored the environs, we soon pieced the mystery together.

The basin and the moored longboat, we found, were only blinds. At the rear of the stockade a path wound through the jungle, ending some four hundred yards to the south at a hidden cove on the far side of the headland. Arched with banyan and liana, this harbor was deep enough to berth a full-size pinnace. Potin had used such a vessel often for exploration along the coast. Last night, it seemed, he had struck out boldly for Madras, with a special passenger aboard. Since there were many islands between Madagascar and the coast of India where they could find water and food, I saw no reason why they would not succeed.

These details were revealed to us from two sources. Somewhat belatedly, the dean recalled how he had helped Potin provision the pinnace for an extended voyage. Later Mozo smoked the eldest of the Frenchman's four wives from a village hut—and we had the story complete. The creature had witnessed the preliminaries to Sir Luke's dash for liberty. At first, as Bonnie had expected, he had been made a prisoner by Potin and threatened with instant delivery to Carter's stronghold. Later *pourparlers* had convinced Metcalf's captor that he would profit far more by assisting his escape.

In the end they had gathered up Potin's few belongings and departed posthaste. The three younger wives had been taken aboard the pinnace as ballast: Jackdaw and the Frenchman's four half-breed sons had made a passable crew. Luck, it seemed, perched on Metcalf's shoulder. Since they had a day's start, pursuit was useless: these coastal skimmers could

outsail any full-size ship afloat. Hazardous though the long
voyage to India might prove, it was feasible for a sailor of
Sir Luke's caliber. By thê same token (if we could take his
note at face value), he would return to these waters in due
course—ready, at long last, to wage war.

Our investigation ended, we returned to the ship and prepared to weigh anchor. I will confess that my first emotion
was one of relief. Potin, I saw, had worked his way deep
in pirate councils: he had accomplished the Company's main
objective, an exact statement of Carter's strength and a map
of Ringo Bay. My own mission, in other words, was ended
before it could rightly begin. Come what may, when I faced
up to Carter and volunteered for his service, I need not act
the spy.

"Was this Frenchman one of your father's captains?" I
asked Bonnie when we had closeted ourselves again in her
cabin. "I thought Ringo Bay was unknown outside the
brotherhood."

"So it was," she said. "I've been absent over two years.
What happened here last night is beyond my comprehen-
sion. This much I do know: Potin was never captain. My
father trusted him—but not that far."

"Could the map be a fraud?"

"Again I can't give you a sensible answer—but the Frenchman was an expert cartographer. I hardly think he'd be taken
in by substitutes."

"Perhaps your father's been deposed," I ventured. "A
successor might wish to strike a truce with the Company."

"No man living could depose Jonathan Carter," she said
quietly. "And gentlemen of fortune make no truces. Either
we rule Madagascar in fact as well as name—or we die fighting. There's no middle ground."

I held my peace on that—but I could not help sharing
Bonnie's bewilderment. It had been natural that Potin should
yield to Sir Luke's blandishments and help his escape. Yet
why would Red Carter give up his secrets to an underling?

"Do we set a course for Ringo Bay?" I asked.

"We've no alternative," said Bonnie in the same resigned
tone. "I'll still be glad to drop anchor—though I'd hoped for
a better home-coming."

Home, to this salt-water Lilith, was only a pirate's fortress
—yet she was returning to it eagerly after her exile, ready to

become a full partner in her sire's marauding. Who was I to warn her that she was choosing the way to death, that such defiance of law could have but one ending?

"Your father can hardly censure you," I said. "Quill was in command when Metcalf left the ship."

"It wouldn't have happened if Jonathan Carter had been aboard," she said. "It's a bad start for his daughter."

Again I fell silent, realizing she was making the worst of the affair as a kind of penance: since she was her father's heir, she could do no less. Nor could I blame her if she looked forward to that inheritance as ardently as any princess anticipating the succession. From Bonnie Carter's viewpoint, her kingdom on Madagascar had been earned—as justly, in its fashion, as England's own conquest of India. Viewed in their broadest aspect, had the victories of the East India Company on foreign soil and Carter's years of raiding from his hidden bayou been too different?

"May I ask how soon we'll reach the anchorage?" I asked.

"With luck, our voyage will end tomorrow, Richard. Ringo Bay is nearer Fort Dauphin than you realize. I must ask you and Dr. Hoyt to stay below when the watch changes. You aren't full members of our company until you've taken the oath. As I told you, only my father can administer it—and we must keep a few secrets until he does."

All that night, and the long day that followed, Tom and I were confined to quarters with a blind porthole. Night had fallen once again when we made port—and, though there was a great stir of feet overhead, our door remained barred until morning.

When we went ashore at last, it was in a longboat with four of Mozo's watch at the sweeps. Before we went topside, the Negro blindfolded us with his own hands—and the blindfold remained in place until we stood in the pirate king's presence. That afternoon, impressions came to me in snatches: a wide expanse of salt water over which the boat coursed, the crunch of shells beneath our boots, a long flight of stairs up which we stumbled, with Mozo's hands at our elbows— and, finally, a plank floor that echoed hollowly to our steps. . . . Now (when I can draw Ringo Bay from memory) I will break no trust if I describe the kingdom before the king.

The corsair's stronghold was situated near the southern

tip of Madagascar, not too far from Cape Sainte Marie. Boxed on three sides by beetling hills and a belt of rain forest, the bay was completely hidden from the sea, thanks to a narrow estuary, whose mouth was smothered in jungle. Finding the entrance without landmarks was virtually impossible; sailing its dog-leg channel was a task to try any captain's seamanship.

Once the roadstead was entered, protection from bad weather (and enemy telescopes) was virtually assured. To the south and west high, rock-ribbed headlands offered added protection. Angry surf spouted here even on the calmest day, and there was not even a pocket handkerchief of beach. Carter had finished what nature began by planting masked batteries on the jungle-crowned heights—with each gun muzzle trained dead on the harbor mouth. So far, there had been no attempt at invasion: it had been years since a merchant vessel had risked a voyage through the Mozambique Channel, which opened under the pirate guns to the north west. As I have remarked elsewhere, the Company convoys gave Madagascar a wide berth on their runs to the Cape.

Within the harbor the scene was one of deceptively peaceful bustle. Members of the buccaneer fleet were always at anchor here—in the act of disgorging cargo, licking recent wounds, or careening on one of the several broad beaches that fringed the roadstead. Carter's warehouses (or *entrepôts*, to use the French word) stood just above the high-water mark. His countinghouse (where profits from each prize were apportioned and the shares assigned) occupied the end of the longest of several piers that marched, on spider-leg pilings, into the very heart of the bay.

Save for the profusion of gun mounts, the scene might have passed for a Company port. Many of Carter's crewmen were renegades from that same Company, which only added to the bizarre resemblance—to say nothing of the fact that much of his plunder (and the majority of his ships-of-war) had once been items on Company ledgers.

The pirate king's own abode stood apart—on a headland at the southern end of the harbor. Its own beach spread like a tan prayer rug to meet the tide, and acres of palm groves surrounded it. Like the other structures on Ringo Bay, it was more bastion than dwelling. In this case a deep moat and drawbridge gave added protection, along with an outer wall of crushed stone (planted with thorn trees and prickly pear) and a star-shaped barbican that flanked the gate.

Another fact was obvious at first view: this medieval show of strength was deliberate—intended to impress the pirate kings' own crews no less than it deterred aggression from without. Long before I had spent twenty-four hours at Ringo Bay, I could believe his daughter's own words. No man in Red Carter's realm would even dream of deposing him. . . .

As I have related, Tom and I were led blindfolded to the portico of his lair before we were permitted our first glimpse. When Mozo took the blindfolds from our eyes, we found ourselves standing on a rattan matting in the midst of a wide veranda. I knew instantly that the figure facing us across a trestle table was Red Carter. . . . For once, the man himself and the fevered images I had drawn seemed to coincide.

He was well over six feet in height, with the shoulders of a bullock and a leonine head that sprouted fire-red hair in all directions. His locks were a scarlet blizzard: his spade-shaped beard seemed a deeper red, and bristled when he spoke. The eyes were a mild china blue: I would learn how quickly they could darken when passion seized him, how they could shower forth visible sparks on the object of his wrath. When he heaved to his feet, he seemed to tower above us both; when he held out a hand to each of us, I could feel myself grow smaller within my own skin. He was naked, save for a pair of nankeen drawers—and his bare feet, gripping the planking with each gnarled toe, were made for a ship's deck. The voice (even when he did no more than purr) could have outhowled a hurricane, just as the massive body could have outridden it.

"Welcome, lads," he said. "Don't tell me who's the saw-bones: let me guess." He rumbled with laughter when his fist tapped Tom Hoyt's chest. "We can use *you* at once, Dr. Hoyt: the *Merry Andrew* is just back from Celebes, and there was a bumper crop of scurvy aboard. Mozo will take you to our hospital when you're bedded down."

"If you like, sir," said Tom, "I'll go at once."

"Those fellows have rotted in their skins for a good four weeks—they can rot a bit longer. Sit down, both of you—where I can study you." He swiveled my way at last, with an intent stare. "I'm also glad to welcome your shipmate aboard, Doctor: judging by my daughter's report, we can use him too."

I forced myself to meet the impish china-blue eyes when he turned my way again. He had fallen silent, as though daring me to unlock my thoughts. The exchange with Tom had been deliberate, I saw: he was giving me time to sort my impressions.

"What are you thinking, Mr. Douglas?" he asked abruptly. "That I bear small resemblance to Bonnie?"

I spoke up, as boldly as I could. "When we met in the New World, sir—I took her for a Portuguese lady. I haven't changed my view—"

"Your judgment does you credit, lad," he said. "Bonnie's both a lady and a sailor—I've seen to that since she could walk. Will you serve with her if the prize money's right?"

I had not expected so prompt an offer. In a way, it was reassuring—yet it troubled me, too, in a fashion I could not define.

"I'm her man, if she wants me," I said. "That's why I'm here."

"And you, Dr. Hoyt?"

Tom shrugged. "I'm a surgeon who loves his trade," he said. "This seems a likely place to practice it."

"Will you each take tenths until you've proved your worth?"

I calculated swiftly, remembering the strange arithmetic of piracy well enough. Half of each prize cargo went to the corsair's owner (in this case, the pirate king himself). Set shares were given to the skipper of the vessel, and to each of his mates. Depending on seniority, seasoned members of the crew were granted one fifth of each hundred pounds of value thereafter—share and share alike, until each sea dog had his just deserts. Finally the apprentices scrambled for what was left, to the tune of ten pounds per hundred.

Piracy (like any trade) paid it real rewards at the top. If the prize was rich enough, a skipper (or even a mate) could retire on the profits of a single voyage. London was said to be full of such ex-rascals, rolling like lords from coach to club in their green old age, full of strange tales from a deep-dyed past. A man of spirit (I faced the fact calmly) could rise swiftly in such company if he put his morals behind him.

"The berth's mine, sir," I said.

"And mine," said Tom. "Will you take our mark today or later?"

"Now, since you gentlemen are agreeable," said Carter, "I'm putting the *Venture* to sea again tomorrow."

I sucked in my breath, hoping my face was still a mask as the knife gleamed in one of his massive fists. The steel had appeared as though by magic. With his free hand Carter took inkpot and parchment from a drawer. When the sheet was unrolled, I saw it was a set of articles, not too different from the contract each sailor initialed before a voyage (or marked with his cross if he was unable to write). The brethren of fortune have their own rituals. I was aware that the present articles must be marked with special ink.

The ritual was a simple one: I am proud to say I stood without flinching while Carter's blade slashed downward, pricking the skin of Tom's forearm and my own, smearing our thumbs in the spurt of crimson, and affixing the thumbprint to the parchment, below the spot where we signed our names. This was the blood oath. I am told it is a ceremony older than pen or ink—a vow few men have broken and lived to boast of the breaking.

I had expected to take it in more ominous surroundings—by candle at midnight, perhaps, or on deck with a file of shipmates watching. There was still no blinking the fact the die was cast. From this moment I was a member of Bonnie Carter's crew, sworn to fight for her until she released me.

I glanced at Tom, who was still staring at the pucker of red on his wrist—and was glad to observe that his face had gone white. When Carter broke out a demijohn and gave us each a tot of rum, Tom downed his glass at a toss. I sipped at mine, careful to keep my thoughts veiled. Our position seemed secure. It was easy to infer that Bonnie's report on us both had been excellent—and that her judgment had been accepted. I wondered if I dared question the pirate king about Sir Luke—and decided in the negative. (To Carter's own knowledge, Metcalf and I had been strangers when the voyage began. I would only expose my hand if I seemed curious now.)

"So we go to sea again tomorrow," I said. "Can you speak freely of our voyage?"

Carter dismissed both Hoyt and Mozo, and motioned me to bring my chair nearer his table. The surface, I saw, was covered with Admiralty charts, studded with pins of different colors. I would find this was his seaman's way of keeping track of his ships—each of which was logged precisely, and its destination noted. Today, however, he ignored the maps. Instead, he took out a plot of the Monsoon Sea, with both the African and Arabian coasts sketched in detail. I saw it was one of the official charts used by the East India Company.

"You've sailed these waters, Mr. Douglas," said the pirate king, as calmly as though we were discussing a routine shipment in the North Sea. "Allowing for the fact that the winds are variable to the north, where would you head for the best hunting?"

The question was a trap—but I knew I must walk in boldly. "It's hardly the season to prey on the Company," I said. "They'll be waiting for the next monsoon to send their convoys south."

"True. What of the Dutch?"

"Dutch ships also travel in convoy," I said. "When we left the Cape, merchantmen were readying for a voyage to the Moluccas. But they'll be under the protection of men-of-war, now that trouble's brewing between England and France."

"Where does that leave us then? I've a dozen vessels away at this moment, dogging the sea lanes to the east—but my daughter's burning to take out her first command. Naturally, I'm eager to see how the *Pilgrim Venture* handles under fire. Can you suggest another hunting ground?"

"There's always the Grand Mogul's fleet, Captain Carter."

"True. It's been some time since I've hunted the Arabian Sea. Are the pickings still fair?"

I saw that he was still baiting me to test my knowledge, and spoke without a pause. "Better than fair, sir. His dhows are often old and hard to maneuver. Besides, they're seldom too heavily armed: they'll expect no attack in the western waters of the Arabian Sea."

"It's a long voyage, Mr. Douglas. What of their cargoes?"

"Sometimes they're rich beyond belief. A fortune in spices. Or jewels and precious metals. Things that take but little space in one's hold—and can be sold anywhere."

"How would you secure such a prize—if you were master?"

"As I told you, the Mogul's dhows are only prepared to fight off coastal pirates," I said boldly. "They'll be fair prey for a vessel that handles as well as the *Venture*. My guess is we could grapple after a single broadside, gut, and be away before they could manage a counterblow. With fair winds, we could take several prizes in this fashion—striking twenty leagues apart, where they'd expect no visitors. Once we'd combed the Arabian Gulf, we might even tap the Red Sea trade—though I'll grant you it's trickier to navigate."

I had spoken as forcefully as I could, and the picture I drew was a fair one. The infidels have always been legal game for our privateers. If I must turn pirate, I felt I could fight them with a clear conscience, as natural enemies of England.

"Bonnie can navigate any waters that are charted," said Carter. "The point is still well taken." He was jabbing pins into the new map now, his nostrils flaring like a hound to the scent. "She'll victual for the Arabian Sea then—and take what she finds there. You'll ship as her second mate."

I accepted the ruling without demur. "The lady won't regret her offer," I said. Naturally, I had hoped for a first berth —but that post belonged by right to Mozo.

"My feeling is you'll do, Mr. Douglas," said Carter. "The next few weeks will test that belief. Don't be confused if I add there's another inducement to succeed. Or has Bonnie explained you're being groomed as a possible consort?"

He had taken me by surprise, and I knew I was gaping. Despite the implication behind his words, there was nothing friendly in his tone: the eyes were hot coals now, burning my hide.

"I'm afraid I don't understand, sir," I said—and cursed my stammering tongue.

"Don't pretend to be stupid. My daughter and I have no secrets. She's said she wants you. I've promised she could have you—if you pass muster on this voyage. I'll endorse no man for her bed until he's shown his mettle at sea."

I was at a loss for words now—and prudent enough to hold my tongue. Fortunately, Carter gave me no chance for speech.

"The girl's turned twenty," he said—and I had the odd feeling he was thinking aloud rather than addressing me directly. "If she means to give this kingdom an heir, it's high time she was with child. Not that *I'll* part with her willingly. You understand that much, I trust?"

"Perfectly, sir," I murmured.

"Since she was fifteen, she'd had her choice of husbands, but none of my lads struck her fancy. Now you've arrived on my doorstep—and she's chosen you. It's as simple as that, Mr. Douglas. What else can I do but put you on trial?"

"I won't deny I'm honored beyond my deserts. But I never dared hope—"

"There's no need to play-act," he said. "You're a man of parts. Are you pretending you didn't see how the wind was setting?"

"I give you my word, sir—"

"The devil with your word, man! You've taken the blood oath. That means you take orders too. First, you'll ship out as a gentleman of fortune and prove yourself. Then, if the girl still wants it so, you'll wed her. *Is that clear? Or must I keel-haul you and look elsewhere?*"

The words were fairly thundered. Now, for the first time, I could measure the enormity of his self-esteem. (How could it be otherwise when his power here was absolute?) In the same breath I sensed that he took no pleasure in the agreement he had offered me—that he would have kept his daughter inviolate, had not his kingly duties dictated otherwise. Finally, and most important, I saw that my life hung in the balance—depending, quite literally, on the answer I made to his question.

"Consider your problems solved, sir," I said. "I'll do my utmost to serve you both."

For a moment more he continued to stare across the table, and his eyes still smoldered with wordless resentments. Then he expelled his breath in a long sigh before he held out his hand. To my surprise, his fingers were icy-cold.

"Spoken like a man, Mr. Douglas," he said. "I trust you meant every word."

"Try me on either count," I said. "You'll see how well I mean them."

His whiskers still danced (like the quills of an angry porcupine), but his eyes had gone back to lazy blue. I settled in my chair. It had been a narrow squeak—but I felt I was safe as he went booming on to other matters.

"We'll discuss one more subject that's close to my heart,"

he said. "Then I'll give you shore leave. What d'you know of a man called Sir Luke Metcalf?"

I had braced for the query—and found I could answer without quaking. "Only that he's a nabob of the East India Company. He sailed with us under a pseudonym."

"Your paths have never crossed before?"

"Never, sir," I murmured. Aware that my life had balanced again on a proper answer, I was shamed to the depths that this answer must be a lie.

Carter dismissed my avowal with a flick of his massive hand. "No matter—though I wish you'd known his true name and warned Bonnie in time."

"I can see that, sir. Naturally, you meant to capture him along with the *Venture.*"

"It was my hope, ever since her keel was laid," he said. "I paid Bob McLane a fortune to set the trap in New York. When Metcalf walked into it, I felt I'd not lived in vain." He rested both elbows on his worktable and stared into space, obsessed by some evil vision he could never share. "You know, of course, that I've devoted twenty years to his ruin?"

"The story is common gossip."

"Twice in those twenty years I almost lured him into combat," said Carter. "We traded salvos in the Malacca Straits in '85: I was ready to board him when a typhoon separated both ships. In '91 I sighted his topsails off Table Mountain and gave chase—but he turned coward on me then, and sought asylum with the Dutch. *This* time, I told myself, the villain's all mine."

He had bounced to his feet, taking the length of the veranda in raging strides. The words had been flung at me—but they were aimed at Metcalf. So loudly were they shouted, they might have crossed the sea that divided them.

"I'd meant to bring him here in chains, aboard his own ship. I'd planned to make him one last offer. The truth—in exchange for a chance to defend his life."

"The truth, sir?"

"A sworn statement—declaring it was he, not I, who robbed the Company of a million pounds. *Then* we'd have met in single combat. If he'd proved the better sword, I'd have died with my name cleared. If not, I'd have been revenged twice."

He pulled up sharp on that, aware that his mind had wandered into the land of might-have-been. Returning to the table, he struck it with his fist, so harshly that his inkpot overturned. Then he snatched up a tattered sheet of foolscap and shook it in my face. I recognized it as the note Metcalf had left at Fort Dauphin.

"You've seen this, of course?"

"I *found* it, Captain Carter."

"It proves he escaped me one more time. No matter. This note is also proof he'll return—and that he'll be spoiling for a fight."

"So it appears, sir."

"Must I tell you why? The viper from hell thinks he's found me out. That he has a map of Ringo Bay—"

"Forgive my stupidity, sir—but isn't that what Potin sold him?"

"D'you think I'd give a *Frenchman* a true chart of this harbor? The map he sold Metcalf shows the entrance to a roadstead a good sea mile to the north. It's long since returned to jungle—but I'll prepare it for his reception when he comes calling. Believe me, it's the last trap he'll enter alive."

I sat back while he roared out his harangue—most of it addressed direct to his absent enemy. Fools' Harbor (as the other roadstead was aptly named) had an entrance resembling the channel that led to the pirates' actual stronghold. Like Ringo Bay, it could be defended by batteries mounted on two headlands. It was Carter's scheme to plant dummy guns on these ramparts, permit Metcalf's fleet to destroy them with a few salvos—then to show the white flag at the harbor mouth. When the Company men-of-war sailed in to accept his surrender, he would blow them from the water with fire power massed along the beach. Should the enemy escape this punishment, a heavily gunned armada (standing by at sea) would be able to destroy any such vessels as remained. . . .

"Will you believe it, lad? I meant to send Potin to Madras next year, to sell that map direct to the Company. Now Metcalf buys it outright—and flings down his dare. *I'll be waiting, you villain! I'll be waiting!*"

The tirade ended in a screech that was not quite human. I backed from his presence as he waved me out. There was froth on his lips, and the wildly staring eyes were fixed on a horizon beyond my ken. A slave had already come forward to wipe the sweat from his master's brow and hand him a glass of rum: Carter's minions, it was evident, had learned to handle these rages.

He was drinking thirstily as I left. His fury had given way to a series of full-throated chuckles as the rum soothed his choler. I enjoyed his mirth still less than his cursing.

Bonnie Carter was walking in the palm grove just outside the veranda. I was glad to observe that she had shed her boots and jerkin for a pale green robe (of the material the French call *peau de soie*). In one hand she carried the straw hat she had bought in Cape Town: a tiny monkey perched on her shoulder. Chattering angrily at my approach, the beast leaped nimbly into the branches of a jacaranda tree. The new captain of the *Venture* gave me a welcoming smile.

"You look a trifle shaken," she said. "I don't blame you."

"You heard his tirade then?"

She glanced back at the fortress as she led me down a path that skirted the harbor. "I could hardly help myself," she said quickly. "He's a little mad at times: Metcalf made him so. But there isn't a greater man alive when he's master of his rage."

"I'll endorse that estimate," I said. "God knows *he's* made me happier than I deserve today."

She gave me a level look that held no hint of coquetry. "He or I, Richard?"

"You, most of all," I said. "Forgive me if I spoke his name ahead of yours. After all, he's king here—and you're the princess."

It was a gallant speech, albeit a sincere one. I had expected a blush and lowered lashes. Instead, her chin lifted still higher—and the proud eyes did not waver by a fraction. I had forgotten that Bonnie Carter was without guile (as she was without coquetry), that she had forsworn most pretenses of civilization. When she chose, she could be a great lady indeed—but she was still the aggressor in our pact. . . . My avowal (to her) had been an unexpected tribute.

"You're willing to be my consort then—if you survive your testing?"

"Gladly," I told her. "Even though there's small hope of taming you."

"Why should you tame me? Why should any man?"

"It's a delusion most men harbor when they marry," I said. "Marriage to a princess, after all, is an exception."

"You won't regret the bargain," she said. "That much I can promise you. Give my father two years more, and he'll have all Madagascar as his kingdom. He can set his own rules then, for half the Monsoon Sea. Or make himself part of the Empire, like Morgan, and end with London's pardon. I can think of worse futures, Richard."

"Will you believe it's you I desire—not your father's plunder?"

Bonnie shrugged off the answer and turned to face the harbor. I stood at her side for a moment without pressing my advantage. Below us the water flashed in the afternoon sun. On the Carters' wharf slaves sang as they finished the unloading of the *Venture*. It was an English tune that rang oddly on this tropic air:

> *He followed her up*
> *And he followed her down*
> *And she had not the power*
> *To flee from his arms*
> *Nor the tongue to answer*
> *Nay, nay, nay!*
> *Nor the tongue to answer nay.*

I saw that a second file of blackamoors was bringing fresh victuals aboard, and quantities of powder and shot. These, I realized with a quickened pulse, were preparations for our voyage. It would be a long haul to the waters where the Grand Mogul held sway. This stolen moment with Bonnie was a chance that would not come again.

"Don't answer no," I told her. "But I hoped you'd desire me too. As a lover, not merely as a consort."

"What is a lover, Richard?"

"Something I won't define," I said. "No man can translate the language of the heart."

"I've read the word," she said. "So far, it's without meaning."

"Then you chose me without love?"

"I must have an heir."

"You'd take me for that purpose only?"

"You can handle a ship as well as I. You've the brain of a born sailor, and the body to match it. I trust you'll make a good father for my son. Could I have sounder reasons?"

"They're cold arguments for marriage, Bonnie."

She faced me in earnest then. "Are you saying you love me?"

"Ever since we met in New York. Can't you return the feeling?"

"I like you, Richard—better than any man I've known. We think alike—I believe we feel alike. Will that help?"

"Like is a word to console old age," I said. *"Love's* the word for youth. Won't you test its meaning?"

"How can I when I've never been in love?"

"Yet you chose me. I'm still asking why."

"I've told you why, Richard. Don't ask for more." But she moved away with the disavowal—and, for the first time, I caught a hint of emotion in her tone. After all, the knowledge that she is adored is the oldest music to stir the female heart. Nothing, not even her father's iron discipline, could stifle that brief echo.

"When does our marriage take place?" I asked.

"The day we return from my first voyage."

"What if I fail to earn good marks as an officer?"

"You won't fail, Richard. That's one thing I'm sure of."

"Today, in your father's presence, I swore to obey you as captain of the *Venture.* To do all I can to make her a happy ship, and a prosperous one."

"So you did," she said. "And I'm glad to have you aboard."

"I mean to succeed as your husband—with love, or without it. But we've yet to plight our troth as man and woman. Don't tell me *that's* a phrase I must translate."

"I've heard the phrase," she said. "I understand its meaning. If it's the custom, you may kiss me."

The monkey was still scolding in the jacaranda tree when I took my first cautious step toward the girl. Despite my resolve, I found my glance had swept the grove—lest some hidden bodyguard was prepared to spring upon me if I so much as touched her. Obviously, my fears were groundless: here, in the heart of Carter's domain, the safety of his daughter was beyond challenge. By the same token, the wishes of that daughter were law—whether it pleased her to cross swords with her father's captains or to grant a first kiss to the consort of her choice.

When I drew her into my arms, she met the embrace fairly—lifting her own arms to circle my neck, letting her chin rest in the cup of my palm until our lips could brush. When I released her, she stood unstirring, her eyes opened wide.

"Is *that* what one calls a kiss?"

"Did you find it disappointing?"

"I was told it meant more, Richard."

"Who told you of kissing?"

"The ancient poets," she said. "Even in Homer the maidens were forever swooning. In Virgil or in Ovid they wept for joy. I had no thought of swooning, and no urge to shed a tear."

"A true kiss must be returned," I said. "Shall we try again?"

She was laughing when she moved into my embrace a second time: I rejoiced in her laughter, since it was proof that her curiosity was stirred at last. I made this buss as feather-light as our first—but, when I claimed her lips, I let my hands stray from her shoulders to her thighs, caressing her gently as I drew her close. Her response was instant, all female—and so sweetly eager. I felt my senses swim.

While that shared embrace lasted, our roles (for the first time) were reversed. Now it was I who dominated and she who gave. Once she had learned the joy of giving, she gave with all her heart. Her body arched against mine to make a singing chord of passion: her mouth (now she had found what kissing meant) was warm and searching on my own. . . . Trained as I was in this game, I released her first and stood back to savor my victory.

"Homer was right," she whispered. "I *did* almost swoon. Make me swoon again."

We were alone in the palm garden, and the branches of the jacaranda made a tent of green about us as we kissed for the third time. Every instinct I possessed (like rampant male devils) insisted I could possess her—as easily as Adam took Eve in the Garden. Yet conscience trained in a Scottish kirk is not so easily routed: even with ecstasy at its peak, I knew my teasing game had run its course. Loving her as I did, it was impossible to cozen her further. . . . Again it was I who broke that hungry embrace—putting six good feet of greensward between us before I found my voice.

"Those, my dear, were kisses," I said, as casually as I could. "D'you see now what they mean—and what they can lead to?"

"Yes, Richard. Shall we kiss again?"

"Not if we're wise."

"I thought the poets lied. I was sure such madness wasn't meant for this world. *Why didn't you warn me?*"

"If I had, would you have listened?"

Her eyes flashed fire then—and I saw she was playing with an idea I had planted.

"There's a Portuguese priest aboard the *Flying Cloud*," she said. "The ship was captured in our last foray off the Cape, and we've yet to arrange his release. If I wish it, he can marry us now."

"I can't be your husband until I've proved myself. That's your father's ruling."

"Rules can be broken, Richard."

"Not this one. He'd have my head if you proposed it—and rightly."

"You said you loved me," she cried—and stamped her foot. But I could see the light of sanity was rising in her mind again.

"Honor's more precious than love," I told her. "I'll show you what love means—*after* we've taken our prizes from the Mogul."

She tossed her head as we met eye to eye: knowing I was lost if I budged, I held my ground.

"Your strength of will does you credit," she said. "I'm not sure I commend it."

"I was strong at Blomfontein," I said. "I mean to be strong tomorrow—if only to prove myself worthy of you. But don't tempt me again, Captain Carter. No man is strong forever."

When she laughed, I felt we had passed the danger point.

"At least we know what awaits us," she said. "As you pointed out, that's something gained."

"Yes, Bonnie. In the words of yet another poet—'tis a consummation devoutly to be wished."

"That poet spoke of death—not love."

"And he spoke rightly. Until your pride dies—until you learn what surrender in a man's embrace can truly mean— you can never call yourself a woman. It's another thing I'll teach you when the time is right."

Again she tossed her head—and her laughter warned me that I'd missed my mark. "I'll remember that threat, Mr. Douglas," she said. It was the master of the *Venture* speaking now, not the girl I had all but seduced. "See you live up to it." She had all but left the terrace on our final exchange: she paused now, in stern profile. "It's a truce then?"

"It's a truce on the *champs d'amour*," I agreed. "We're already allies aboard the *Venture*: The Douglases don't give their word lightly."

"Have it your way, if you must," she said. Then, with a wordless cry, she turned to me again, flung both arms about me, and kissed me, long and savagely, on the mouth. There was no tenderness in that kiss—only the desperate urgency to show that even here she was in command.

"May I ask what that proved?" I asked when she stepped back.

"Nothing whatever," she said. "Until our next meeting —on what you call the field of love—I'll leave you with the last word. And thank you again for your enlightenment."

She was gone with the avowal, walking with the light, sure stride I knew so well—for all the world as though she already trod her own quarter-deck.

CHAPTER 10

The Aureng Zeb

THE day after I exchanged kisses with Bonnie, the *Pilgrim Venture* set out on her first voyage of piracy.

We left Ringo Bay on the morning tide, with our new captain on the quarter-deck and a sailor in the bowsprit shrouds to call soundings in the dog-leg channel. Again, as second officer on a ship I had once commanded, I found myself in the ratlines, directing the shifting of sail as we ran down that narrow seaway. More than once I was sure we would split apart on the flanks of the headlands—until Bonnie (shouting an order at the last moment) brought our nose on course. In the end we ran for blue water with all our canvas taut.

Long before the first watch changed, we were rolling up the Mozambique Channel with a stiff easterly breeze. Our only other route would have taken us clean around Madagascar—and such cautious seamanship was beneath the dignity of Red Carter's vessels, now he had staked out these waters as his preserve. Bonnie took pride in setting a Channel course, since no merchantman afloat (and few rival buccaneers) would have ventured to run between island and mainland.

My position aboard was unchanged. Indeed, when I was on some errand of my own (or lying in my bunk between watches) I was hard put to remember that the ship was now a corsair in search of plunder. Since we flew the Jolly Roger only when entering a friendly port (or engaging a prize) we could still have passed for an honest merchantman. Our flag locker contained the ensigns of all nations, and it was the captain's fancy to break out an English standard on this leg of our voyage. There was small chance of meeting a Company ship or a Dutchman, but the precaution seemed worth while. True, we were inviting attack from the French —or from coastal marauders. But the gun crews were itching for just such a brawl, if only to show their prowess.

I had hoped for a personal word from Bonnie that first day—or a council with the other officers, where I could demonstrate some knowledge of the problems she would soon be facing. But my deck duty ended without a summons. Before turning down the companionway, I ventured to pause at the quarter-deck ladder. Mozo was at the wheel: Bonnie sat in the captain's seat, a chart across her knee. In her boy's garb, with one booted leg across the other and her hair lost in a tightly bound kerchief, she was a far cry from the girl who (only yesterday) had returned my embraces so ardently. . . . When she felt my eyes, she gave me a crisp salute—and no more. It was my signal to go below.

Tom Hoyt sat on his bunk, reading a copy of our articles. (At the last moment, Carter had decided to send him with us for the experience—though his services would always be in demand at the shore hospital.)

"Don't scowl so blackly, my friend," he said. "I'm aware that you're earmarked as the captain's bedfellow. Did you expect to be called to her cabin the moment you're off watch?"

"You needn't be so explicit, Tom," I growled.

"She'll test you in good time. Try to be patient."

"Never mind my future," I said. "It's the present that concerns me. This will be a tricky voyage at best—the moment we've cleared the Comarros."

"Our master's aware of that, Dick. She's ordered daily gun drills."

"Even as a gunner's mate I'd feel more useful than I do today."

"Patience, I said. And above all, stop resenting the fact that a woman's in command."

"I'd resent it less if she asked my help. After all, this won't be my first baptism by fire."

"I'll tell you what you *really* resent," said Tom. "She's proved she can outsail most men—granted?"

"Of course."

"Why should she call on you for advice—now we're about to go into battle? With her training, she can probably outfight you as well. Or is that too bitter a pill to swallow?"

I smashed a fist into the bulkhead. "She'll need advice soon enough," I said. "What's more, I'll make a separate wager: this ship won't outlast her first engagement unless I'm on the quarter-deck."

"Fortunately for you, I'm not a betting man," said Tom. He tossed the articles into my hands and held up a palm for silence. "Let's argue no further on the skills of your enamorata, in love or war. Tell me what you make of *this* book of rules."

I read through the paper without losing the sense of impotence which plagued me. The first provisions dealt with the division of prize monies, a subject I have already discussed. Despite my mood, I could not keep down a grin as I read the fifth article aloud:

*"Should a man attempt to run away, or harbor a secret
of any kind from the brotherhood, he will be marooned
forthwith. His provisions shall consist of a water bottle,
a horn of powder, twenty rounds of shot, and a musket."*

"Shall we make a clean breast of everything?" I asked.
"We're both fair shots. We could survive—even if they put
us ashore on the Comarros."

"If she learned the truth about us, Captain Carter would
hardly be satisfied with marooning."

"We're of no further use to Sir Luke," I pointed out.
"He's learned all he needs to know, and he's preparing to
attack. Shouldn't we get free if we can?"

"Wild horses couldn't drag you off this ship," said my
doctor friend cheerfully. "And if your conscience is still
rumbling within, pay it no heed. When you signed that
blood oath, you transferred your loyalties. Why pretend
otherwise?"

I lowered my eyes to the articles, unwilling to argue the
point further. There was much truth in the remark. For
better or worse, I was committed to this voyage—and to
Bonnie. I could not force my laggard morals to rise in wrath.

Other items in our contract dealt with theft (pilfering
was punished by marooning, major thievery by shooting).
Forty stripes were the usual punishment for insubordination
—and for smoking between decks. Ten pounds was listed as
the standard compensation for the loss of a limb in action,
twenty for the loss of sight.

"Read the last article aloud," said Tom. "It has a certain
application to the present."

*"If, during a voyage, a member of the brotherhood
should chance upon a woman, and indulge in fornica-
tion without her consent, he shall suffer death by hang-
ing."*

"As you see," said Tom, "Red Carter thinks of everything."

"Let's not belabor the point," I said. "The lady's quite
safe from me—and knows it well."

"Are you safe from *her?*"

"What d'you mean?"

"Suppose this *is* a trail voyage for you—in every sense?

What if you're tested between the sheets and found wanting? It's the captain's privilege to invoke that article—and who'd dare say her nay?"

"I think we've joked enough," I said.

"Would that I were joking, Dick—but I'm not. From what you've told me, you're between the devil and the deep. Falling in love's a risky business in any language. Loving a pirate princess who can hang you at any moment is enough to try a man's soul."

North of the Comarros (an archipelago of palm-studded islets above Madagascar) we set a course for the open sea and went rolling on, with favoring winds, to our next landfall. This was the mountain mass of Socotra, a fair-sized island off Cape Guardafui. Beyond was the Gulf of Aden, which gave in turn to the Red Sea. It was Bonnie's intention to begin her hunting in this area before pushing farther north.

So far, I had yet to tread the quarter-deck when she was on watch, though I had taken several tricks at the wheel when Mozo was in command—and, of course, gave the orders when I was the officer in charge. As it chanced, I had the deck when we sighted our first prize. I will not deny that the long-drawn cry of *Sail-ho!* from our crow's-nest sent a shiver down my spine. Fortunately, I remembered my place in time—and turned to knock on the captain's door just as Bonnie herself came into view.

"Where away, Mr. Douglas?"

"Dead ahead, Captain."

She was in the ratlines with a single catlike bound, a spyglass at her belt—mounting to the height of our topsail before she took her first squint at the northern horizon. Her eyes were sparkling when she dropped down beside me and tendered the glass.

"Name it if you can," she said.

We were bowling north-by-northeast, in freshening weather, at close to fifteen knots. The horizon opened as I climbed: even before I reached our first yardarm, I could discern the white blur of a sail with the naked eye. I climbed on until I was just below the crow's-nest, where I conferred with our lookout, then studied our prospective quarry with care. Bonnie was pacing the deck impatiently when I returned.

"Even for a Scot," she said, "that's a dour face you're wearing."

"She's an Indiaman," I said. "But she's convoyed by three booms."

"I'd call them coastal dhows, not booms."

"This convoy is boom-rigged." The point was worth making. The Arab coastal dhow, a light-draft vessel with lateen sails, was often heavy in the tail and easily outmaneuvered. The boom, however, was double-ended—with a built-up sternpost and a raked bow that gave great speed, and permitted an adroit ship handler to change course in a twinkling.

"Thunderation take your booms!" said Bonnie. "Can you name the Indiaman's home port?"

"She looks to be one of the Mogul's ships," I said. There had been no mistaking that blood-red standard.

"Judging by the shortened sail," said Bonnie, "she has only a prize crew aboard."

I nodded my agreement. The boom is a craft much favored by the pirates of the Trucial Coast. The Indiaman was almost surely a prize, and the three-ship convoy seemed to be shepherding it to one of their strongholds in the Gulf of Aden—but we were too far off, as yet, to be positive.

"If she's a prize," said Bonnie, "she's worth retaking."

"Undoubtedly," I said. "The Mogul uses dozens of these Indiamen on the run to Suez. I've known him to send cargoes worth a hundred thousand pounds."

"She didn't seem heavily armed."

"I doubt if she's armed at all," I said. "The gun decks are often stripped to make extra storage space. Usually, they hug the coast until they reach Aden."

"Of course this may be her original convoy."

"It's far more likely *they're* at the bottom of the Arabian Sea," I said. "I'd give ten to one those booms are corsairs, since they fly no colors. Not that the point's worth arguing. We'll have a war on our hands if we sail amongst 'em."

Bonnie's eyes strayed to the English flag that whipped bravely at her own mizzen. "So far as they know now, we're a Company ship," she said. "As such we mean no harm. Hold course, if you please, Mr. Douglas. We've time for a look at the chart."

She returned to her cabin, emerging at once with an Admiralty map, which she spread for my inspection. This, I perceived, was to be my first testing.

"As you see, we've two routes open," she said. "One is to make westing at once and enter the Gulf at Socotra. The other is to hold our present tack and risk a fight. Which would you suggest?"

The answer was simple. Only the most intrepid of masters would have ventured to run the narrow channel between the island of Socotra and the mainland. True, some brethren of the coast had found rich pickings in the Babs (which the Arabs called Bab el Mandeb, a strait at the mouth of the Red Sea itself). But this area could be approached only with the monsoon. At other seasons the dangers of foundering were great.

"I'd hold course and sound this convoy out," I said.

"So far, we think alike," she told me. "Send word if the escorts show their colors." Again she was gone with the words, popping into her cabin like a jack-in-the-box. Had the deck of the *Venture* belonged to a British ship of the line (and had I been the greenest of ensigns), she could not have addressed me more formally.

In the next hour I stole an occasional glance through the half-open door. Our skipper was working hard at her log, which she had kept meticulously complete, in the precise, schoolgirl hand she had learned in Boston. The glimpses I had had of that ponderous, copper-bound book had shown but routine mention of my name. I could not help wondering how high she would score today's advice.

News of a prospective prize had spread through the ship. Mozo and Jack Ketchell (who had been promoted from bosun to third officer) were on deck before their off-watch ended, each with his glass trained on the sea ahead—and volunteers leaped to every shroud when I ordered the yards shifted. Indeed, I was forced to speak sharply on occasion to keep the men from overmanning the lines. It would never do to advertise our interest in advance.

When Bonnie came on deck again, we were a half mile upwind of the nearest boom. The vessel was sailing a tight triangular course to protect the lumbering Indiaman's stern. The sister ships formed the remaining points of the triangle: we could not risk a closer approach without coming into gun range. Nor did I doubt now that the three smaller vessels were pirate-manned, though they had boldly broken out French colors as we drew nearer. The sons of the Prophet are ever ignorant of Europe's political shifts: they could hardly know, as yet, that war between France and Britain had erupted once again. Or that the forged letters of marque (which they carried to preserve the fiction they were privateers in the Sun King's service) would protect them no longer, if we were, indeed, the honest English vessel we seemed.

Once again I climbed the mast for a more detailed study. The three escorts were top-heavy with guns: such scavengers were built to strike swiftly and make the first broadside count. Their three swarthy skippers (clinging like great-beaked birds to their halyards) were studying us intently. Evidently, they were as yet unsure of our purpose: there had been no warning shot—but each of their gunners stood at the *qui vive*.

Bonnie was at the rail when I descended. "What's your opinion now, Mr. Douglas?"

"She's a prize from the Mogul's fleet," I said. "There's only a skeleton crew aboard her—and, judging by the way she wallows, she's loaded deep. There isn't a round shot aboard. Boxes and bales are jammed into both her gun decks. You can see them through the ports."

"It's hard to picture an easier capture," said Bonnie.

"She's a duck in a millpond—if we can wipe out the three booms."

"How would *you* take her, Mr. Douglas?"

I glanced around me, realizing that both Mozo and Jack had climbed to the quarter-deck. This, obviously, was my second challenge.

"There's a way, Captain Carter, if you'll risk it," I said. "May we discuss it in your cabin?"

Bonnie cast a glance at the seamen who crowded both rails, eager for a command to quarters. "Follow me, gentlemen," she said—and stalked once again into her cabin. She did not face us at once as we followed. Instead she made another notation in her log, sanded the page, and slammed the book shut. Even now I felt she was testing my patience. I stood unstirring just inside the door and held my peace.

"Speak up, Mr. Douglas," she said. "Until you've proved yourself otherwise, you're among friends."

"My plans are on the daring side," I told her.

"So are most sea fights when the odds are three to one."

"In your place I'd sail straight through the convoy. I'd put extra men on the yards and shift course constantly. Coming into their midst on a zigzag, we'd be sure to confuse 'em. By engaging the nearest boom first, we'll use the Indiaman as a shield. Then, when we're ready, we'll hit both the others point-blank. With proper timing, we can put all three out of action in two passes."

"Daring's a mild word for such a ruse," said Bonnie. "How would you vote, Mozo?"

"I'd prefer a more even odds," said the Negro.

"And you, Jack?"

"Mozo's right," said the Englishman. "We could stop a round shot where it'd hurt—while we were still outgunned."

"Both objections are valid," said Bonnie. "I'm still voting with Mr. Douglas. Break out our colors, Mozo. And you, Jack, send your gunners to their stations. We're holding course—and asking for a fight."

When our eyes met, I felt myself take fire from her endorsement. True, if our plan miscarried, we were risking a fearful aftermath. Yet I could not but feel she would assume the blame if luck deserted us.

"Since the plan is yours, Mr. Douglas," she said, "you will take the deck. I'll give contrary orders, if needed."

I remembered to salute before I left the cabin, but I could not quite keep down a grin: my spirits were bounding as I took command again—for the first time since Cape Town. A cheer ran down the deck as I gave the order to move into action: there was no question that these sea dogs would serve me to the last gasp.

Mozo and Ketchell had taken their posts—the former at the bowsprit to gauge the first hostile shots, the latter to the gun deck. I needed no more than a passing glance for these activities. Thanks to constant practice, each man alow and aloft knew his job. . . . Even in the brisk following wind I could smell the oily blaze in each of the pots where round shots were heating. The gunners stood above their matches, primed to snap into motion. Powder monkeys hung at the rail, awaiting the command to open ports. Still others waited at the pulleys for the order to ease the cannon into firing position.

Similar activity was going forward on the enemy escorts. A howl of dismay sounded across the narrowing strip of sea when the black flag of our profession replaced the English ensign. The first shot, when it came, was only a grotesque warning—a high, arching ball that skittered into the water a hundred yards off our larboard bow. Fired from a rusty howitzer, it could be followed by the naked eye, so feeble was its propulsion. I guessed it was one of the stone cannon balls still used by the infidels against lesser prey and hoped it meant the enemy was short of more effective weapons.

Sailing at our top speed, breaking course at two-minute intervals, we were still a shifting target—and our own gunners would have an excellent chance to sink or disable the nearest escort vessel. Once that objective was attained, we must move with lightning speed. It was my intention to come about in the shadow of our prize, cross her bows, and smash broadsides into the two remaining booms before they could return the fire. No other tactic was feasible, since we were so sadly outnumbered. If one or more of those escorts came within grappling range, it would go ill with us: the Trucial pirates are past masters in a fight at close quarters.

Bonnie had not come on deck when the first shot whistled across our bows, followed by a spatter-dash volley from the boom's stern gunners. The enemy was still feeling us out, hoping to establish his trajectory and catch us later in a straddling fire. Sending my first order to the gun crews, I rejoiced that he had not, as yet, divined my own strategy.

On the weather rail a score of matches flared as a powder monkey raced down the deck with a brazier. In another moment the same procedure was repeated alee. Our bow gunners (warned by Hans) had prepared to fire on order: the nearest boom was already looming in their sight.

"Hold your fire till we're abaft," I called.

"Steady she is, sir," Hans shouted.

Round shot was plummeting into the sea on both sides, and several of the hits were uncomfortably close. The master of the escort vessel was aware of my purpose now, and shouted imprecations from his perch in the rigging. . . . There was a stir at our cabin door, and Bonnie came on deck at last to stand beside me with folded arms and a set smile I would remember later. Busy though I was (and counting the seconds before I gave the order to open fire), I risked a glance in her direction. The brief taste of command had been heady: I had half forgotten I could be deposed at a word.

"All shipshape, Captain Carter."

"The deck's still yours, Mr. Douglas."

"The gunners have orders to aim for the sternpost," I said. "Everything hangs on disabling the boom with a single shot."

"So I observe," she said. "In your place I'd sail a point closer to the wind."

I corrected my helmsman with a smothered curse at her eye for seamanship. The distraction, brief though it had been, had permitted the *Venture* to ease off a bit: it was vital that we roar down on our enemy with our bowsprit leveled at his rudder chains.

The pause that followed seemed never ending. Less than two hundred feet of sea lay between us now. Heeled over as we were, we would never be more vulnerable to a shot between wind and water—and such a blow could end the fight before it was fairly joined. I held my breath as a ball splintered the coaming of our forward rail. A second shot, hissing out of the blue like some evil banshee, missed the quarterdeck by inches before it geysered into our wake. Still holding course, I dropped to my knees at its passage—certain, for the moment, it would splinter the wheel beyond repair. Bonnie, still defiantly upright beside me, laughed aloud at the near miss.

"Keep her nose down, Mr. Douglas! Give the gunners a clear sight!"

I accomplished this simple maneuver easily—taking the full force of the wind on my main and foreyards and driving the bowsprit into the heart of the next roller. White water spouted over our foredeck and I bellowed the order to fire. As the spume cleared, the parrot-beaked silhouette of the enemy sternpost seemed to hang above us. Hans was the first of the two swivel gunners to fire: the other gun roared before the first report could die, blanketing our bows in a nimbus of smoke. I ordered the helm over just in time, as we shot through the cloud.

Both shots had found their target. There was only a gaping hole where the rudder had been—and the enemy mainmast, cut clean away, had spilled its sail into the water, fouling the hostile gunports as we ran past.

"*Fire!*"

The broadside, delivered almost in unison by the eighteen guns that lined our weather rail, would have foundered a vessel twice the size of the boom. There was no time to measure the exact damage, since we had already gone winging alee of the Indiaman, but the screams of the crew spelled out the impact.

"*Load—and stand by!*"

The command was needless. The gunners (there are no finer marksmen on earth than your seasoned buccaneers) had already sprung to their task, aware they must deliver a fresh broadside when we emerged from our ambush. I eased off a point, giving them what time I could. The Indiaman, now less than a biscuit's toss upwind, seemed to fill the sky. I studied the disposition of her men, noting that less than a dozen faces showed at the rail. As I had surmised, the Arabs had put no more than a jury crew aboard, hoping to bring their prize to land without mishap. Had their gun deck been manned, we would have breathed our last before we emerged from her shadow.

The vessel herself was an ancient vagabond who showed yards of seaweed beard with each roll of her bows. Despite the stiffening breeze, she was barely moving—and, compared to the *Star of Bengal*, she was a decrepit hulk indeed. The Arabs, by and large, are slovenly shipmasters: it was easy to see that she had not been careened in many months. That barnacled exterior, however, was only a blind to mask the riches within: it had always been the Grand Mogul's custom to use such hoary argosies to transport his wealth to Suez. Her name—the *Aureng Zeb*—blazoned in Arabic on her stern, was advertisement enough of her value.

Our next move called for co-ordination. Before we had darted into the shadow of our prize, I had marked the position of the two remaining booms exactly. Since they had been shut out of the battle so far, I counted on them to be ready—and so they were, guns trained well ahead of the Indiaman, eager to blast us from the water when we emerged from the protection of those cliff-high decks. Naturally, they expected us to run clear. Instead, I put our helm hard to larboard, almost before we had drawn level with the bow-

sprit of the *Aureng Zeb*. In another instant we burst into
the open sea again, shaving the Indiaman's bow by a whisker
—precisely as a race horse, breaking fast, might cross the
path of the others.

It was a desperate tactic, and I had counted on its surprise value. As I hoped, the skippers of the two remaining
booms reacted as prudent seamen should—putting up their
helms to avoid a head-on crash, and opening space between
them.

"Stand by to come about!"

Again the order was scarcely needed. The ratlines were
black with sailors when we went bulling into that narrow
sea lane. Feeling the stab of Bonnie's eyes as she continued
to stand silently beside me, I forced myself to hold back
my next crucial order, to gauge the position of both enemy
vessels seconds after we made our swing. Then, just as we
had passed the first boom and seemed certain to pile up on
the second, I shouted my command into the yards.

The helmsman leaned once again upon the spokes. Coming about in that narrow space (like a dancer spinning on
her toes to hold the center of a stage), we slowed to a full
stop in a matter of seconds. Our targets were dead on our
muzzles. The enemy ships, with all sails straining, could
not slow their headlong rush. Our larboard guns spoke first.
The crash of the broadside had not died when I signaled to
the starboard battery.

Both targets shuddered from end to end under those twin
fusillades. At point-blank range there was no chance for re-
taliation after our lightning-swift strike. Of the eighteen
round shot belched from each gun deck, nearly all struck
home. I have sailed in booms on the Malabar Coast; most
of them are floating eggshells—relying on speed rather than
the strength of their timbers in combat. Before the smoke
had cleared, I was sure both our broadsides had been mortal.

In another instant we had taken the wind on our starboard quarter and run away from our battle smoke. When
we heard no answering fire, I ordered the yards braced for
another attack and charged our quarry a second time, in case
a *coup de grâce* was needed. Any one of our three adversaries might show fight: I had seen enough of this rough-
and-tumble to be cautious. But I needed only Bonnie's victory

shout (in which the whole crew joined) to tell me our sweep was complete.

I raised my glass to confirm that hasty judgment. The first boom had sunk without a trace. A second was foundering: the sea around her was dotted with swimmers making for the third vessel, which was listing badly under shattered spars, though she appeared seaworthy. Most of her cannon had already gone overside in an effort to right her balance—and the crew was rigging what sail they could. Should we leave them unmolested, I knew they would run for the Trucial Coast, a day's sailing to the east.

The action had taken less than a half hour. The *Aureng Zeb* was ours now—and the token dropping of her mainsail as she awaited capture was final proof of our success.

Another hour was all we needed to secure the fruits of our victory.

With Bonnie once more in command, we circled the crippled boom just once, to make sure she had no fight left. By that time the survivors from the other vessel had managed to scramble aboard. Mozo (who spoke fluent Arabic) ordered her to heave to, while we sent a warning shot across the bows of the Indiaman. When the *Aureng Zeb* had dipped her colors, we ran broadside and grappled her while Bonnie and her first officer went aboard, under cover of a score of muskets. . . . In a matter of minutes the last of the Arab crew had tumbled into their boats and raced to join their fellows aboard the damaged boom. Once we had tested the sails and rudders of our prize (and made certain our adversaries had not opened the bilges) we permitted the overloaded vessel to take to her heels—which she did in a limping fashion indeed.

I had expected an explosion of cursing as the enemy abandoned the field, but they decamped in silence—and with all possible speed. Evidently they could not quite believe their lives had been spared, and were eager to leave us before we changed our minds. Had our roles been reversed, I am sure they would have butchered us all.

At Bonnie's order, Mozo took charge of the *Aureng Zeb* —and the prize crew that would sail her back to Ringo Bay. Anticipating such a chore, we had shipped nearly twice our normal complement: Mozo chose his companions for the homeward voyage—taking apprentices for the most part, with a few old salts to bear a hand in heavy weather. The Indiaman would be in little danger, since we planned to convoy her to waters northeast of Madagascar. It would mean a loss of four days' hunting, but with so rich and defenseless a prize it seemed a wise precaution. Besides, we planned to make a day's westing after we had left the larger vessel, to fill our water casks on one of the larger of the Comarros, and to repair such minor damage as our hull had suffered.

We made no attempt to estimate the exact value of our capture. One of our stewards (a cockney who had once been an auditor for the East India Company) had been added to Mozo's crew list. Watching the fellow climb aboard the *Aureng Zeb,* with his quills and his ledgers slung round his neck in a canvas sack, I knew he would soon tot up her riches to the last halfpenny. Later the totals would be entered in Carter's books at Ringo Bay—and each man's share apportioned when our voyage ended.

There were hours of daylight remaining when we broke free of the Indiaman, with our own mainsail still furled, and watched her spread a tower of canvas for the voyage south. Because of her advanced years we gave her a fair start before we followed in her wake. Had she been less heavily laden, we might have paused to clear the worst of her seaweed beards—but time was too precious for such niceties.

Bonnie had given me but little notice once she had taken back her quarter-deck. At four I had gone off duty in favor of Ketchell—and stopped at the sick bay to watch Tom patch up the last of a half dozen powder burns (our only casualties in the engagement). The master's summons came when I was downing a double tot of rum in the wardroom, in a solitary celebration of my triumph. I had half expected a night of riot aboard the *Venture,* and a round of toasts to my seamanship—but there had been no compliments so far save for a few handclasps from my brother officers. . . . I was beginning to realize that captures of this sort were routine among Carter's buccaneers. With a convoy trick to plot (and a double lookout against possible marauders), there was no deck space for the wassail I had so romantically pictured.

The captain of the *Venture* lolled in her chair, her booted heels on the desk and the log before her. Its cover, I saw, was closed, the key in the lock that protected its pages from unwanted visitors. Bonnie gave me a nod of welcome and pushed a demijohn across the chart table.

"Take your tot, Mr. Douglas," she said. "You've earned it."

"I've already toasted our victory," I said. The cabin door stood wide, and the helmsman was within earshot. Not that his presence mattered. At such a moment Bonnie could build a wall between us too high for mortal leaping.

"Drink it again then," she said. "You've a good head on your shoulders. I don't think it can be dislodged by rum."

I watched her narrowly as I poured out a glass and tossed it down. She had already dropped her feet to the deck, and now sat bolt upright. To save me, I could not tell if she was smiling or frowning when her eyes brushed mine.

"I've noted today's action in our log," she said. "Perhaps you'll find my remarks instructive—you can see for yourself."

I moved politely to her side as she turned the key in the heavy brass lock and opened the log for my inspection. Her entries for the day filled most of a closely written page: point by point, they described the attack precisely as I had carried it through. There was the head-on charge that crippled the first boom, the use of the Indiaman as a screen—and, finally, the reversal of course that brought the *Venture* between her two remaining targets, to administer the last deathblows.

"May I ask when the captain made these entries?"

"Before we came in cannon range," said Bonnie. "Your battle plan and mine were identical. I said I'd correct your orders if they went amiss."

"In that case why was I allowed to direct the action?"

There was no doubt she was frowning now. For the moment, she looked almost forlorn—like a child whose only toy has been snatched away.

"I had my own orders—from my father," she said. "He wanted you tested under fire."

I could understand her resentment well enough. Itching to capture her first prize singlehanded, she had been forced to try my mettle instead. Today's entries in her log had been her only comfort—the written proof that she, too, could have done as well.

"Did you feel it prudent to trust me that far?" I asked.

"Of course. I shall so enter it in tomorrow's log—when you take Mozo's place."

I kept my aplomb with some effort. "Are you saying I'm your first officer?"

"From this moment, Mr. Douglas. Does that restore your self-esteem?"

"May I thank you for your confidence?"

"There's no need for thanks," she said crisply. "So far, you've exceeded our expectations. Let's hope a good beginning means a good ending."

"If the captain pleases—" I said, and paused, in some confusion. It was clear our interview was over: I would prolong it at my peril.

"Yes, Mr. Douglas?"

"If the captain pleases—she's left out the best part."

"Meaning—?"

"I'm proud of my promotion," I told her. "And prouder still if you feel I did passably today. But I'm proudest of all to learn we think as one—when it comes to taking prizes."

"That will do, sir! You're dismissed."

I saluted smartly and left the cabin—remembering to march out backwards, as it were, if only to prove I was still taking orders.

CHAPTER 11

Action in the Laccadives

IT IS not my intention to log that voyage of piracy in detail after we completed our escort duty and cheered the prize crew of the *Aureng Zeb* on their way. Suffice it to say that our plans for careening were abandoned the following afternoon, when we sighted a heavily laden dhow, gave chase, and brought her to heel with a single warning shot across her bows. Again a prize crew was put aboard and the enemy sailors sent packing in their own longboats—save for their captain, who was held aboard as hostage, lest the others give warning of our presence in these waters.

From this cringing fellow we learned that good hunting awaited us to the north since a whole string of these vessels had set out recently from Mocha, en route to Suez. A storm had broken up the formation, driving some of these craft aground on the African coast: our newest prize had been blown off course and fallen into our hands by luck. . . . Near as we were to Madagascar, Bonnie decided to send the dhow to Ringo Bay without escort—and once again we crowded on all sail in search of other booty.

Thrice in the next fortnight we made captures—once in a running gun duel that forced the infidels to drop their colors, twice in outright grapplings and boardings for harder won victories. As first officer it was my duty to direct this all-important maneuver while Bonnie gave orders for the actual boarding from her stand on the quarter-deck. . . . Once our first wave of steel had surged overside, I led the second wave, with the captain herself accepting the surrender. Your Arab will fight like an eager terrier when the odds favor him—but these scurvy seamen had no liking for such an onslaught. Within minutes of the boarding most of them had flung down their scimitars. The few who resisted were cut down without mercy.

Our total plunder on these prizes equaled (though it did not exceed) the cargo of the *Aureng Zeb*. A rough estimate indicated that we had already taken booty to the value of nearly two hundred thousand pounds—which meant that each of us would reap a splendid award for the venture. Best of all, we had lost no more than eight men in all five actions —though the necessity of shipping so many prize crews south had seriously depleted our complement. The damage to our hull had also been minor. But there was much accumulated work for our carpenters, and the growth of seaweed and barnacles on our keel (an inevitable result of long voyaging in tropic waters) warned us that we could no longer postpone careening.

Bonnie had been slightly injured in our last boarding—a freak accident that reflected no discredit on her. On this occasion, as we moved aft to accept the formal surrender of the vessel, she had slipped on a spray-soaked deck and wrenched a knee—badly enough to keep her off her feet thereafter. . . . When it was decided that we must seek out the first safe landfall for our repairs, she was still lying in her bunk. The sprain was mending nicely, but Tom had insisted she remain there until our work on the hull was finished.

By this time (and I make the statement with no false modesty) I had given my proofs as first officer. Since I had no choice, and since there was no other way to win her favor, I had simply turned buccaneer, using all the wit I possessed to make my position aboard the *Venture* secure. As a result I was in complete command when we set a course for the Laccadives—and (what was more significant) took my watches with no animus from the rightful skipper. Even in my rare moments of self-doubting I had come a long way from that nightmare moment when the ship changed hands. Nowadays my conscience scolded me only in dreams. My only war, so far, had been against the foes of England. I could excuse such sins in my waking moments.

As to what would come after (when we returned to Ringo Bay, as we must, when the *Venture* was seaworthy again), I refused to think clearly.

At the time, our hunting had led us far north. We had crossed the shipping lanes of the Mocha fleet, reaching a point midway between Malabar and the Trucial Coast of Oman. The Laccadives are a coral atoll group of perhaps twenty islets. We chose one of the larger among them, slipping through a break in the reef and dropping our hooks near a shelving beach of snow-white sand that was ideal for our purpose.

Three days of hard work were enough to scrape our hull bone-clean—and more than enough for Chips (the master carpenter) and his apprentices to repair all topside damage. When the last tool was stowed and we had floated clear in the tide, I proceeded to a safe deep-water anchorage and gave the crew shore leave *en masse*, save for a few oldsters to stand watch. There was a sizable native village on the far side of the island; its inhabitants had traded with corsairs over the centuries—including the services of their women, which had been freely offered from the moment we entered the lagoon. Pigs had been roasting in the pits since morning, in anticipation of our visit, and palm wine would soon be flowing freely. After the discomforts of weeks at sea I felt it was best for the men to ease their minds and bodies in this primitive fashion. Only the master of the *Venture* was forbidden sleep tonight, along with the lookouts he had posted in the crow's-nest and a spot of high ground on the island's spine.

Bonnie was sleeping soundly when I paused at her door. Each night at sundown she had taken a small quantity of the mysterious white powder Majunga had given Mozo just before his surgery. The drug (if one could call it that) was a powerful sedative, and she had used it freely since her fall to ease the pain of her knee. . . . I passed on to the deck, obscurely glad that she could not hear the sounds of revelry ashore. I had needed all the wiles of command to keep the men at their tasks for those three sun-drenched days while venery and alcohol awaited them. I would have been hard put to explain tonight's relaxation of discipline in words she would understand.

On the captain's bench I wrapped myself in a boat cloak to escape the drenching dew that would fall by morning, and sought such repose as I could. It seemed that I had dozed but a moment when Jack Ketchell's hand was on my shoulder.

"Sorry, Mr. Douglas. But there's a monstrous big ship offshore. She's showing fore-and-after lights, bold as brass."

I hurried to the ratlines and followed him to the crow's-nest. As he had said, a vessel was cruising outside the harbor mouth, following an off-and-on course in the cloudy night. Evidently she meant to drop anchor in the lagoon, once there was enough light to navigate.

"Can you make her out, Jack?"

"She could be an Indiaman. Light's too bad to be sure."

I cursed softly in the dark. Instinct had warned me that we had crowded our luck to career here—and crowded it still further with this night of debauchery, richly earned though it was. If the ship was an enemy, our condition would be desperate on the morrow. This, after all, was a port of call for pirates of every stripe. The mere sight of the *Pilgrim Venture* (smart with new paint again, and ready for sea) would be enough to set any skipper's mouth watering.

"We'd better round up the crew, Jack."

"I sent the bosuns ashore already, Mr. Douglas. But they'll need some time, if I know sailors."

"Take the whole watch, and sluice 'em down if they won't

waken easily," I said. "I'll stand guard until dawn. We're in no danger until it's light."

Thanks to the size of the shore patrol, we had most of our crew aboard again, while the last of the shadows still lingered above the harbor. The clouds had lifted meanwhile, and I had a clear view of the vessel's silhouette against the stars. As Jack had said, she was almost twice our bulk—another Indiaman, judging by the flaring of her bows and the houselike dimensions of her stern. Her presence in these waters, and the way she had approached the anchorage, could have but one meaning. This was a pirate vessel—fitted with an armament as formidable as the fortress she resembled. Once she had marked our presence, we were trapped beyond salvage. Sailing that same tight triangular course, her master could bottle us here for days or weeks, until desperation goaded us into making a run for the open sea. Or he could come charging into the harbor with the tide, confident he could outgun us at such close quarters. . . . It was my guess that he would follow the former course, once he had discovered our presence—and trust to our common sense to show a white flag and proclaim our surrender.

Two of the longboats were lashed together, at my orders, under a common platform. Wth eight fuddled oarsmen at the sweeps, I sent Hans and two gunners ashore, with twelve-pound cannon, to a point above the entrance to the reef. Here a dense stand of palm seedlings made an ambush of sorts. There was time to install this makeshift battery before the sun rose. The element of surprise was still in our favor—and I had no intention of permitting the Indiaman a peaceful entrance to our haven if he could be discouraged.

It still lacked a half hour to dawn when I dropped into the captain's gig, with Ketchell at the rudder and two of our best men to row me. I was decked in a frogged coat, with a cocked hat to give added dignity. Until we were sure of our adversary, I had no intention of wasting powder. After all, we flew the English standard at our peak and could pass for an honest merchantman en route to Bombay. The Indiaman might be a Company ship, replenishing her larder on the last leg of a voyage.

While I waited for muskets to be brought aboard the gig, I swallowed a hardtack biscuit, and washed it down with rum and water. Anchored as we were, with our bowsprit pointed toward the reef, we could rake the passage with our guns. These, joined with the masked battery onshore, would be enough to discourage our unwelcome visitor, should he attempt to force an entrance. I took what comfort I could from these precautions—but I fear we were a glum quartet of mariners when the gig danced through the pass and into the open sea beyond.

Viewed at water level, the Indiaman seemed huge enough to blot out the fiery promise of morning. She was a good quarter mile distant, lounging along with a reefed mainsail and less than half her canvas drawing. Her master was waiting, all too obviously, for full daylight before negotiating the difficult channel to the lagoon. It was equally obvious that he had not yet seen the spars of the *Pilgrim Venture*— since the sunrise was behind him, the island itself still wrapped in shadow.

The stern transom of our visitor was hidden, so I could not spell out her name. Sweeping the gun deck with my glass, I made sure that there was a cannon muzzle at each port. All of the seamen on deck seemed to be lascars—and the officer in charge on the poop (a burly fellow in pantaloons and a flaring crimson sash) was far too swarthy to be either English or Dutch. He had just noticed our presence outside the reef, and had trained a spyglass upon us. As the sun rose, the ship broke out her colors, a gaudy pennon which I could not identify at once. I handed our own glass to Ketchell, who rose in the thwarts for a better view.

"Can you name those colors, Jack?"

"No doubt about it, Mr. Douglas," said the second mate hoarsely. "She's served by lascars, and her officers are Indian too. The flag's the Angria pennant."

Ketchell's words solved the mystery, on the worst possible terms for us. The Indiaman was part of the fleet of the pirate Canoji Angria, a scourge in these waters for the last ten years. I knew from Company reports that he had several stations (or factories, as they are called) along the Malabar Coast south of Bombay. The Laccadives were within easy reach of these bays—and he would not be the first buccaneer king to use a captured merchantman for piracy. The picture was complete when I saw that several of the gun crew were scurrying to train a cannon on the lagoon. They had evidently just seen the spars of the *Venture,* and meant to send us a warning of their intentions.

"Reverse course and head for the pass," I ordered, and my oarsmen obeyed with alacrity. We were scudding between the protecting arms of the reef when the cannon boomed, lifting a spout of white water behind us. Even had the Angria's ship's gunners been equal to ours (a fact which I doubted), there was but small chance of a hit at that range, but I was giving them no opportunity to test their marksmanship. We did not slacken our pace until we had muzzled the hull of our own ship again.

There was no second shot, but the enemy had already changed course, for a test run toward the pass. A glance toward the western end of the island told me our land battery was mounted and ready. I saw with approval that Hans (anticipating my next command) had already broken out two of our heavy broadside cannon and mounted the guns in tandem, beside the slender, long-range bow guns. With six muzzles trained on the harbor entrance, we had a fair chance to remain in sole possession of the lagoon.

I sighted down each of the cannon in turn, with Jack Ketchell at my elbow. The guns were jammed side by side, just aft of the bow. The combined weight had brought the bowsprit close to water level, giving us an excellent trajectory, should the Angrian dare to venture within range. Already, I saw, she was bearing down upon the reef—ready to test our defenses and her own firing power.

"Can we sink her at this range?" I asked.

"Only with a lucky hit."

"We'll try a double charge and risk blowing up the cannon."

The enemy's first challenge came hurtling across the reef while the extra charge was being rammed home. The ball skittered into the lagoon, a safe distance from our anchorage but too close for comfort.

"In another round they'll have our range," Jack warned.

I nodded to Hans, who put his match to the touchhole of a bow gun. The powder spewed into flame and the gun thundered, rearing on its carriage like a balky stallion from the recoil of the double charge of powder. From the masthead a gunner's mate shouted that the shot had gone clean over the Angrian's mainmast. Even at that range a lower trajectory would have scored a direct hit. . . . It was a temptation to risk a second double charge, but I resisted it.

"Load the other bow chaser with an extra half charge," I ordered—and mounted the ratlines with my own spyglass to watch the second try. This time, the ball struck the sea, a scant ten feet from the enemy's bow. As I had hoped, he shifted course instantly and ran away on the opposite tack, without risking another shot. Until they had assayed our strength more exactly they would continue to stand offshore and await our next move.

"They're coming within range of the cannon on the point," shouted the man at the masthead. "Shall I signal 'em to shift aim and fire?"

I shook my head. The chances of a hit were good, but it was unlikely that the shore battery could inflict mortal damage at the range. Besides, I meant to conceal my extra fire power for the nonce. It was a trump card I could use later.

"Stay on watch and keep the pass covered," I said. "I'm going to report this to the captain."

Bonnie was in her bunk, with her injured leg propped on sandbags and a chart on her knees. As always, the drug had left her mind quite clear when it wakened. Contrary to other opiates I had known, it sharpened the faculties rather than dulled them.

She received my report of the action with a curt nod. During our weeks at sea we had developed a formal give-and-take relationship that had functioned admirably, even in the heat of combat. Without challenging her command, even by inference, I had contrived to give her the benefit of my experience—while relying on her own wit to shape our ultimate plan.

"Our situation doesn't seem too desperate," she said. "Not if we can hold them off this easily."

"They're still in command outside the reef," I said. "And time's on their side. We can't last indefinitely in this anchorage—and we'll need all our provender for the long voyage home. Besides, they may send to Malabar for re-enforcements. Then they could put men ashore and attack us from both sides."

"Couldn't we slip through the channel in the dark?"

"Not without soundings: we'd be sure to ground."

"Is there another break in the reef?"

"That's what I'm about to investigate—with your permission."

"Permission granted, Mr. Douglas—and good luck."

Ten minutes later, taking the largest of the longboats, and putting a leadsman in the bow, I set out for a tour of the lagoon. Like many reef-enclosed harbors, this one was crescent-shaped, with its two points shaping the actual land boundaries of the roadstead. The coral reef formed the remainder of the circular boundary. Here and there, as the tide fell, it projected above water like a sleek brown wall. For most of the distance it creamed with surf, a warning of the jagged surfaces waiting to impale any ship foolish enough to attempt a crossing.

Picking our way just inside the coral arc, I searched hopefully for a spot where the water appeared blue rather than green—a sure sign of depth, since the color indicated that the sun was not reflected so quickly from the white sand of the bottom. Near the far end, perhaps a hundred yards from the point, I noted such a spot. On the lagoon side it seemed wide enough to permit the passage of the *Venture*. The real test, of course, would come at the reef itself, where the water was shallowest.

We put the longboat into the pass, negotiating it slowly, and using the lead to measure its depth from lagoon to coral. The bottom shelved up rapidly to the backbone of the reef itself: even at high tide I estimated that our ship would barely float. There was no sign of coral spurs in the lagoon itself—but to make doubly sure, I stripped to my pelt and plunged overside to explore firsthand.

The water was clear and warm. I swam slowly downward, giving myself time to adjust to the pressure that always comes at such depths, and keeping an eye out for sharks, or the still more deadly morays, the great eels that inhabit these reefs and can snap an oar with their teeth. Luck was with me here, for I encountered no sign of marine life, save for a school of rainbow-hued fishes that scattered as I approached the lagoon's floor. The sand was grainy to my touch, but clear of coral outcrop.

Knowing I might not get another glimpse of the pass from the underwater side, I swam on—ignoring the increasing pain at chest and eardrums. There was still no sign of outcrop when I reached the ocean side. Here and there, I noted, the scour of the ebb had cut gullies in the shelving sand, but none was continuous. If we risked the passage, we would still run the chance of grounding where the sand shelf was highest—but I was confident we would clear it partially, at the very worst.

The pressure was now all but intolerable, and I set my feet firmly against the bottom and rocketed to the surface. Jack Ketchell gave a cry of relief when I burst into view and swam slowly toward the boat again. Dizzy as I was from my long submersion, I could not focus my eyes too clearly. Until the vertigo passed, boat and sailors seemed to spin in a grotesque circle against the sky.

"I was about to join you," said Jack. "I was afraid you'd tangled with a squid down there."

"We've a second channel," I said as I clambered over the stern of the boat. "If we use our wits, we can navigate it. Still, we'd best explore the rest of the reef, in case there's another opening."

A painstaking search of the lagoon convinced us that the spot we had chosen was the only exit. During the exploration I lay back in the thwarts until the sun had dried my body. When I donned my clothing, my plan was fully formed: I had no doubts that Bonnie would approve it.

We held our council in the captain's cabin, just before noon. Both Hans and Ketchell were present at my invitation. My scheme would call for an extra effort on the part of each man aboard. I knew that both could speak for their watches.

"The stratagem I propose is threefold," I said. "First, we must kedge the *Venture* into deep water, between dusk and dawn, so the enemy will have no notion of her departure. Second, we must devise some means of convincing him we're still at anchor here. Third—when we are through the reef—I'd like to take one more prize before we sail home. By that I mean the Angria ship."

"It sounds like a tall order, Mr. Douglas," said Jack.

"So far, this crew has been expert at handling tall orders. I'd hate to spoil our record. May I have the captain's opinion?"

Bonnie spoke up from the chart-littered bunk. "The captain's cursing her luck that she can't take part. I needn't tell you gentlemen that Mr. Douglas has my confidence, no matter what he proposes."

I took the accolade with due modesty. "The kedging operation won't be too hazardous," I said. "Providing it's carried out quietly. There must be gallons of lard at those cooking pits after last night's feast: we'll use it to grease blocks and metal, so we'll have no creaking capstans. Jack will be in charge of the longboats: we'll drop two kedge anchors from strongbacks. It's sinew-cracking work, but the distance isn't too great. If we put our hearts in it, we'll clear the pass by dawn."

"They're bound to scout in closer once it's dark," said Jack. "Won't they guess we're on the move?"

"That's our second stratagem," I said. "They haven't yet heard that masked battery on the point. When it's time to move, I'll order a gun fired there at intervals. Meanwhile we'll hang ship's lanterns in the palms to simulate riding lights. Unless their skipper has cat's-eyes, he'll think our shots are coming from the *Venture* to warn him offshore."

"He'll still be primed for an attack," said the second officer.

"Not if it comes at dawn from the west. If he sails last night's course, he'll be fixed on the old passage, a good mile to the east. We'll bear down on him just before sunup, when the light is worst. Knowing his position, we can hit him on his blind side—when he still thinks we're bottled here. In the open sea we can outmaneuver him at every turn. If he's crippled at that first volley, we can call the game thereafter. If not, we can always cut and run."

The vote for my project, as I had expected, was unanimous. Bonnie detained me for a moment after the others had hurried out to begin their preparations—which would be both long and arduous. She did not speak at once, contenting herself with flinging the charts across the room, then struggling to her feet as best she could, with the aid of a crutch and my supporting arm. For a moment more, she stood at the stern window, staring out at the spout of waves on the reef—and the dark silhouette of the Indiaman, still idling beyond the pass, just out of cannon range.

"Don't mind my tantrums, Richard," she said at last. "But I'd give an arm to command our strike tomorrow."

"Let's pray we get that far. If we straddle the reef, we may have to abandon ship."

"You'll get through somehow. You always do."

"No man's luck can last forever," I said. "I still prefer the gamble to remaining in this cul-de-sac."

"And so do I, no matter what the odds," she said quietly. She held out her hand and clasped mine. It was a man's handshake, the salute of an equal to another: on shipboard our captain had always been as masculine as her garb, and there was no blurring of that hard-muscled image today. "Would you think me vain if I say no one could handle tonight's affair better—including myself?"

"I can't think of a finer compliment," I told her.

"Compliments be damned—it's the gospel truth. Get about your business, man. You've much to arrange before nightfall."

Bonnie's remark was an understatement: I was on my feet until sundown, with scarce a moment's respite. Though each of us had sprung to his task with a will (spurred by the double incentive of deliverance and plunder), there were a score of details to oversee while daylight lasted.

First, I sketched a free-hand map of the reef and the course we planned to negotiate. Then, in the gig, I explored the passage one more time and placed a buoy in its exact center, to serve as a navigation point in the darkness. Now that the tide was low, I could measure the width of the channel much more exactly, and saw that we had searoom to spare. According to my calculation, the tide would be at its flood by midnight (when I hoped to warp the *Venture* into place).

Returning to the ship, I paused at the point to give the gun crew their instructions. Beginning a half hour after sunset, they were to fire across the original passage at irregular intervals. Making a rough estimate of the length of the *Venture*, I placed lanterns among the trees: when they were lighted they would create the illusion of a ship at anchor. The firing of the guns, I explained, would suggest that we were guarding against the chance that the Indiaman might slip into the lagoon in the dark. To complete the stratagem (and to save precious ordnance), I instructed the gun crew to use green coconuts (which were scattered abundantly along the beach) as missiles. In the night the sound of their impact on the water would not be too different from actual cannon balls.

It was almost dark when I climbed the Jacob's ladder to our deck. There was barely time for a snack with Bonnie, and a last-minute review of our schedule, before I was called topside again. Already it was pitch-black, as is characteristic of nightfall in these latitudes. As I ascended to the deck, the false riding lights winked on down the point and the first cannon sounded.

The *Venture*, of course, showed no lights when we began our kedging—and there was some stumbling and cursing as the cables were stowed in the longboats. We lifted our hooks while the lines were paid out. I crossed my fingers as the capstan bars went round: to my intense relief, they turned without a squeak. The ship moved easily, confirming my belief that she would not be too difficult to handle in the backbreaking ordeal that lay ahead.

Once we were fairly underway, I moved ahead of the boats, to lead the sweating cavalcade in the captain's gig. It was a necessary precaution, since the buoy would be difficult to find in the starless dark. As it was, I needed a half hour to locate it. By that time the slow-moving vessel (a slightly heavier wedge of darkness in the night) had begun to move into the passage.

Following my whispered order, the men rested on their oars a moment, until I had fumbled my way to the reef to study the tidemark I had left that afternoon. To the best of my judgment, the sea was nearly at its flood. We had no alternative but to enter the pass, knowing that the next two hours would determine success or failure.

The operation had gone according to plan, so far—but I did not allow myself to become unduly optimistic. Things would be simple if the *Venture* continued to float clear. If she grounded in the sand-choked spine of the reef, we might be trapped beyond salvage. The thought hung like a cloud on my mind while the most difficult part of the kedging began.

When the cable Jack was paying out from his longboat tightened, showing he was at the end of his line (though no more than a third of the distance across the reef) the kedge anchor was dropped from its strongback. A whispered signal passed back to the bow of the *Venture*—and the capstan began turning. Bit by bit the vessel inched through the pass, until the kedge itself was reached. . . . The second longboat had already moved forward, carrying its own line still deeper into the pass. When the maneuver was repeated without mishap, I began to breathe a trifle easier.

It was hard work, both for the men at the oars and those who manned the bars. I could hear the whispered oaths of Jack's men as the original kedge anchor was brought aboard and rowed into the darkness, toward the glimmer of the open sea. If my estimate was accurate, this third try might be the last, freeing the *Venture* from her tight quarters. I crossed my fingers once again as the line tightened.

The sound of labored breathing on deck told me that the capstan hands were putting their hearts into their task. Almost half the line had been brought inboard when I sensed, rather than saw, that the ship had grounded. A moment before, she had been a slow-moving shadow against the night. Now, shivering down her length, she had simply stranded— and the men leaned against their bars in vain.

I brought the gig alongside Jack's boat and whispered an order to take all lines aboard, along with the kedge anchors. Then I dropped overside and (following the side of the *Venture* with my finger ends) swam down her length. She had come within an ace of clearing. Perhaps ten feet aft of her waist the keel had grounded on one of the treacherous humps of sand I had discovered on my morning exploration. She was wedged there—deeply enough so that it would be useless to reverse our course.

Climbing to the deck, I surveyed the island, and the lagoon we had just quitted. On the point the cannon were banging away at intervals, and the bogus riding lights glowed brightly. Our deception was perfect in that quarter—unless, by unhappy accident, one of our dummy charges should land on the enemy deck and reveal the nature of our trickery.

It was heartbreaking to stand with success in our grasp. There was still a way to free us, and I began giving orders as I shuffled into my clothes again. Hazardous though the method was, I had seen it used before.

Under my directions, the bosuns broke out four cannon from our broadside batteries and trundled them forward on their carronades. Lashed firmly to the foremast, they were inched into the bowsprit coaming, one by one. Six seamen (three on each side of the bowsprit) were sent into the shrouds to add their weight to the ordinance. Watching a plumb line I had hung above the capstan, I saw it had begun to incline gently—a sure sign we were moving, though the motion, so far, was too gentle to be decisive. When a fifth cannon was added to the balance, the *Venture* moved with a rush, sliding down the steep pitch of the bottom like a toboggan on a hill.

The vessel's timbers screeched, but held firm. For an instant, as the bowsprit plunged downward, I feared that the weight had overbalanced us as we slipped free. The six men in the shrouds had already begun swimming for their lives. Sinews cracked on the foredeck while their shipmates did their utmost to keep the cannon from plunging overside. . . . Then, like the thoroughbred she was, the *Venture* slowly righted. The cannon, responding to the laws of gravity, changed in a trice from deadly weights to manageable wheeled engines. We were in the clear, heeling gently in an offshore wind, with the coral trap behind us.

A dozen tasks remained before we could lift a sail. It was a ticklish job to restore the guns to their proper places. The kedging cables had yet to be stowed and the anchors returned to their housings. Even when we raised a jib and staysail, and began to plot a course just outside the pass, it was necessary to send back to the lagoon and order our masked battery to bring their guns aboard. By the time these cannon were added to our armament and the last boat was snug in its chocks, barely a half hour of darkness remained before dawn.

I had sent Chips into the bilges with a lantern to make sure we had sprung no timbers on the reef. Now I drank down the pannikin of rum the ship's cook gave me and munched a biscuit. It was the first pause I had allowed myself since we left our anchorage, and I could feel weariness seep into my very bones. Yet perhaps the worst of our ordeal still lay ahead. I had promised the crew that we would engage the Indiaman as a reward for their efforts. It was time to put that promise to work.

The Angria captain had done me a favor by keeping his riding lights burning—which allowed me to stake out the position I wanted. With the promise of dawn, the breeze freshened steadily. I had already ordered the yards of the *Venture* braced around, and the sails thoroughly wet (since wet canvas holds the wind far better than dry). This, of course, meant hoisting dozens of buckets to the highest yard-arm and dumping them on the sail below. But the high-pitched hum of our rigging proved we were jealously guarding every bit of the wind which would soon send us roaring down on the Indiaman—the monstrous enemy who, a few hours ago, had held us in the palm of his hand.

My plan had the virtue of simplicity. I meant to keep to windward of the Indiaman—and, using the *Venture's* mobility to the utmost, to rake her with my cannon in two passes. This, I hoped, would be enough to disable her mortally—or, at least, to force her to strike her colors. At the moment, she was hove to, perhaps a mile offshore—which made her a perfect target if we could approach her unawares.

Unfortunately, the element of surprise was lost when the wind shifted, forcing us to come about and take a new tack before we could begin our run. This complication destroyed our timing since the sun had already lifted above the horizon and revealed our presence. We were well to windward, however, a factor I hoped to maintain. At the height of the conflict we would still bar wind from the enemy sails, making him even clumsier than usual.

I could see that the Angria skipper was a fair seaman. Already he had begun to pile on canvas, and was trying hard to wear around us in an attempt to take the weather gauge. We were prepared for such a try and reversed our own course, putting the helm hard to larboard. Immediately the enemy made a second attempt to wear around us. As a result, on our first pass, we were now on opposite courses, within long cannon shot of one another.

I had no intention of wasting a broadside at that range, but did hope to lure my opponent into wasting his. Therefore I had the bow guns run out on a diagonal as we approached and sent two round shot whistling his way. The first struck short—but the second (largely by luck) landed on the forward deck. Spent as it was, it did but little damage, but it served its purpose. Seconds later smoke erupted from the Angrian's starboard bank of cannon. The thunder of the detonation reached us only a trifle ahead of the missiles themselves, all of which fell short. Before they could reload, or bring their stern chasers to bear, we were well out of range.

It was now our turn to wear the *Venture* round with all speed—a maneuver we accomplished with far more skill than our adversary. I have said that the enemy skipper was a fair seaman—but he now revealed he was far from expert. A master strategist could have forced me into a ticklish position once he had me astern—merely by keeping a trifle off the wind, and thus extending the time of my approach as he brought his maximum armament to bear on me. This deliberate use of a leeward position against an opponent eager to join battle has often proved its worth in naval warfare—but the Indiaman had already lost her chance to make full use of heavier fire power.

Instead, as we bore down upon her, she continued to pile on canvas. We were approaching this time from the starboard. The moment we came in range, I started the bow guns firing across the poop deck—seeking to cut the rudder chains or, failing that, to silence the stern chasers. The first shots were clean misses, and we took some damage from his nine-pounders as we approached. The third shot produced a great gust of smoke. I judged that we had struck the reserve powder charges that serviced his stern cannon.

We were now coming into range, with a chance for a broadside. Knowing we were outgunned, I had no intention of taking this risk. If I had judged the enemy rightly, he would follow the usual tactics of combat, letting us come parallel to his gun deck before firing. Gambling on this outcome, I had taken charge of the port battery for our pass, and had instructed the gunners to fire two by two, at my signal. It was a radical departure from accepted tactics, but I felt it was worth the risk.

"Reload as fast as you can," I added. "Starting at the bow and moving back. I want at least two shots from every gun as we overtake him—but none except at my order."

Standing between the two forward carronades, I studied the mountainous flank of the Indiaman as we began to draw abreast. Her squat cannon seemed to look down my throat, at this angle—but I knew it was too soon, even now, for the first match.

"Steady all!"

"Steady as she goes, sir!"

"Fire!"

The first two guns spoke in unison, dead on their opposite numbers aboard the Indiaman: there in the cramped space of the gun deck the detonation all but floored me. I managed to scramble aft, between our next two cannon, to repeat the fragmented volley. Just after the third pair of guns had spoken, I felt the *Venture* quiver like a horse with a spur in its flank, and knew that a mizzen spar had been shattered. Since it was our only damage so far, I judged that all but one of the enemy guns had been silenced in that first tier of cannon.

Our gunners, stripped to the waist and black with powder smoke, were reloading at lightning speed, eager to smash home a second salvo, now that they had grasped my strategy. Twice more I saw flashes from the enemy ports. I felt the *Venture* shudder a second time as a ball crashed into its target—but we did not alter course by a hairline.

When we completed our run, I was glad to note that the Indiaman was losing way rapidly as we took her wind in our straining sails and continued to pound her hull with every gun we could bring into action. Her captain fought desperately for the wind as he strove to bring his ponderous ship around. Then, as we moved past him, the sails filled again—so suddenly that the Indiaman yawed violently, heeling over almost on her beam ends and showing a considerable width of barnacle-crusted bottom.

I had not counted on a wind-and-water shot, and roared at our helmsman to bring us round. In another moment our stern chasers had lowered dead on the enemy. Both shots tore gaping holes in her bottom in the split second before she righted.

The pass had been made in a matter of minutes, but my refusal to trade broadsides, the spiking of the enemy guns with round shot, and the final deathblows at the water line had already decided the action. When we came about for another pass, I saw that there was but little fight left in my adversary. Even at that distance I could hear her take water through her ripped planks like a stricken whale. Along her starboard gun deck nearly all the ports had been reduced to fire-gutted holes, with the deck itself a shambles.

The battle could have gone on, had her crew possessed

more courage than is usual with lascars. Had she been staffed with seamen of our caliber, with a wily captain on the poop deck, she might have held us off—since her larboard battery was intact, as were her bow guns and at least one of the cannon astern. But the spiking of the other battery, and the bubbling tumult that filled her hatchways as the sea poured through her splintered bottom, filled officers and men with the same blind panic. The crew was already milling about in hopeless confusion, fighting for a place at the rail as her boats were lowered. Then, screaming their hate at us and cursing one another in the same wild babel, they abandoned ship by the boatload, leaning hard on their oars to put distance between us.

We had won the field in that single pass—and the ship would be ours in another moment if we could keep her afloat.

I waited prudently upwind, keeping out of range of the port batteries in case there was still a round of shot in their lockers. I doubted it, since the gun crews (or, rather, such of them that had survived our pounding) were also deserting their posts, no less shamelessly than their own officers. Wallowing though she was, I felt we could grapple her— but it seemed unwise to close in until I could be sure most of the crew had cleared.

"Shall we fire on the boats, Mr. Douglas?" asked Jack. "My gunners haven't smelled powder yet."

I shook my head, having no taste for wholesale murder, though it is common practice among gentlemen of fortune. Regardless of his race, your true buccaneer believes in the extermination of a competitor—especially when he is a sitting target. Watching the enemy boats scatter, I saw that they were bearing mostly to the eastward. I surmised that they would take refuge among the smaller of the Laccadive Islands until they could be rescued by one of their own corsairs from Malabar.

"We'll close with the Indiaman in another moment," I said. "There's no time for that sort of revenge."

"She's a dying ship, Mr. Douglas."

"Dying but not yet dead," I said. "If we move in now, we can careen her."

"She seems about to founder."

"Only because those cowards were too confused to man the pumps." I cupped my hands for what I hoped was the order that would end the action. "Gun crews on deck! Prepare to board!"

In another moment some fifty men had come boiling up from the gun decks, each with a cutlass in his fist and *pistolas* primed: there is nothing the average buccaneer enjoys more than an order to board an enemy when that enemy is clearly *hors de combat*. We had already come about, and were bearing down on the sinking hulk at our top speed. In fact, I was obliged to order the topsails backed at the last moment to avoid a collision that could have sent us both to the bottom. As it was, we came together with a jarring crash. Men were dropping to her decks all down our length long before the grapplers sank home.

There were scarcely a dozen of the Angria pirates aboard, and most of these took to their heels as we bore down on them, to scull away for their lives in the last longboat. I had kept to our own deck, letting Jack Ketchell direct the boarding. Now I ordered him to bring the Indiaman around until she could heel with the wind. Meanwhile I had cast off our grappling irons, and stood a short distance abaft of her until I was sure the two splintered planks were above the water line. Once this was done, it was possible to man the pumps and keep the hulk afloat, after a fashion. Though she would never be seaworthy after the drubbing she had taken, we could bring her easily into the lagoon. With lookouts posted at all hours against possible reprisal, we could salvage what we wished.

In the end the gutting proved an easy task. Once she was beached in the lagoon, the Angrian's very bulk was a point in our favor. The *Venture* had only to approach her outboard in deeper water, unload from her waist, and pass such plunder as we fancied from deck to deck.

The cargo was not too badly damaged by the salt water— and was rich enough to justify our attack. There were bales of Ceylon tea, Chinese brocades, silks and spices, precious woods, and jeweled handiwork in both gold and silver. What delighted my shipmates most, however, were ten chests of coins (some of them minted in India) amounting to almost eighty thousand chequins, a piece worth about ten shillings. In addition, we found gold ingots which we valued at over twenty thousand pounds. All in all, I estimated the total value of our haul at well over fifty thousand pounds. It was a fitting climax to a lucky voyage. Best of all, thanks to our lightning-swift attack, we had lost not a single man.

By the time we were ready for sea again, Bonnie was well enough to come on deck. The cheer that greeted her announcement of our homeward voyage would have gladdened any commander's heart. In this case I knew it was the tribute of a loyal crew—though I can hardly deny that each man aboard had estimated his share in the enterprise exactly. Tom's share and my own were modest enough, though my promotion as first officer would give me an added share in every prize since the *Aureng Zeb.* . . . What really unnerved me, however (even as it set my pulse pounding with longing), was the sure knowledge that I had acquitted myself well, that my testing was over.

My marriage would take place on our return to Ringo Bay. Bonnie left me in no doubt of that (an hour after our departure from the Laccadives) when she called me to her cabin and pointed to her last entry in the log:

> *Mr. Douglas has proved an admirable first officer in every way. His strategy that resulted in the capture of the* Aureng Zeb *was identical with my own. His behavior under fire and in boarding actions showed both courage and initiative. The capture of the Angria pirate was carried off with brilliance, as log entries above will demonstrate beyond cavil.*
>
> *It is the captain's opinion that Mr. Douglas is well suited to any duties he may be assigned in future, afloat or ashore.*

I knew I was blushing as I read the final sentence and trusted the mahogany tan I had acquired in these tropic waters would cover the worst of it.

"If I interpret this praise correctly, Captain Carter—"

Bonnie cut in sharply. "No praise was intended, Mr. Douglas. I am stating a fact for the record. As you know, my father's ships are logged as carefully as any you have sailed."

"May I ask the nature of the shore duty you had in mind?"

Her eyes did not waver at the impertinence—but the hard look she gave me was warning enough that this was no moment for romance.

"Only my father can answer that," she said.

"Do you have any special recommendation?"

She got up from her worktable on that, and her eyes were still unsmiling as she moved to the cabin door to study the luff of our mainsail.

"Nothing has happened on this voyage to change my original opinion of you. Now I've signed this log, my wishes are official. Will *that* do you for now, Mr. Douglas?"

"Nicely, Captain Carter," I said, with my best salute. But I could tell by the set of her shoulders (and the fact she had not yet turned from the cabin door) that she was not ready to dismiss me.

"Perhaps I should enlighten you on one point," she said—and I could see she was forcing coldness into her tone, with some effort. "I've given you your head on this expedition. Those were my orders, and they've paid off handsomely. But you'll never be one of our captains in fact as well as name. Shall I explain why?"

"Are you suggesting that a consort should know his place?"

"Precisely. You've given your proofs—that's all I'll ask of you. Your function hereafter is to provide our family with an heir. While we await that result, you'll be shorebound."

"And *you*, Captain?"

"I, too—more's the pity," said Bonnie. "There'll be time enough later to show what I can really do with a ship that's all mine."

Again it was a statement of intent, with no overtone of bitterness—but I knew she was raging within. On this voyage she had followed Red Carter's wishes to the letter—standing aside to watch my performance alow and aloft, and giving me unstinting praise in her logs. It was still a bitter admission (now that the voyage was ending) that each of our actions could have succeeded without her. Bitterest of all to write that our final capture (through no fault of hers) had been carried out in her absence from the deck. . . . I moved forward to comfort her—and remembered my place just in time.

"Being a woman has its drawbacks," I ventured, "as you've already remarked. Being a princess in the bargain, with a dynasty to establish, can be even more onerous. The special duty we've been discussing need not last forever. With luck, you can put to sea again in a year's time. Assuming, of course, that I'm to be our son's nursemaid as well as his tutor."

"I'm glad you're broad-minded, Mr. Douglas," she said. "Most men would rebel at such a role."

"Being a royal consort has its drawbacks too," I said. "I'll accept them gladly if I can give you what you really wish."

CHAPTER 12

The Eagle's Nest

MY WEDDING night (I confess it freely) was an occasion where romance and reality coincided. Not that events jibed with my fancy. I had pictured a vast pagan ritual—Red Carter's battle-scarred bullies massed as witnesses, tom-toms beating, torches flaring against a midnight sky. . . . Measured against such dream images, the actual ceremony was a pallid anticlimax. It was the aftermath that exceeded my fondest hopes.

The wedding itself was short, simple—and dignified. There were two of them in all. The first was a private affair in the pirate king's own quarters. Here Carter officiated as a sea captain, reading the service from an English Book of Common Prayer. The second ceremony took place in the seamen's chapel on the dock, with the captured priest in charge—a bit of popish mumbo-jumbo I accepted with what grace I could. Carter's captains, many of whom were of the Catholic faith, had insisted on a church marriage as well. . . . But once again I run ahead.

Carter himself had given no formal notice of my return from voyaging.

When we dropped anchor in Ringo Bay, his stevedores had come out (as they always did) to help unload our booty. The sight of the *Aureng Zeb*, moored to a repair dock at the far end of the harbor, did little to raise my spirits—

nor did the three captured dhows. . . . The activities of the vast roadstead—and the fact that the *Venture* was but one ship of many there—had restored my distorted sense of proportion instantly.

True, our hunting trip had been a success: my reward awaited me on the morrow. But my sense of sleep-walking persisted when I took over the harbor watch—and stood at attention with the crew while Bonnie (as befitted a corsair captain) went ashore in the gig to make her report.

Awaiting my own summons, I slept aboard that night. Tom had gone in to drink with Jack Ketchell, but I was in no mood to join them. There was no word from Carter's fortress castle the next morning, nor the morning that followed. So far, I had been given no shore billet: it seemed wiser to remain on the *Venture* rather than approach the pirate king, hat in hand, to ask for orders. . . . On the third day (just as my impatience was about to choke me) the gig put out from the castle dock. Bonnie, still in her buccaneer garb and looking serene as the brand-new day, was in the stern sheets.

There was a shore watch on duty, and I ordered her piped aboard. Keeping a straight face, I saluted smartly—and, at her gesture, followed her into the captain's cabin. When I closed the door, I realized that her jaunty air had been but skin-deep.

"I'd have sent word earlier, Richard," she said, "but it was only today that my father endorsed my plans."

"I trust I'm still part of them."

"How could you not be?"

"Has something gone amiss then?"

"Of course not. He's accepted you as my consort. It's just that I'd made a decision on our wedding—or, rather, our wedding journey. *He* had other thoughts. I've had hell's own time changing 'em."

Red Carter, I learned, had already prepared our quarters, on the top floor of his dwelling. Immediately after the ceremony that would make our union formal, he had demanded that we settle there—so that I might begin at once on a course in bookkeeping that would make me useful ashore. Bonnie, however, had demanded (no less insistently) that we enjoy a month-long honeymoon, at a hunting lodge he still maintained on the African coast.

The argument between father and daughter had been long and furious. In the end the daughter had prevailed. She had agreed to reduce our absence from four to three weeks. In view of Metcalf's threatened attack, she had also agreed to take me to the Eagle's Nest (a retreat in the hills above Ringo Bay) rather than to the mainland.

"He wanted to send a dozen guards," she said. Now she had won her point, she seemed more amused than angered. "I told him I needed no army to manage a husband. After three days of sulks he consented."

"Apparently your father still doesn't trust me."

"He trusts you completely, Richard. And he approves of you—as much as he approves of any man. But he can't bear to surrender me."

"He let us voyage together."

"I was in command then. Things will be different at the Eagle's Nest if I see the future plain."

I felt my heart leap at this avowal—since it was her first admission she was prepared to yield to my male dominance.

"Most fathers find it hard to lose a daughter to a husband," I said cautiously. "Why should yours be the exception?"

"He doesn't intend to lose me, Richard. You've been engaged by him as a bookkeeper—and a stud." She had the grace to blush at the last word. "You'll have no other duties here."

"In that case why did he let me take the *Venture* into action?"

"To prove you were a shipmaster, of course. No daughter of his could wed a man who wasn't a born sailor. But that voyage is in the logs: it's past history. Tomorrow, as I say, you'll have but one function at Ringo Bay. If *he* had his way, you'd be sent packing, once you'd performed it."

"Why shouldn't he have his way? He's king here."

"Not in my bedchamber. I'll have the kind of wedding trip I choose. When it's over, I'll enjoy my husband, after my own fashion."

"Even when he's given you an heir?"

"For shame, Mr. Douglas. D'you think I'd abandon a man who fulfilled my dearest wish? Or destroy him, like some female spider?"

"Nothing you do would surprise me," I told her. "But I'll say this, here and now. Your choice of the Eagle's Nest as our honeymoon house seems a perfect compromise. I'll look forward to our twenty-one days there."

"And so will I, Richard."

"When do we set out?"

"My father is waiting now to read the marriage service," she said calmly. "If we can hurry him a bit, we'll be there by nightfall."

As I have noted, our two weddings were run off with a minimum of formality.

Carter (still in the work clothes he had donned to help with a careening) recited the poetic words from the prayer book as baldly as some rural judge. When he finished, he did not suggest that he (or I) should kiss the bride. Bonnie and I had gone straight from the *Venture* to his sanctum: I was wed in my own sailor garb, and she still wore the jack boots, dead-black tights, and leather jerkin that were the symbols of her command.

Only two concessions were made to the moment. At the door of her father's castle she had cast aside the belt that held her cutlass and *pistolas*. And when our hands were joined at the finale of the service, she untied the knot of her bandanna and let her hair stream about her shoulders. . . . The hair was still uncovered (in defiance of the edict of Saint Paul) when we repeated our vows in Latin before the priest's altar. Ten minutes later—still kissless—she stepped into the captain's gig again, at its mooring post on Carter's wharf.

Her father had accompanied us to the church, since protocol demanded it—but there had been no other witnesses. The dock was deserted when we three marched down its length side by side. Indeed, I am certain he ordered it cleared —as though he were unwilling, even at this late moment, to admit before his men that Bonnie's will had prevailed.

I offered him my hand when I joined my bride in the gig. It was a chancy thing, for he had not spoken a word beyond the recital from the prayer book. Our eyes had met just once in chapel, when the priest had ordered me to place the ring on my wife's finger. . . . Now I was the son-in-law of Red Carter's own choosing—and yet, even as his busy brain admitted my usefulness, I could feel his hatred break through.

The look he flung at me as he towered above us on the dock was murderous—though he did accept my hand. For an instant his fingers crushed mine in a viselike grip, as though he had half a mind to drag me from the gig and declare the whole business null and void.

"You're to return at once if Metcalf attacks," he growled. "Remember, daughter, that's a promise."

"We'll be back posthaste if his sails show in the Channel," said Bonnie. "Don't forget we've a bird's-eye view from the Nest."

"Make sure you signal me with the semaphore," he said in the same mastiff growl. "You might also signal your safe arrival."

Bonnie had made herself comfortable in the gig. Her booted legs were stretched out before her, and she had just cocked her black sombrero at a saucy angle over one brow. Before she spoke again, she laughed up at her sire—and the mirth was like a sword between them.

"For the next three weeks," she said, "we'll be far too busy for semaphores." She nodded at me with a proprietary air—but I knew better than to speak again in this battle of glances between daughter and father. I was, after all, but a helpless bystander, caught in the cross fire.

I dropped the oars into their locks, uncertain if I should row away without Carter's permission. In the end it was Bonnie who signaled to me to put the gig in motion. I pointed the prow toward the eastern shore of the harbor, where a jungle trail would lead us (after some hours afoot and on muleback) to our special eyrie in the hills. As I rowed, I glanced over my bride's shoulder at the motionless figure of my father-in-law. He was still frozen to the dock, his arms akimbo, staring at our lengthening wake.

Bonnie sat at her ease in the stern, her chin lifted in defiance of his wordless anger. But she did not speak until we were in the shadow of a banyan on the eastern shore— a colossus among trees that spread its roots over a full acre.

"Don't be afraid of him, Richard," she said. "Whatever his crotchets, he's fair. If he regrets his bargain now, he'll see it through."

"At the moment," I said, "I'm too happy to think of to-morrow."

"Should I be happy too?" she asked. "I'm not—so far. I'm just numb—if that's the proper word. As though I'd been struck between the eyes yet felt no pain. Is that usual among brides?"

"So I'm told," I said.

"Did my mother feel this way—when she married? Did yours?"

"It's quite likely," I told her. "Pay it no heed—it will pass, once we're at the Nest."

Tying our painter to one of the score of banyan roots, we took to the narrow trail that snaked eastward through a saw grass marsh (I saw at once why Bonnie had been married in her jack boots). On my shoulder I carried a traveling case, which was her only baggage, and my portmanteau. My own spirits were numb enough while we threaded the green, heat-drugged growth. Of all the wedding trips that anxious couples have taken since marriage was invented, this one seemed the oddest.

"We'll walk for just under a mile," said Bonnie. "There's a native village at the first fork—they'll have our mules waiting."

The prediction was confirmed when we entered a ragged clearing in the rain forest and found a brace of fine mules tethered before the chief's hut. Out of deference to Carter the entire village had retired: among this island people it is considered bad fortune to look upon a bride's face before her husband has possessed her. Nor did we encounter a soul after we had saddled our mounts and begun the long and steady climb into the hills. Save for the chatter of parakeets, the forest seemed empty today. This could have been our private Eden. It was easy to believe the jungle trail led straight to the Tree of Life.

We rode out of the rain forest in the hour before dusk, traversing open, parklike slopes a good thousand feet above sea level. A little later we reached a region of stunted bush, where the rocky trace we were following seemed made only for goats—though our mules picked their way with ease.

So far, I had avoided looking back—and had ceased to protest when Bonnie continued to lead the way, pausing now and then to take my bridle when the path grew dangerous. Finally she reined in on a ledge that was wide enough for us to come abreast—and we stared down together, in silent wonder, at the world we had left behind.

At that height the bay seemed remote as a mirage. The jungle slope (now far below us) looked impenetrable: I could scarce believe we had just threaded it. Carter's ships, riding at their anchor chains, seemed mere toys, the fortress castle a mass of baby's blocks, forgotten in the sun. To the west the Mozambique Channel glowed like burnished steel, empty as the day the first native proa had braved it.

We had spoken only in snatches during our grueling climb. Now, when it was nearly over, I put a hand on Bonnie's as it lay on her saddle horn.

"It's not an original thought," I told her. "But this Eagle's Nest must be an outpost to heaven. At least we've climbed high enough."

"We've another half mile," she said. "Most of it is uphill." She had made no move to withdraw her hand—and the quick, weary droop of her lashes told me she was ready to be kissed. I contented myself, for the nonce, by lifting her hand and brushing my lips against the palm.

"Shall we go on?" I asked. "This is no place to be caught by darkness."

"We've time to spare, Richard," she said. "It's steep climbing, but the trail is wide. You'll find it easy riding."

She proved her words in the next half hour, when we left the timber line and emerged into a region of cliffs and green, sloping meadowland. The scene reminded me, oddly enough, of our own Scotch Highlands, lacking only the scent of heather. For a space the path skirted the deep blue border of a lake that Bonnie said was the crater of a dead volcano. Then it serpentined through tumbled boulders and emerged on an airy plateau no larger than an English croquet lawn.

Even before we dismounted, I saw we had reached the crest of the mountain. The chalet that crowned it had been well named the Eagle's Nest. It dominated its blue fastness —and stood on the edge of its thousand-foot cliff, foursquare to any gale that blew.

On the reverse slope there was a corral for the mules, and a steep acre of pasture where they could graze. After I had carried our baggage to the portico and stripped the saddles from our mounts, I lingered outside another moment, to give Bonnie time to open the windows of our honeymoon haven. I have called it a chalet advisedly: it was an exact replica of a Swiss *Berghaus,* with the same weathered timbers, the same steep roof, and identical carvings on porch and doorsill.

The porch (it was no more than a shelf) looked out across the distant bay and the shining floor of the sea. Here I found the semaphore that Carter had mentioned—a thing of pulleys and metal arms capable of spelling out messages to the fortress once a glass was trained upon it. Beside it stood our own telescope, on a brass tripod, with a tarpaulin housing to protect it from the weather.

Bonnie was humming inside the chalet. A glance through the open door told me she was busy in the larder, where a pair of venison steaks had been hung to serve as our first wedded meal. Still reluctant to disturb her, I stripped off the cover to the telescope and focused it on Carter's castle. The lens was a powerful one: the portico of the fortress leaped into view instantly. As I had expected, the pirate king was pacing there, hands rammed into pockets, red wilderness of whiskers bristling. As I watched, he whipped up his own glass and studied the mountaintop. Evidently he disliked what he saw, for he turned aside with a snort of displeasure.

I faced the doorframe as Bonnie emerged from the single bedroom the chalet boasted. She had discarded her boy's garments and wore the sheathlike robe of *peau de soie*.

"Was his glass trained on the mountain, Richard?"

"So it seems," I said. "Now he's studying us again. Shall I signal our arrival?"

"He knows we'd arrive safely," she told me. "He knows why I brought you here. Why should he hate us—when we're following his orders?"

I made no attempt to respond to the question. Instead, I took her in my arms for a kiss that broke the last barrier dividing us.

"Shall I carry you over the threshold?" I asked. "It's the custom on a wedding eve."

"Do, by all means," she murmured. Her lips sought mine again before we could enter our honeymoon house.

I have already said that our three weeks of *lune de miel* were perfect. How does one describe perfection—when not even the poets can snare fulfillment in a phrase?

From that first white night of love I knew that our minds and hearts had been merged no less firmly than our bodies.

Communion so intense is a boon granted to but few mortals. Had I died on the morrow, I would have gone gladly—in the knowledge that I had given the same breathless happiness I received. Yet, when I wakened the next morning, with my wife in my arms, my joy was even greater. Desire is a night-blooming cereus, a flower that flourishes by dark. Love is a hardier blossom—and it can be sweetest by day.

Bonnie had wakened as contentedly as I.

"Why didn't you *tell* me?" she asked. "I'd no notion marriage was like this."

"It's something no man can tell a woman, Bonnie. She must learn it herself."

"You might have given me some notion," she said, nestling deeper in my embrace.

"If you've had it, you know," I told her. "Words are wasted otherwise."

"I'll never be the same again, Richard."

"Nor will I."

"All that's gone before is without meaning," she said. "Yesterday I thought of you as my lieutenant. A brave fellow and a clever one—but a man who took my orders. Now it's *I* who await commands."

"You'll find me a gentle master," I said as I bent to kiss away her look of happy bewilderment.

"Try me, Richard. There's nothing I won't do for you."

"Already you've given me everything a woman can give a man," I said. "And let's have no more talk of commands. You're my wife—not just a princess. Once you've made that admission, nothing else matters."

"I'm your wife, now and forever. Just let me *prove* it, my darling."

"Very well, since you insist," I said. "I'll give just one command, then hold my peace. Never reveal what you've just told me. It's a secret we must keep from every man at Ringo Bay. Above all, from your father."

"Why my father? He *wanted* this marriage."

"Your father wants an heir," I said. "Not a husband for his daughter. He'd have our heads if he knew the truth."

"I'm not afraid to speak the truth. Why shouldn't he know you've made me into a woman?"

"Because he's trained you to think and fight as a man," I said bluntly. "Because you *are* the son he never had—and, like all fathers, he won't give up the dream picture for the reality."

"What must I do then?"

"Nothing could be simpler," I said. "When we return to Ringo Bay, you must go on as before."

"Only if you're beside me, as an equal."

"We both know that's impossible, Bonnie."

"Why? From this day forward we share and share alike. Isn't that what marriage means?"

"Only when we're alone," I told her solemnly. "Only if Red Carter never guesses our true feelings."

"Is it shameful for us to love one another?"

"A princess has no right to love," I said. "Not if the lover comes between her and destiny."

"How could you, Richard?"

"To your father I'm an outsider. Why should I share your future? Only yesterday you told me he'd never permit me to sail a Carter ship again. My task is to keep the books."

"That was yesterday," she said, with a sigh of pure content. "How could I guess *then* what you'd mean to me?"

"True enough. Yesterday you were an unawakened girl, with a man's strength and a man's way with a ship. You saw life through your father's eyes—you accepted his values. It was a form of bondage—but you were a willing slave. Now he means to keep you bound. For your good, of course. In his fashion he loves you too."

"How can he pretend to love me if he treats me thus?"

"Remember the life he's led," I told her. "Remember his credo is founded on hate. Until he's destroyed Sir Luke Metcalf, he won't rest easy. But he's a builder too—for all that need to destroy. His empire is built on death and plunder: the fact remains, he created it for you, and you alone. Someday he hopes to bequeath you the whole island. When he's gone, he believes your legend will surpass his own. Take away that vision, and you rob him of his reason for being."

"The deadly lady of Madagascar," she murmured, with her cheek against mine. "Is *that* what he'd make of me?"

"I've said it was his dearest wish. You'll cross him at your peril."

"It was my wish too, only yesterday," she said. "Now it's only a crazy vision—unless we can rule here together."

Again I silenced her with a kiss. *"That's* a vision we can never share. Your father's bound to think otherwise."

"I'll beard him when we return. I'll say you'll go mad if he keeps you on the beach. Perhaps he'll make you a captain after all, once we've crushed Metcalf."

"I'm afraid even that's too much to ask."

"Let me try, at least."

In the end I yielded to Bonnie's pleas—if only to give her peace of mind. It was enough, for now, to know we stood together, with Red Carter as our common Nemesis, that Bonnie was my wife in every sense. I could hardly ask her to change her whole way of thinking overnight—nor could I ask for the same blind loyalty she gave today. Deliverance (I told myself solemnly) must come in the end. Meanwhile I could only bide my time—and pray, with all my heart and soul, that her guilt-ridden past might be redeemed by a different future.

I had expected those weeks on the mountain to stretch into a blissful eternity. In sober fact, they seemed over before they had fairly begun—so busy were our days, so silver-swift our nights.

In the mornings, we rode on the hillside trails—hunting for deer or smaller game, or resting in the shade of a dell to read from the stock of books the chalet boasted. Often we swam in the crater lake, plunging into its crystal heart in a vain search for the bottom. Sometimes we were content merely to drowse away an afternoon in the sun and wind while we built air castles, as lovers will. . . . Even a three-day storm (when the wind howled round the eaves, and rain pelted like hail on the shuttered windows) failed to dampen our ardors. Snug in our nest, with the *Odyssey* open between us, we chanted the sonorous Greek meters into the teeth of the gale, drank down the last of the cellar —and fell into each other's embrace.

Now and again, when Bonnie slept late, I tiptoed down the portico to study the harbor through the glass. There was no further sign of Carter—and I judged he had gone to Fools' Bay with his cannoneers, to prepare for Metcalf's reception there. For the rest, I found it easy to forget my father-in-law. Easier still to admit that my dedication to Bonnie's fortunes was now complete. No matter how this war with the Company might end, I would not change sides again. If Metcalf should win the day, I would fight him, as wholeheartedly as I had fought the pirates of Angria. If our paths crossed in that battle, I would oppose him with dirk and cutlass, as furiously as I had fought in that New York alley, when he was a menace without a name.

A short while ago I would not have faced that decision without something like terror—positive that I had damned myself forever in the sight of God and man. Today I merely shrugged off my scruples—and went shouting after my wife, as joyously as a stallion in April, when she ran naked from our eyrie to win another footrace to the lake.

When our three weeks were nearly ended, torrential rain delayed us still further. Bonnie assured me that the jungle trail would be a quagmire until the sun had dried it, and I was only too glad to accept her judgment. This time, the rain fell for almost a week without ceasing—and once again we laughed off the threats of Jupiter Pluvius in each other's arms. Our stock of food was adequate. It was still a pleasure to reread the *Aeneid* and the *Odes* of Horace while the storm made the world outside a misty dream.

All in all, it was thirty-one days after our arrival when we prepared to ride down from the mountain. Morning fog was lifting from the tops of the nearest trees when I saddled the mules and returned to the portico for a final survey through the telescope. To my amazement, I saw that the first of a dozen ships had begun to negotiate the dog-leg channel to Ringo Bay. All of them were Carter's vessels (if I could judge by their black flags) and all were loaded with cannon, lashed side by side on their decks.

Bonnie confirmed my estimate after her turn at the glass.

"Those were the guns intended for the ambuscade," she said. "Why are they returning so soon? Does it mean the fight's over and Metcalf a prisoner?"

"It seems highly unlikely," I said. At this elevation we could spy on both harbors with the telescopes. Bemused as we'd been with our own sport, we had not noted the buccaneers' departure for Fools' Bay. Nor had we witnessed their preparations to return until now—when the first ship was already past the harbor defenses.

"Should we have left sooner, Richard?"

"How could we, with the heavens opened?"

"My father will never forgive us if we've missed a fight," said Bonnie.

"It's my opinion we've missed nothing," I told her. It was a reasonable assumption: though we had ridden far on the trails, we had never left the mountainside. Some echo of a bombardment would surely have reached us, distant though we were.

Bonnie's eye was fastened to the glass. "I'm inclined to agree," she said at last. "From the looks of things, the trapper has gone home empty-handed."

When she gave up her place, I swept the bay one more time, returning to the Carter fortress after I had counted some thirteen ships in all. The pirate king was pacing his porch in full uniform. As I watched, he whipped up his own telescope and focused it carefully on the mountaintop. When he observed that we had already trained our glass on the castle, he gestured emphatically at the semaphore on his porch rail, then moved toward it to spell out a message. Once again I gave the telescope to Bonnie: so far, I had not been honored with the pirate's code.

"There's pen and ink inside," she said. "You can write down what he's saying."

Now she had the telescope, I could discern nothing but the brown mass of the fortress. The figure on the portico was too small to take on identity—and the metal-armed device he was manipulating (though it gleamed in the early sunlight) could not be seen with the naked eye. There was already something ominous about the moment. My wife, now that she was dressed for the trail, seemed to belong to me no longer as she repeated the message, letter by letter. . . . Was it my fancy, or had her voice already deepened? Had she returned to Red Carter's cosmos even before he issued his first command?

" ' *Come down at once,*' " I wrote as she dictated. " '*Attack expected tomorrow.*' What does that mean?"

"I wish I knew, Richard. But there's no doubt we've outstayed our leave." Her eyes were shining when she moved to our own semaphore and began to signal a reply to her father's message. They had gleamed with the same fire when we grappled the *Aureng Zeb.*

"What are you telling him?" I asked.

"That we'll be at Ringo Bay in two hours. Less, if the

trail is really dry." She was working the semaphore at top speed, and seemed but half aware of my presence. "Watch him through the glass, Richard. See how he's taking it."

I focused the telescope on Red Carter. Not even the powerful lens could pierce his red blizzard of whiskers, but I knew he had smiled when he pocketed his own spyglass.

"He seems a happy man today," I said.

"He's always happy when a fight's brewing."

"And happier still when you've joined it?"

"We'll both take part in this one," she said. "Trust me that far, Richard. But we must hurry."

"Lead the way," I said grimly. "I'll follow."

When we had ridden out of the corral, she reined in and put her hand on mine. Then, leaning across her saddle, she kissed me briefly. It was not a lover's caress. Rather, it was the salute of one comrade to another on the eve of battle.

I set my teeth and followed her as she left the corral at her mount's best canter—a bone-shaking gait that would have unseated most riders.

CHAPTER 13

War to the Death

Mozo awaited us at the Carter dock. Sculling at my fastest pace across the last yards of open water, I let the gig run up to stringpiece under its own momentum and turned to study his face. I could read the bad news there before he spoke—addressing Bonnie, not myself, when she rose to toss him a line.

"Your father expects you at the harbor battery, *Señora Capitán*," he said in the lisping Castilian that emerged so oddly from his huge body. "We're setting up the defenses of the outer bay, and he wishes your advice." The *señora*, I saw, was a deference on Mozo's part to Bonnie's marital status. Otherwise, from his viewpoint, the chain of command seemed unaltered.

"Give us the worst," said Bonnie. "We've a right to know."

"I was told to bring you at once, *señora mia*—"

"*Caramba contigo!*" she shouted. "We want the facts now, Mozo! That's an order!"

"If the *capitán* pleases, I will talk while we cross the bay."

Bonnie nodded a curt permission to this compromise— and we followed the Negro across the pier. A longboat awaited us there, with eight brawny fellows at the oars. I leaped into the wide stern beside my wife: Mozo half knelt against a thwart to tell us his story. It emerged in bits, as it were, against the screech of eight oarlocks straining as one against the hard crash of the blades.

Even as he related it, I saw that Ringo Bay was lashing up for war. During our descent from the mountain the ships that had ferried the cannon had slipped their cables and put out to sea. Of the vessels brought in for careening, only two remained, and these were slender dhows, of no use in combat. Each of the warehouses was shuttered, its sentry posts black with muskets. At the castle fortress the drawbridge was raised, the portcullis down; not a head showed on the barbican, but I knew that each gun was manned. . . . The story Mozo told us gave meaning to these sinister preparations.

For the past fortnight the batteries at Fools' Bay had rusted on their carronades while their gunners awaited an attack that did not come. Rumors had flown fast between Carter's castle and the decoy harbor. In the end he had sent pinnaces up the Channel to scout the seaways to the north: they had returned with no news of the enemy. Meanwhile the buccaneers' navy had made its rendezvous at a point just off the mainland, awaiting its signal to storm down on Metcalf. These ships, too, had worn down their patience in mock war games. . . .

"We had planned to trap them," said Mozo. "We staked everything on that plan. Ringo Bay was undefended while we massed our power at the trap. Instead, its jaws almost closed upon us."

Word had come at last that Metcalf's ships were bearing down from the west, that they had put boldly into Fort Dauphin at the height of the week-long storm while he perfected his own plan of battle. It had been Mozo's task to uncover that plan, a perilous tour of duty he had carried out brilliantly. With a picked squad he had gone overland to the enemy anchorage, to swim among the ships on a black midnight and spy out what he could. The news he brought back had been dire—but it had given Carter his chance to return to a prepared position while there was still time.

First (and most startling), Mozo had found that the map Potin had sold to Sir Luke had been exposed as a fraud even before the latter could reach India. An unnamed spy, working in the buccaneers' midst, had finally brought in a true chart of Ringo Bay—complete to the soundings in the dog-leg entrance and a count of the guns on the headlands. (Mozo had seen this map with his own eyes when he risked his life to climb the rudder chains of Metcalf's flagship and peer through the chartroom window.)

Metcalf, it seemed, had paused in Madras just long enough to lock up his false informer. Then, armed with the information he had been years in seeking, he had assembled his fleet —and come keening south for the kill with the first breath of the monsoon. Knowing that Carter would expect an attack via the Channel, he had chosen the western approach, relying on the storm to cover his movements.

"Where is he now?" I asked.

"*Quién sabe, señor?*" Mozo spread his hands in a gesture of despair. For the first time, I saw how tired he really was. It had been a bone-breaking task to redeploy a force intended originally for attack—which would now be used in a desperate defense against superior force.

"Haven't you scouted his movements?"

"We had no ships to spare. All our sail now lies across the Channel. When Metcalf strikes here, they'll move to assist us—but not before."

I glanced at Bonnie, and saw that she had grasped her father's strategy. The armada waiting in the shadow of Africa was our only remaining trump. Were its anchorage revealed prematurely, Metcalf could engage it first, before his attack on Ringo Bay.

"What of those careened dhows?" I asked. "Can't they be used as lookouts?"

"The *jefe* says no." Mozo glanced up at the beetling headland, into whose shadow we were gliding. "Now he is sure the attack must come, he feels it is God's will. If we can hold if off until our ships arrive, well and good. If not, we'll go down fighting—and the ships will drum up plunder elsewhere."

Again I glanced at Bonnie, who nodded in tight-lipped agreement. The Negro had stated the dilemma that faces all gentlemen of fortune—the need for a haven in a world where each man's hand is against them. Ringo Bay had been an ideal sanctuary when Red Carter's rule was undisputed. Now his rule was challenged, his ships had but one choice—to lurk at a distance and await the outcome of this war to the death. Should the fight go against us, they would never risk an engagement with the flower of the Company's navy.

"How many men have stayed ashore?" asked Bonnie.

Mozo glanced at me: I saw that Carter had forbidden specific answers in my presence. (Why should a mere consort share the secrets of the high command?)

"All we could spare from the ships," the Negro said.

"How many cannon?"

"Your father will answer that, *señora*."

Bonnie stamped her foot. "My husband has the right to hear everything."

"Forgive me, *capitán*—but Señor Douglas must return in the longboat to await you at the castle. You may join him there tonight."

I held up a soothing palm before Bonnie could speak. "When we were ordered off the mountain this morning," I said, "we were told the attack would come tomorrow."

"Such is our prayer," said Mozo. "Sir Luke won't stand offshore forever, with the weather clearing."

Again I spoke ahead of Bonnie to forestall her wrath at this bland admission that Carter's message had been a ruse to bring her back. "Find out what you can," I told her. "Help all you can—that's what a daughter's for. Then return to me tonight. I'll wait at the castle, since that's your father's wish."

If my wife was disappointed by the tameness of my words, she kept her opinion to herself while the boat grounded at the landing stage behind the headland. Here a series of ladders gave access to the batteries from the harbor side. I could hear Carter bellowing orders above us: after Mozo had announced our arrival, he moved to the cliff's edge and stared down at us, with no sign of greeting. Considering his present peril, he seemed wonderfully calm: I had guessed he would grow increasingly cool as danger thickened, like all born fighters. . . . Finally, he gave me the briefest of nods, then leveled a finger at the stair. The gesture was a command, meant for Bonnie alone.

The boat continued to nuzzle the landing stage while her eyes held her father's. I feared she would refuse to obey, with all refusal would entail. It was only when my hand closed on hers that I felt her tautness ease.

"Remember our talk at the Nest," I said. "Obey his wishes while you can."

She left me then, bending to kiss me after she had stepped out to the landing stage. I was sure she was raging within—and watched anxiously as she ran lightly up the last of the ladder and joined her father at the cliff's edge. For an instant they stood there eye to eye, without exchanging a word. Then, giving him the coolest of salutes, she moved with him toward the nearest battery.

I had expected to find the castle an armed prison. Instead, it was deserted, save for the guards in the barbican. Mozo left me with the suggestion I mount to the roof if I wished to study the preparations for battle. (It seemed an odd concession, in view of the secrecy Carter had insisted on—but I knew the Negro sympathized with my plight.)

After I had explored the castle to the last corner, I realized the gravity of our position fully. Carter's rooms contained a cache of food and a stack of mattresses where he had slept while he deployed his forces. The room above (intended for Bonnie and myself) was also stocked with food and wine, and there was still another mattress on the bed. Aside from this the place had been stripped bare, and there were iron shutters on every window. This was no longer a home (if it had ever been) but a donjon awaiting siege.

The fact that the donjon was unmanned told me the battle would be decided elsewhere—on the headlands above the harbor, or in the sea before it. If Red Carter was forced to barricade himself here, he would be fighting a hopeless cause.

The bridal quarters opened directly to the roof of the pirate king's own portico: this flat expanse served as a kind of Oriental terrace, with a fine view of the bay, the castle gardens, and the apron of beach below them. Above (with access provided by a recessed stair) was the roof of the castle itself, a spot Mozo had mentioned as an even better vantage point. I was not surprised to find it a replica of a ship's deck, complete with compass and binnacle. At its far end a tall mast had been stepped into the floor, with a set of ratlines and a crow's-nest.

Eager as I was for a look, I was careful to climb but half way to the nest, keeping a weather eye on the guards in the barbican. The men lounged at their posts: the mate in command cast a sharp glance at me, then returned to the map he was studying. Mozo's orders to give me the run of the castle, I gathered, had been accepted literally.

The crow's-nest was the summit of Red Carter's world. Accustomed though I was to ship's rigging, I felt my head swim as I surveyed the airy vastness around me. For a moment I wondered if I had contracted a fever after our long spell of rain. My pulses steadied while I observed the frantic preparations afoot on the headlands. Viewed from this height, the men swarming over the gun mounts resembled busy ants. Like the insects of that regimented kingdom, each was fulfilling an assigned task.

Some fifty guns had been placed on the north side of the harbor pass, with half again as many on the southern headland. It was evident that Carter meant to stake his all on the contest for the channel and hoped to rock Metcalf on his heels there. Such an outcome would give his fleet time to close in before the enemy could force a landing. (I could only pray that they would crowd on sail when news of the battle reached them: much would depend on the speed of Carter's herald.)

I estimated that two hundred men had been kept ashore. Most of them would service the guns. Should Sir Luke secure a foothold on land, there were less than fifty marines to repel boarders: these hardy fellows, I noted, were engaged in a solemn practice game of their own, with Ketchell in command. They would give a good account of themselves if it came to hand-to-hand combat on the beach—but their numbers seemed woefully small. Once again I realized that Carter had preferred to keep his ships well manned: the action here would be a holding operation until help came by sea.

During most of the long, hot afternoon I continued to sit in the crow's-nest—brooding over our chances on the morrow (if the attack should come then), and liking them less with each fresh survey of the field. Now and again my giddiness returned—and I felt sure I would soon be in for a bout of ague. . . . I must have dozed, for I was wakened by an angry exchange of voices, and realized it was Bonnie and her father, disputing on the captain's veranda.

Even when I descended to the castle roof, I could not catch the drift of the quarrel, nor did I feel I should venture nearer. In the end Carter stormed from his sanctum, to board the gig that awaited him on the beach. His arms were burdened with muskets, so I judged he had returned here to collect the last of his ordnance. The explosion I had overheard must have been the finale of the quarrel that had simmered through the afternoon.

The thundercloud on my wife's brow, when she sought me out, confirmed that opinion.

"Are *you* confined to quarters too?" I asked.

"Yes, Richard. I refused to fight for him tomorrow unless he'd give you equal rank. This is his answer."

I felt my heart leap, though I was careful to conceal my joy. At least she would have no baptism of blood when Metcalf struck.

"Remember that I warned you," I told her. "Be glad your punishment isn't more severe."

"He gave you to me as a husband," she cried. "Why won't he trust you in battle?"

"Because he'll let no man challenge your authority—your husband least of all."

"I think it goes deeper," she said. "I think he hates you—because I love you. Can you tell me why?"

I held my tongue: the reason for Carter's refusal to number me among his captains was obvious, but I could hardly state it openly. Loving Bonnie as he did (and why should I blame him if that love was twisted?), he could not share her.

"Let us not go into his motives," I said carefully. "He's our commander, and we're in a state of siege. Until the siege is lifted, we must do his bidding. Do we still have the freedom of the castle?"

"Of course. I gave him my word we'd remain here until the fight's over."

"Then I'd suggest we sup while the light lasts," I said. "And get what rest we can. We'll have little enough tomorrow."

Bonnie turned to stare across the bay at the twin headlands and the cook fires beginning to wink among the batteries. Watching her fist beat a tattoo on the stone balustrade, I could measure the wavering of her allegiance before she turned to me again. With that motion, the fist became a hand, extended to close warmly on my own.

"You're right, of course," she said. "We must save our strength. Meanwhile we'll have a clear view of the battle when it comes—even if we can't take part."

I slept but fitfully because of my fast-rising fever. With the dawn (when the boom of cannon roused us both), my head was swimming. I smiled at my sorry state, reflecting that luck was still with me: had Carter yielded to his daughter's pleas, I would have been useless to him this morning.

Bonnie regarded me anxiously while I stumbled from bed to floor—but I put her questions aside, insisting it was a touch of ague and that I was already on the mend. I would have given much to summon Tom Hoyt, but Tom had already set up his field hospital across the bay. Today my doctor friend would have no leisure to cure the ills of a noncombatant.

When we had prepared a hasty breakfast, we carried it to the castle roof—aware we had already missed some vital elements of the action, since the booming of our cannon was now continuous and there were heavy answers from the sea. From the crow's-nest we had a complete view of the battleground, and could form a rough surmise of our chances. Even as we trained our telescopes on the headlands, there was no mistaking the gravity of the situation.

We would discover later that the Company fleet (a round two dozen men-of-war) had made their first pass at the harbor mouth before sunrise, raking their stationary targets at close range. Carter had not risked a reply in that uncertain light. On their second pass the men-of-war had sailed a tight course—too far offshore to offer us an easy target, yet keeping us within range of their murderous thirty-pounders. They continued to follow this course as we observed them.

Marauders who had previously explored the dog-leg approach to Ringo Bay could not even guess the location of our batteries until they were exposed to their fire. Today, with the position of each gun charted, the Company vessels could place their salvos exactly. Many of our carronades were already smashed, the gun crews blasted at their posts. Still others were silenced as we watched—but worse was to come. A few moments after our arrival at our observation post the stern gun on Sir Luke's flagship, arching a hot shot above the southern headland, exploded a powder magazine at the cliff's base. The detonation that followed rocked the castle walls, and sheared away a huge segment of the headland itself.

The opening the explosion had blasted gave the enemy a clear view of the harbor: our warehouses were already in their sights, and the castle would be a fair target, once the shore-batteries were silenced. At the same time, since the channel was also exposed, the run from sea to bay was now but a simple problem of navigation.

Our gunners fought back with double fury after that lucky hit. A reserve line of cannon were trundled into place and serviced by fresh teams. But it was now grimly evident that the battle could have but one ending unless help arrived. . . . For the next two hours our fortunes hung in the balance. They rose briefly when three of the men-of-war, risking a closer run, sank under our fire. They fell when Sir Luke (enraged at the loss) ran into the very shadow of the headlands to deliver a point-blank salvo. It silenced an entire battery, though he limped from the scene with a broken mainmast and his deck a welter of splintered iron.

Thereafter our assailants moved cautiously, contenting themselves with long-range duels from which they could emerge the winner. Now and again an intrepid master would bear down on the harbor mouth, take such punishment as we could deliver while he blew up our cannon with methodical precision, then retire with decks aflame. Twice in the hour before noon we sent such targets to the bottom. The enemy strength was thus reduced to nineteen ships (all of them damaged to some degree) when our deliverance came.

Intent though he was on our destruction, Sir Luke had not neglected to post lookouts. The first warning came from his own crow's-nest while the roiling smoke of battle still obscured the harbor mouth. It had been a whippy day when the action began, with an offshore wind ideal for maneuver. As the day wore on, the breeze had lightened, making the run for the channel difficult. Now, as though favoring us at last, the wind strengthened, lifting the smoke in a trice and showing a horizon white with our sail.

Ship for ship, the two fleets seemed evenly matched—with the advantage on our side, since we had the wind. Trapped between the land and the converging enemy, the Company vessels seemed to hang irresolute against the curtain of fire laid down by our sea-borne cannon—and the still deadly salvos from the shore. Their hesitation was to prove fatal, losing them the last chance to seize the initiative—or, failing that, a chance to run for safety.

I continued to hold my breath when a second magazine exploded, sending another huge segment of headland tumbling into Ringo Bay and leaving us virtually defenseless. But it was the last landward shot before the battle ended. Thereafter it was Metcalf's turn to defend himself.

Had he elected to fly for open water and fight a classic naval battle there, he might have won the day. He was outgunned as things stood, boxed in enfilading fire—and (as the struggle entered its last phase) forced to grapple in a wolf-iliad of hand-to-hand combat. Here, as he found too late, he was no match for the screaming devils who swept over his gunwales.

In a matter of minutes (or so it seemed) half our enemy had struck their colors. Flags continued to drop all over the Company armada as ship after ship was grappled and boarded—even when it was evident no quarter would be given. Of the nineteen ships that contested the field, no less than fourteen were taken outright. The others, spreading what sail their damaged rigging allowed, ran up-Channel for their lives.

Our counterblow had been so stunning, I was still breathless with wonder when the battle smoke settled: even my raging fever was forgotten for the nonce. At my side Bonnie stared across the disputed harbor mouth as though she, too, could not credit her senses. While we gaped, the Company's flagship (her colors shot away and her masts in ruins) wallowed into her death throes and sank in a rush of flames.

Her assailant, I noted, had cast off her hooks just in time. It was appropriate that she should be the *Pilgrim Venture*.

My glass, sweeping the vessel I had once commanded, told me that several prisoners had come aboard. Some of them were still fighting back, after a fashion—and were cut down before my eyes. Others were pistoled without mercy when they threw down their arms. In the end only one figure towered among the dead and dying—and there was no mistaking his identity.

I had not thought that Sir Luke Metcalf would let himself be taken alive—but there he stood in silent defiance, as though already resigned to his fate. When I remembered the ancient pirate custom of trial by combat, I half guessed why he had yielded. The surmise became a certainty when Red Carter (black as a Kaffir from powder smoke, his porcupine beard bristling in the glare of noon) scrambled from the ruins of his battery and lifted a cutlass in salute. As the *Venture* neared the harbor mouth, Metcalf raised a fist in answer.

"Can you believe we've won?" asked Bonnie.

"I fear it's a Pyrrhic victory," I answered.

Try as I might, I could make no better estimate of the battle. It was true the enemy had been beaten off with appalling losses—but our own damage was even more severe. Unlike the Company (which could mount a second attack when it chose), we had no reserves to draw on. With four-fifths of our cannon silenced and the very ground where they stood blown sky-high, Ringo Bay was a haven no longer, but a wide-open target, vulnerable to the first invader who approached it.

"It's still a victory," said Bonnie. "The kind of victory my father would have bought at any price." She pointed to the *Venture* as she spoke, and the solitary prisoner who loomed at the rail.

"What comes next?"

"They'll meet on the beach," she said. "With sword and dirk. He's planned that duel for twenty years. Today he'll have it on his terms."

"No wonder he's a little mad," I said, with my eyes on the harbor mouth. The *Venture*, leading its file of battered ships, had just entered the Channel. On the headland Red

Carter continued to stand at attention, like Hercules against the sky.

"The madness will pass when he cuts his enemy down," said Bonnie. "That's one thing I'm sure of."

"Suppose he's the one to fall?"

"Then I'll fight Metcalf in turn," said Bonnie calmly. "That's buccaneer law."

"I won't let you."

"You can't prevent it, Richard. I'm second-in-command at Ringo Bay. These men would never obey me again if I failed to prove my courage."

"Couldn't I fight in your stead?"

"They wouldn't permit it," said Bonnie. "Nor would I."

I argued the point no further, realizing I was faced with an impasse that transcended logic. Bonnie would have fought Spenser without turning a hair the night she took over on the *Venture:* it had been pure chance he had died by his own hand. The gods of fortune had brooded over our voyage of piracy—giving her command, but leaving the killing to others. I closed my eyes and breathed a prayer to those same fickle deities. If Bonnie shed no blood today, I might find ways of saving her tomorrow. Or so I told myself as I sat atop Carter's castle waiting for the last act of his tragic drama.

The surviving corsairs anchored in the bay before they brought Metcalf ashore. They stripped him to the waist, and threw knife and cutlass at his feet, while Carter was making his own blade sing. There were no seconds for this duel, and no umpire. Metcalf's captors had simply rowed back to the *Venture* after they put him on the beach, to join their fellows in the ratlines as spectators of this finish fight. In the end the two men charged one another without preamble, in silent fury, like steel drawn by a common magnet.

After the first clash of blades I found I could not quite watch the combat after all: my head was ringing with the fever, and the whole scene had begun turning in slow spirals, like some garish nightmare. In sober truth (knowing what must happen if Carter fell), I would not have watched the fray even had my brain been clear. Covering my eyes with my two hands, I let it come to me in snatches.

Bonnie, seated beside me in the crow's-nest, told me nothing as the duel proceeded. The howls of the audience on the ships proved only that Carter had the upper hand for the nonce—but the long silences between, broken only by the constant ring of steel on steel, suggested the two old enemies were well matched. . . . The end came suddenly, with a wild outburst of cheers to tell me who the winner was.

I uncovered my eyes in time to watch Metcalf go down in a welter of blood, dead as a mackerel before he could spread-eagle on the sand. Red Carter had triumphed one more time—but it was another Pyrrhic victory. Before the cheering died, I saw that Sir Luke's dirk had found its mark seconds before Carter had delivered his own stroke.

The pirate king coughed just once before the cutlass fell from his hand. In another moment, he had sprawled on hands and knees beside his fallen rival, and I could see the glint of sunlight on the blade that had pierced his side.

They brought him to his own room to die, and stretched him on the mattresses that had served as his bivouac.

Bonnie and I stood at his side while he breathed his last. The eyes he turned toward me now were as kind as they could ever be. The explosion of hate that had finally destroyed Metcalf, it seemed, had burned the madness from his mind. When he whispered for us both to come closer, his voice was almost gentle.

"It's yours now, Bonnie," he said. "Yours to the last marlinspike. See you use it well."

She was weeping when she put her hand in his. So was each man among his captains. All of us knew this was an end, not a beginning.

"Do you want the priest, Father?"

He summoned a laugh of sorts, an echo of the Jovian mirth that had once shaken these same rafters. "Hardly, daughter. I don't deserve shriving, I'm afraid. Just remember I've made my peace with fate. And I'll die content if you have your heart's desire."

"I have that now," she said. "Please believe me."

"I meant to give you all of Madagascar," he said. "I wanted your name to be feared from Madras to the Cape. Perhaps it's too much to hope for, after today. You can still have Paradise."

"*Paradise,* Father?"

"Mozo knows the way: he's made the voyage with me. So does Ketchell. They'll chart your course."

Bonnie smiled and held his hand between her own. Their words had reached me from a great distance—for the fever had crept over me in that last half hour, and now threatened to swallow me entirely. Yet even in that state of trance I felt Carter's mind was clear as he hesitated on the threshold of death. When he spoke for the last time, his voice rang with certainty—and his eyes, moving again to find me, were quite tranquil.

"Keep Douglas with you, Bonnie," he said. "Make what you will of him. He's a good man."

CHAPTER 14

Flight and Pursuit

IF I have described this war to the death through a veil (and left Red Carter's dying instructions to his daughter suspended in mystery), I can plead illness as a cause. While the death rattle was still sounding in Carter's throat, I was staggering from the room with Tom Hoyt's arm around my shoulders. In another moment, I had collapsed on my own bed, letting the fever take me where it would.

As delirium goes, mine was short-lived, and my life was never in danger. For the next week (when they had the leisure) Tom or Bonnie nursed me—as I thrashed on the mattress in the gutted room the pirate king had called his princess' bridal chamber. Even after the fever eased, I was too weak to ask questions—and too thankful to be alive to wonder at the strange silence that hemmed our fortress castle.

I had no way, so far, to soften Bonnie's grief for her father's death: nor had I the words to solace her for the ruin of his empire. It would hardly have consoled her to say that Carter and Metcalf had been destined to cut each other down from the moment their careers had clashed. Their first encounter in Madras and their duel on the beach of Ringo Bay were twin acts in the same drama.

Sir Luke (I could see it clearly now) was an evil genius who deserved his quietus. Jonathan Carter (who might have risen to greatness had the fates ruled otherwise) was but another proof that they who live by the sword shall perish by the sword. Or so I reasoned, now the man's blind passion had destroyed him outright.

He had thrown down the gauntlet to law and order—and the law (in this case, the East India Company) had picked up the challenge. He had repulsed the Company's attack and slain its leader. But Ringo Bay, and all it stood for, were doomed and damned. All that mattered now was when the next and final blow would fall.

When I left my bed at last, my health was far from mended, though my mind was sound enough, now it had won through the misty night of delirium. I could do no more than lie in a chair on our terrace—passing the time as best I could while I awaited Bonnie's coming. When I found an inkpot and a great stack of foolscap in Carter's *escritoire,* it seemed natural to take to writing, if only to give me useful employment in those hours of indecision. The log of my own voyaging (from Glasgow to the New World, from New York to the Cape and Madagascar) was far in arrears—and I felt it was worthy of record. The manuscript I leave behind me, whose final chapter I am now inscribing, has been the result of that tidy Scotch impulse to state my case as fairly as I can.

Even on the terrace (with only a glimpse of Ringo Bay, when I found the strength to lift myself for a moment and look out across the parapet) I could understand the silence. Twenty of our corsairs, including the *Venture,* had survived the action. Most of them had anchored here for a time, while broken gear was replaced. Today the harbor was empty: the warehouse doors gaped wide, and the guards had long since left the barbican. . . . Save for the presence of the dhows, and the few sailors who worked in their rigging, Ringo Bay was a roadstead fit only for ghosts.

When Mozo brought me my invalid's ration of broth and biscuit, I made no effort to question him on the mass exodus: the reason was plain enough. When he helped me to my bed in the hot siesta hour, I slept on that knowledge as best I could. I was only half awake when Tom Hoyt came in with my medicine an hour before sundown—a decoction of Peruvian bark, which he used as a sovereign specific for all fevers.

"You'll live, it seems," he said after he had examined me. "Not that I had doubts on that score—the Scots are a hardy race. Still, it will relieve your wife to hear you're out of danger."

"Where's Bonnie now?"

"At the sick bay, nursing the wounded. She'll be with you soon."

I closed my eyes on the image. Our losses had been most stark, our sick list a long one. I knew both Tom and Bonnie had worked like Trojans to save all they could.

"Tell me what's happened here," I said. "I'm strong enough to listen."

"If you don't mind, lad, I'm leaving that to Bonnie."

"Where are the ships?"

"Plying their trade, I suppose. Or moved to safer anchorages."

"If Bonnie's crew have gone, Ringo Bay is hardly safe for her."

"That's another thing she'll explain," said Tom. "Not that I mean to sound mysterious—but some imponderables can only be discussed with those we love."

"It isn't like you to be sentimental, Tom."

"It isn't like you to be dense," he said. "We'll put it down to your recent illness." He left me on that note, with a mocking grin which told me nothing.

I was pondering his last remark when Bonnie joined me at last. In the past week this was the moment of the day that had made my sorry state bearable. Tonight (though I was mending) I still felt oddly helpless when she took my hand in hers and kissed it gently. My confusion deepened when I saw her eyes were brimming. I had yet to see her weep—save at her father's deathbed.

"Don't talk tonight if you're exhausted," she whispered. "It's my turn to speak."

We smiled at the shared joke. While my fever raged, I had babbled of a hundred things I could scarce remember now.

"Why do you weep?" I asked. "For the dead—or the living?"

"For you, Richard," she said. "These are happy tears: I know you'll soon be well again. In another month this business at Ringo Bay will seem a bad dream to you—and nothing more."

I fought off my forebodings, glad that my sickness explained the slight tremor in my tone. "Are we giving up the harbor then?"

"Would you try to hold it, in my place?"

"Hardly," I said. "I've racked my brains to invent some way to defend it—and come up with nothing."

"There is no way, Richard. Ringo Bay belongs to the past."

"D'you weep for the past, too?"

"Only for my father's ghost," she said quietly. "I think it's at rest now." She wiped away her tears, and smiled for the first time.

Seven days ago Jonathan Carter had been given a sailor's funeral, along with the eight captains who had died in the last bitter defense of his domain. It had been his wish that he be buried from the deck of a vessel under sail. Bonnie herself had read the service while the *Venture* sailed up the Mozambique Channel and back to the shattered harbor. It had been her last act aboard. The next day, our corsairs had spread sail and gone about their business.

Tom had told me that much when I was well enough to listen. Try as I might, I could offer Bonnie no comfort now.

"Don't tell me you'll surrender your kingdom?"

"Yes, Richard," she said in that same tranquil tone. "It's a kingdom built on the bones of victims—like the great Khan's empire. I can't kill to hold it: all that's behind me now."

My heart leaped at that simple statement. And yet, weak though I was, I did not risk showing my exultation.

"You'll give up this life entirely then?"

"What else, now my father's gone?"

"Then it was he—and he alone—who held you here?"

"Once you called it a form of bondage," she said. "When he died, I saw how right you were."

I had meant to devote my life to severing that bond. Now, it seemed, death had cut it with a single stroke—and Bonnie herself had learned the lesson. Love had done what hate could never do. Overnight she had discovered the difference between right and wrong.

"What of your captains?" I asked. "Will they let you resign your command?"

"Most of my captains died defending Ringo Bay," she said. "The others will hunt elsewhere, on their own. We settled our contracts while you lay ill: they took what was left in the warehouses as their shares."

"Leaving you with nothing?"

"Not quite nothing, Richard. Mozo and Jack Ketchell refused to go with the rest. So did Majunga, Hans—and a score of others. We'll survive nicely."

"Of course we will," I said—and strove to rise from my bed. My head was swimming, yet my brain was clear enough. It was an odd sensation—as though I were floating on a cloud, able to measure my impulses as accurately as though I had second sight.

"Rest quietly," she whispered—and laid her cheek on mine. "And have no fears for me. You've opened my eyes to the future. I know how to redeem myself."

"We're sharing that future, Bonnie."

"Yes, Richard. We'll share it, in ways you never dreamed. You won't be poor—that I promise. Remember, you were the one sailor in Christendom brave enough to wed the devil's daughter. You deserve a special reward."

She seemed to float away from me then—as definitely as though she possessed a cloud of her own, as though we addressed each other across a blue infinity. Her words came to me clearly: the illusion was not unpleasant.

"There's a trove at Crater Lake," she said. "Just below our Eagle's Nest. Mozo can find it in an hour. I'll send him there tomorrow with pick and shovel—and a mule train to bring it down. All in all, I'd say it amounts to half a million pounds. Few husbands have earned such a dowry so quickly."

"I'll take no reward from you, Bonnie. What's mine is yours."

"Use it as you like," she said as though she had not heard my protest. "When you've become an Admiralty lawyer, you might reopen my father's case before the Company—prove that Metcalf, not he, was the thief."

"We'll clear his name, if it's in me," I said. "But we must go to London for that."

"I can't return with you, Richard," she said. "It's the one thing you must see clearly."

"Why not? You've given all this up."

"Would you see me hanged as a pirate?"

"Your only acts of piracy were against Moslems—who are fair game for Englishmen. The rest was your father's doing, before you came of age. He's squared his account with the Almighty. Why should you be punished?"

"Are you forgetting I took part in a mutiny aboard the *Pilgrim Venture?*"

"Quill was ringleader then."

"I took command after he was killed; I delivered the prize to Ringo Bay. Face the facts, Richard—I'm still the devil's daughter, and I reformed too late."

"We can start a new life in Scotland," I said. "The world need never hear of Ringo Bay."

"The world has ways of learning one's past," she said. "It's folly to play the hypocrite."

"Have it your way," I said. Free as my mind was, I could not argue with her hard-won logic. "If you're turning your back on England, I'll share your exile."

"You needn't throw your life away—just because you were cozened into marriage with me."

"I married you with my eyes open wide. It was the best bargain I ever made. Don't think you'll cancel it with an acute attack of righteousness."

She did not speak for a moment, as she continued to sit at the foot of the sickbed with her hand in mine. Instead, her eyes opened wide—as though she could see into the depths of me and read my inmost thoughts. What she saw, I gathered, had not pleased her.

"I know who you are, Richard Douglas," she said. "Who you *really* are. I've known since you went out of your head with fever and spoke the truth."

Despite my strange withdrawal (the sense of floating in a limbo where no man could harm me), I could feel my face muscles tighten.

"So you know I was in Metcalf's employ," I said at last.

"Tom Hoyt's admitted it. I'm glad you're honest too."

"That was before we took the blood oath," I said. "Before

I found I loved you. I'm not the first man who changed sides."

"Only you haven't changed," she said. "Your real home is Scotland, and it's half a world away. I've yet to discover mine."

"We'll discover it together, Bonnie. The world is wide. We'll find a country we can share."

"We can't, Richard. I won't let you share my exile. It's been reward enough for me to share your love."

"Where can you go? How can you live without me?"

"Life will be easy enough on Paradise," she said. "I've yet to visit it—but I'll take Mozo's word it's heaven on earth."

I recalled the strange mention of Paradise Red Carter had made on his deathbed.

"And just where is this heaven on earth?" I asked.

"It's an island in Oceania," she said. "Over the years we've stocked it as a refuge. You'll see it mentioned on no maps—most of those waters are still unexplored. But Mozo can chart a course there, and so can Jack."

"Is it a pirates' haven then?"

"No, Richard. But my father planned to retire there when his buccaneering was over—when he'd deeded all Madagascar to me. Now it's I who must use it as my sanctuary."

"Why can't we share it?"

"We shared one Paradise, at the Eagle's Nest. I've no right to ask that you join me in another."

"Not even if I demand it?"

"Think on well to what I've said tonight," she told me as she rose from my side. "No man can make his own rules in the world and expect the world's acceptance. My father tried and failed. Would you do likewise?"

"If you'd asked it, I'd have turned pirate," I said. "I'd have finished what your father began here. Why should I fear exile?"

"Sleep on it, my dear," she whispered as she bent to kiss me. "And when you do, remember Red Carter's last words. He said you were a good man. Your head will clear in the morning: you'll understand his meaning."

"My head is clear now," I said.

"So you say tonight, Richard. You'll know better tomorrow. Sleep on it—and don't speak another word."

"How can I sleep, now I know your plans?"

"Remember the drug we gave Mozo—that night off the Canaries? You've had the same dose tonight, along with your Peruvian bark."

So the mystery of my light-spirited clarity was explained. I closed my eyes in drowsiness for a moment—then opened them in a panic, half fearing that Bonnie had already left me.

"Don't you love me?" I whispered.

"I'll always love you," she said. "That's why I'm sailing to Oceania. So you'll be free to return to Scotland."

She had moved to the door as she spoke. I called out to her desperately—begging her to return to my side, if only for a moment. Too late, I realized that Majunga's potion had taken hold at last, for my voice was but a wordless echo within my brain.

When I wakened again, the day was far advanced. There was no need to ask Bonnie's whereabouts: a sixth sense told me she had left Ringo Bay with the tide.

I lay back on my couch and groaned aloud—but my despair was of short duration. Even now the drug imparted a singular tightness to my spirits, a *joie de vivre* that lifted me above my sense of loss. . . . A moment later I heard sounds outside that cheered me in earnest: the clink of oars in their locks, the bark of Mozo's commands at the pier's end.

Drained as I still was of my strength, I could not rise unaided from my bed. But there was no need to look as I heard the procession of bearers move from dock to castle, to deposit their burdens in the captain's room below my own. I knew what those burdens were as surely as though I had been standing in Carter's sanctum.

Mozo's bearers made ten trips down the mountain (I counted them carefully) before the last sack was brought to the stronghold. By then I was on my feet once more—walking a bit in the palm garden each morning with Tom's support, or taking my ease on the terrace while my pen set down the other chapters of this narrative. . . . Bonnie had gone in one of the two dhows—but the other, reserved for my own transport, still rode at anchor across the harbor while Mozo and his crew finished her outfitting.

The giant Negro was my friend: I knew he would await my pleasure. I had no intention of leaving Ringo Bay until my health was fully mended, my story set down to the last word. Meanwhile, so long as white flags flew from our ruined headlands and the sea beyond was empty, I did not fear a second visit from the East India Company.

Now that I have glanced over what I have written, I can see that my history (like most tales of man's striving) is a blend of comedy and tragedy: as I said at the outset, mine was scarcely a hero's role. I have inscribed it as fairly as I could, sparing myself nothing. As I approach the ending my pen falters for the first time.

A man's conscience, after all, is part of the heritage that links him to the gods. Mine had suffered badly. At times, indeed, it seemed all but extinct. Still, I can offer no apology for the final act that closes this record of deeds and misdeeds. Given the chance again (I cannot stress this too often), I would not have done otherwise.

I will set down the last scene of the play without comment, before I quit Madagascar, letting the lines speak for themselves. Only the reader can judge if I have acted wisely. (Somehow I feel sure my manuscript will find its readers. If it does not justify me wholly, it will explain me in a fashion that leaves no room for doubts.)

It was a full fortnight after Bonnie's departure when a fist hammered on my door. I had expected Mozo. But it was Tom Hoyt, not the Negro, who stood before me—looking a bit the worse for wear (as he always did at a day's end) but coherent enough.

"The inventory's completed downstairs," he said. "Counting the bar silver, we've close to a million under lock. Nearly five hundred times what Metcalf offered when he hired you for this mission. Count it yourself—or will you take my word?"

"I'll take your word, Tom. Will you see it's handed over safely?"

"The Company will see to that when it calls here again," said Tom. "Confound your scruples, Dick—won't you take it beyond their reach?"

"Using what for transport?"

"The dhow, of course. Why else d'you thing Mozo's lingered here?"

"To take me to the Cape," I said. "Those were Bonnie's orders, as you well know."

"Why not ship the plunder too? She wanted you to have it, as your reward."

"Reward?" I exploded. "Why should *I* be rewarded?"

"Are you denying you turned a lady pirate into a woman?"

"Why'd you let her go?" I demanded. "I was too ill to stop her—you might have acted in my stead."

"No one could have stopped her, Dick. When a woman's in a sacrificial mood, mere man can only stand aside—and hope for the best."

"You could have tried, at least."

"Listen carefully, my friend," said Tom. "From the moment she discovered what love meant, Bonnie had but one wish."

"To give up this life?"

"Put that another way—to prove she deserved your love."

"So she proved it by leaving me?"

"Exactly. By starting life afresh, as an atonement for Red Carter's sins. By giving *you* your freedom, so you'd not be burdened by that guilt." Tom's grin had widened: he was almost beaming now. "Remember, she ran but small risk. Once you were well again, she knew you'd follow her."

"How can I? Will Mozo take me?"

"If you like, Mozo will sail you up the Clyde and stand by until you've made yourself a laird. Or he'll set a course for Paradise. With a fortnight's head start, Bonnie will soon be established there."

"What are you trying to say, Tom?"

"Only this, my prince of numbskulls. When your girl set out for Oceania, she was only testing you. You passed your *other* tests with high marks. Why are you failing this one?" My friend the doctor guffawed at my wide-eyed stare before he thumped me between the shoulder blades. "Don't look so feazed, lad. Just give me your sailing orders—is it Glasgow, or Paradise Isle?"

"Need you ask?" I felt, for a moment, that my fever was returning, and settled in the nearest chair until the tumult in my blood had subsided. "When the next armada arrives from Madras, you can give 'em my regrets."

"Sorry, Dick. I won't be here. I'm coming with you."

"You can't leave your field hospital."

"I discharged my last case two days ago. When that dhow

weighs anchor, Ringo Bay will really belong to its ghosts. I find ghosts poor company—even with a bottle."

"What of the loot?"

"It's under lock—it'll hardly run away, since you insist on leaving it."

"Don't tell me you'll be happy on a Pacific island," I said.

"I'll be happy nowhere for long," said Tom Hoyt. "That's the curse of an itching foot. Still, I think I should linger there awhile. This Paradise, I take it, is on the primitive side. In any case, I don't trust native midwives."

I had gone to the veranda rail to look across the water at the dhow, already beginning to tug at her anchor as the afternoon breeze freshened. As complete understanding of Bonnie—and Bonnie's last stratagem—burst like a rocket in my brain, I turned to Tom Hoyt with a great shout of happiness.

"Are we already expecting an heir?"

"Beyond a doubt, Dick. I told your wife as much before she departed."

"Why not tell *me* too?"

"Because she swore me to secrecy. She wanted no weapon to hold over you. Unless you followed her freely, she'd planned to raise your son alone."

I have told my story—and, I trust, my reasons for leaving what one calls civilization, for want of a better word, to venture into the unknown.

The captain's sanctum is in order. I leave this stack of manuscript in plain view—together with a letter to the representative of the East India Company who calls here. The letter (written in the Company code) tells him of the hiding place of the treasure in the castle: it repeats the reasons why I am surrendering it.

I fear my story has no moral—save the obvious one that love conquers all, since it is stronger than hate. Someday Bonnie and I may pay civilization a visit, to see how it has fared in our absence. Meanwhile, I trust, we will both do well enough.

————

Keep Up With The BESTSELLERS!